I0680289

INVISIBLE

INVISIBLE

BY D.R. FULLER

Text © 2014 D.R. Fuller
Published by White Meadow Books
Cover image "Oak Tree Sunset" © Martin Eager, Runic Design. Used under Royalty Free Image License.

All rights reserved. No part of this book may be reproduced or stored in a retrieval system by any means, be it mechanical, electronic, recording, or otherwise, without written consent of the author, or an authorized representative thereof as designated by the author. For information regarding permissions, please review our contact information on our website at www.whitemeadowbooks.com

ISBN 978-0-9853160-7-5

Library of Congress Control Number: 2014934560

Printed in the United States of America
Year First Printed: 2014
Second Edition: 2018

To Florence, my eternal wife and companion. Thank you for choosing me and allowing us to be one.

ACKNOWLEDGEMENTS

I WANT TO THANK FLORENCE, my eternal companion, for the wonderful life we have shared that inspired much of INVISIBLE, and our children and grandchildren who all helped in various ways to make it come alive. An extra special thanks goes to my publisher, Destyni Shirley, for her encouragement, without which it would never have been published. I also want to thank Clara, one of my beautiful granddaughters, for allowing me to use her portrait on the front cover, and her sisters for their creative work in modifying the existing cover. This story is indeed a family project.

CONTENTS

PROLOGUE

ART LISTENED AGAIN AS the weatherman forecasted triple-digit temperatures. Perhaps it was a case of shooting the messenger, but he really detested the guy, especially since he was positive there was a hint of humor in his voice. Then, before switching back to the sober-minded newswoman, he said, "But Sandy, it's a dry heat." Art grimaced at the resulting laughter.

It was only mid-morning, and the stifling heat was already oppressive. With sweat dripping down his stubby beard, he leaned back in his '52 Dodge pickup, wishing for the hundredth time he had installed a fan on the dash. Of course, the thought of having air conditioning did not even occur to him; his truck barely ran anyway. The strain would have sent the old girl straight to the junkyard.

Stockton was a small dusty town just south of Tooele and southwest of Salt Lake City. It was not his home, but after Vietnam, he had ended up there by default. As a veteran and most men were veterans back then, he had hired on with the Department of Defense at an Army depot ten miles to the south. It stored World War II chemical munitions, very nasty stuff. Stockton became his adopted home after they finally started tearing down Deseret, a small town built for the workforce. Eventually, he bought a humble one-bedroom house in Stockton and had lived there ever since.

Arthur Brown never married and as a rule, stayed to himself. Some said it was the war; others suspected he was just plain crazy. For Art's part, he did not much care what people thought. His hitch in Vietnam had just about purged him of any respect for his fellow man. He had seen atrocities there that plagued him with nightmares ever since. He hoped the passage of time would somehow dim the horror — it never did.

Today, he still worked at the depot but spent much of his spare time going over the mountains mining silver. He liked to fancy himself a prospector. Deep down inside he believed he would eventually find the mother lode, notwithstanding the fact that the mining boom had ended in the last century. In his saner moments, Art figured if anything was crazy about him, then that had to be it. He had attempted to shake it off countless times, but it always came back like a bad addiction.

1

His main equipment was an old World War II metal detector purchased from an Army Surplus store in Salt Lake. Of course, there were new ones on the market, but money was always a problem, something he hoped striking it rich would solve.

This morning had been no different from any other except for the increasingly stifling temperature. Art should have left earlier, instead of deciding to have breakfast at The Silver Pit, a local restaurant. Had he done so, he would have been well on his way by now.

Sid, the proprietor of The Silver Pit, was not much for conversation but was a decent enough cook; this was to Art's liking on both accounts. Unfortunately, after Art thanked Sid for breakfast and settled back into his solitude, a young man entered. He gave the dining area a brief look before casually walking over to Art's table. His name was Frank Coburn, and he was a reporter for the Tooele Transcript. Art hated having to talk to the fellow, but not being a rude man by nature; he invited him to have a seat.

Frank was preparing an article on Stockton's history and was researching information available from the residents. Surprisingly, the young man was easy to talk to and had a pleasant personality; but of course, Art did not have much for him. No, he never voted and was not interested in local government in the least. Yeah, he stayed to himself and tried to keep a low profile. No, he was not married, nor had he ever been. No, he was not Mormon. No, he had no plans on becoming one, and no, he did not want to know more about them.

Art was just getting into the conversation when the young man got the picture, which was that Arthur Brown lived in Stockton, but was not part of Stockton, Utah, or even the world anymore.

Frank eventually excused himself after thanking Art for his time and went over to talk to Sid. Art did not hear what was said but smiled to himself when Sid turned around and entered the kitchen, leaving Frank staring at the closed door in obvious embarrassment. The young fellow would have to develop a much tougher hide if he wanted to survive in the news business.

Now, Art sat in his rapidly overheating oven wishing he had not delayed his departure. Pulling out onto the road, he headed up into the local hills to one of his favorite spots, an abandoned mining town called Jacob City.

He kept a good record in his journal of the ground he had already covered, and there were plenty of readings, but all he had ever been able to find had turned out to be old rusty mining equipment. Standing there looking over his next area, he felt that the predicted one hundred plus temperature was beginning to manifest itself viciously. Sweat dripped down and collected in the rag tied around his forehead. His shirt was already soaked but did little to cool him off.

"Come on, Art, get a move on it! The silver's not gonna dig itself out!"

Turning on the detector, he placed a small silver coin on the ground and tuned it. It had been difficult in the beginning, but his ears eventually developed a greater sensitivity to the sound made by the iron scrap he normally located. Of course, he still had to investigate it, always thinking it might be hiding silver beneath it. It never did, but there was always the chance.

His search detected nothing for almost two hours, and he was about to take a break when an unusual response sounded out of the small speaker! It was such a surprise that his first thought was the instrument had suddenly stopped working, squawking out its final death rattle: BONG! Every time he moved the coil over the ground, it gave the same response. Excitement and confusion filled his mind as he dropped a silver coin to recheck the detector. The search loop again passed over the coin and again: Bing, Ping. It was not silver. His educated ear told him at least that much. The signal strength meter appeared useless as well. It was maxing out the gauge, even with the sensitivity turned nearly off. His confusion increased.

He replaced the silver coin with a rusty disk and performed another test. Ping. Ping. Again, he dropped the silver one and compared the silver and iron targets together. Bing. Ping. Bing. Ping. Brushing them aside with his boot, he again checked the target. BONG! BONG! He had never come across any targets that sounded even remotely like this. There were times when the pitch varied slightly, but nothing like this. He verified the location one last time before marking it with several stones.

Stepping back, he again looked at it. The buried object may not be silver, but he no longer felt disappointment. At least it was not iron. He also knew the sound of gold, which was a lot like iron. This thing was like nothing he had ever come across.

Setting down his metal detector, he hurried back to the truck to get his pick and shovel. He hoped the object was shallow enough to dig up without much trouble. If he dug a hole about a foot deep and took another reading, perhaps the difference in intensity might indicate the actual depth. Usually, he could get a rough idea of the depth with the meter, but it didn't seem to be working correctly. If all else failed, he would just have to go with his instincts.

Puffing from exhaustion, he returned to the stones. Looking up, he saw that the sun was as high as it was going to get; the heat was almost unbearable. Removing his handkerchief, he wiped his face and tried wringing out some of the sweat, but it was so dry that the rag refused to give up its moisture. He replaced it on his head and kicked the stones off the target area.

"I don't know what you are, but I hope you'll be nice and not give me a hard time." Art was starting to feel a little lightheaded and knew it might be a sign of heat exhaustion. He would have to get out of the sun soon, but this was too exciting, and he was a sucker for a mystery.

Raising the pick, he brought it down dead center of where he thought the target would be. The pick entered the ground for about four inches before coming to a solid stop. Still normal, a larger stone could be blocking him. However, as he continued to strike, it soon became evident that the stone may be too large to break up. He was making no progress.

Picking up the shovel, he began removing some of the loose gravel. The sun's blinding reflection immediately caused him to drop the shovel and rub his eyes. He attempted to regain his bearings, but something else was wrong, something more ominous. His head was spinning and throbbing with pain. Looking at his arms and shirt, he saw he was no longer sweating. His medical training immediately told him what the problem was. He had heat stroke!

"No!" he exclaimed. Heat stroke was not good! He needed shade; he had to cool off. His truck was close but far too hot. Looking at one of the town's near-by dilapidated buildings, he staggered over to the truck and grabbed a jug of water before approaching it. As he entered an open door, he poured the water over his head and body. The building was not cool inside, but it was cooler than outside. The musty odor told of years of non-use, though he did see a filthy mattress on the floor. Looking at it was the last thing he remembered.

Slowly, he became aware of the surrounding blackness and the throbbing pain in his head. At first, he did not know where he was, but the sickening smell and huge headache brought back the memory of vomiting. Feeling around, he realized he was lying on the mattress and knew from his time as a medic in the war that it was a miracle he was still alive.

"Idiot!" he tried to say, but his throat hurt him too much to do more than groan. The moon was out, and he was able to see the doorway a few shades lighter than the surrounding interior. Feeling his arms, he discovered that he was sweating, a good sign. He contemplated whether he should go to a hospital. Somehow, he had survived; getting himself checked out was not a bad idea.

With some effort, he was gradually able to regain his balance and stand up. He felt weak, dehydration no doubt. Again, he lambasted himself for being such a fool for not recognizing the danger signs. He knew better. That thing had made him forget caution and had nearly cost him his life. In fact, it should have. His mouth was gritty and dry, and he did not know how long he had been out, but he needed water.

Staggering to keep his balance, he made his way back to the truck and grabbed another jug from behind the seat. He drank as much water as he dared before closing his eyes and resting his head against the cab. He figured he should clean himself off before climbing inside. Sid's cooking covered him, and it had for sure lost its appeal.

Removing the handkerchief from around his head, he stripped down to his boxers and used the rag and water to wash off most of the vomit. It was not going to remove all the smell, but he should be able to get to the hospital without giving it a permanent home in the truck.

Throwing his clothes on the truck bed, he climbed in and once again rested his head, this time against the steering wheel. He thought about what he should do. His headache had settled down, and he was beginning to feel normal again, also a miracle.

After about ten minutes of staring, he wondered why he had not left yet. Obviously, he had to clean up and visit the hospital, possibly rest a few days. Continuing to stare out the windshield, he again thought about the buried object.

After another moment, he finally said to himself, "You're one sick puppy. There's no way you're going to try to dig that thing up tonight in your skivvies, in the dark no less!"

Almost without realizing it, his hand slowly moved to the ignition switch. Another moment passed before he turned it and listened to the engine's soft rumble. The moon was up, and he could almost see the small pile of rocks. In all the years he had done this, he now understood that he had never expected to find anything. Now that he had, he felt an intense possessiveness for it. It may not be silver or anything monetarily valuable, but something inside told him it was special to him. Whatever he had been searching for, he had found it.

Turning on the headlights, he moved the truck closer to the dark depression until he was in front of the metal detector and his scattered tools. Stepping down in his boxer shorts and shoes, he slowly walked forward into the headlights. The hole in the ground beckoned to him like one of Ulysses' sirens. A shiver ran up his spine as he continued to stand there, and he could not help but look nervously behind himself for a moment. Why was he waiting? Instead of reaching for his shovel, he knelt and slowly began removing the gravel-sized rocks. As he reached the object that had prevented his pick from going deeper, he felt a slick surface and quickly removed his hand as if he had touched something slimy. However, that did not make sense; it was dry ground. The headlights were not allowing him to see into the shallow depression.

Going back to the truck, he retrieved his flashlight, and again, standing over the shallow hole, directed the beam downward. His eyes, now accustomed to the dark, were again blinded by the reflection.

"Whoa!"

Kneeling, he moved more gravel from its surface before carefully directing the beam of light back into the hole. The object's surface was completely smooth and shiny like a mirror. He had never seen anything reflect light like that, not even a mirror, and the surface was super slick as if it had no resistance. It reminded him of nothing he had ever seen before. He may be some old fool who liked to search the mountains for treasure, but he was experienced enough to know this was something different, something very different.

Art's military training buried for years by running and hiding from his past jumped into high gear, and he knew he had to let someone know about this, and it was not going to be the local police department.

By morning, still only wearing his boxer shorts and shoes, he sat next to the empty hole, looking at the sphere before him. It was roughly the size of a basketball with a mirrored surface, and he could find no sign of damage from his pick. Although it did not appear to weigh more than a few pounds, getting it out of the hole was very difficult. Art could almost understand how something could be so hard that a pick would not make a scratch on its surface, but it raised the hairs on his neck when he tried to grasp the sphere. The surface had no resistance — zero. It reminded him of when he played with magnets as a child and how, if he put the like poles together, they pushed each other away. As he tried to get a grip on the sphere, it felt like there was nothing there except a force pushing against his fingers, making the surface so slick that he could not get a grip on it. Only after making the cavity large enough, was he able to get his hands under it to lift it out. Getting his jeans, he fashioned a carrying bag by maneuvering the sphere into the waist and tying the legs over. The pants still smelled of vomit, but he knew this was more important than bad smells, or even a bearded man in his boxer shorts. He quickly placed the improvised carrying case into the truck and headed down the mountain. When he got to the highway, he did not head toward Stockton, but toward the military depot. Someone there would know what to do with it.

She felt as much as heard the steady thump. It had given her a sense of security for as long as she could remember; it represented home, and she lived for its consistency. Occasionally, she synchronized her light fluttering to match it but just briefly. Sometimes, she would count the nanoseconds that separated each beat and graphed the fluctuations. It didn't match her precise rhythm, but she loved the variations and plotted predictive analyses curves to see if she could guess at future variations. Of course, the thumping was not the only sound that filled her world. A multitude of reverberations echoed through her. The steady rush of fluids that accompanied each thump, gases passing over variable surfaces, liquids of varying degrees of viscosity moved in and out of restricted passages, more solid elements passing over each other in a cascading symphony of pops, slurps, and snaps. Hers was a beautiful world of sound and pressure, and she loved it. Suddenly, she paused as understanding began to fill her consciousness. Occasionally, at irregular intervals, the rushing gases took on a wonderful cadence, sometimes rhythmic, but more than that. The recurring consistency that accompanied it left her universe and returned later. Sometimes the returning sounds were modified in ways that could not be accounted for by her world. It was as if something existed beyond her universe. Could there be others? She systematically collected and correlated all the occurrences she could identify, both past and present. Repeatedly, she evaluated the evidence until she was positive. Now she remained perfectly still as wonder and amazement touched her understanding. Her rapid fluttering synchronized with her world's consistent thumping, and her mind perceived the data outside her universe for what it was. She listened as her world responded to the other universe.

"Oh, John, I never believed it would work."

Then from the other universe--

"It's wonderful, Lu. Hey! Why the tears?"

Again, from hers--

"I'm so happy! We have our little one, John. We have our baby."

CHAPTER 01

EVELYN WAS THE DAUGHTER of John and Luwanda Jefferson. Her father was a research scientist, her mother a sports broadcaster at a local radio station. This was the full extent of her family. There were others, of course; she had seen photographs but had no memory of their visits. A few, now passed on, had seen her as a baby. The others lived in faraway places and were too poor to make the trip. There were seldom any phone calls. When a call did come, conversations with Evelyn were limited to a few "How are you" and "Be good and work hard" comments.

Her father worked at Stone Labs, Inc. Most of what he did was confidential; he was a federal government contractor assigned to work on sensitive projects. She remembered asking her father about it in grade school, and he said he built flying saucers and little green men to fly them. He was quite the comedian, but her teacher failed to see the humor. She recollected the incident initiating a "parent-teacher" conference, which never actually materialized.

At seventeen, Evelyn was active in the school's athletic programs and very competitive. She liked swimming and track, but gymnastics was her favorite. She was also never satisfied unless she was pushing herself to do one hundred percent of what she was capable. Like her mother, she had her trophy case full of achievement plaques.

Academically, she was a straight-A student with a perfect attendance record. She was equally comfortable with math and science as with literature and writing. Moreover, her memory — well, there were some things about herself she never told others, not even her parents. Evelyn did not see them as things to be particularly embarrassed about; she had simply come to an understanding early in life that if she was better at everything, it made others uncomfortable to be around her. She decided that being too different was often negative. She was, therefore, careful to pick only those things that seemed less likely to offend.

In addition to her academic skills, she was beautiful, or at least she thought so. Her hair was deep brown, kept short for the swimming, and her airbrushed complexion had never looked less than perfect. If anything about Evelyn looked strange, it was her eyes. While no one would have indicated that her eyes were anything but beautiful, the color was a bit too green and perhaps too penetrating. On those rare occasions when someone did notice, designer contact lenses were the cover story.

Of course, Evelyn felt comfortable with how she looked. Although never complimented by anyone except her mom or dad, she felt she looked as good, if not better, than the other girls did. Additionally, she was never stuck-up or rude. She tried to help when she could, and never took offense at being ignored. No, it was not her appearance. She knew other girls that were pretty, but not popular. And, it was not her attitude. It was when she added her appearance to how well she did athletically and scholastically, that she began to feel something was not right. It was not so much that she wanted attention (though an occasional date would have been nice), it was more because she was able to see the bizarre significance of it.

She was never intentionally ignored, but often overlooked or tuned out. It was like being on the sidelines at a sports event where everyone's attention was on the players on the field and not on you. She had never been very popular, but during her high school years, this problem seemed to have gotten worse. There were never any dates, and even when her friends did get together, Evelyn was often forgotten. Later, they apologized and appeared to be sincerely embarrassed. If this had only happened once or twice, she would have written it off as an unfortunate oversight. However, it was becoming consistent. No one had an explanation for it, and indeed, others began avoiding her from the embarrassment. She needed some serious advice. Turning to her mother was only natural.

Sunday mornings were slow to start for the Jefferson family. No one got up early except to see if someone else had fixed breakfast. Pancakes were normally the Sunday breakfast special, but doughnuts or sweet rolls did occasionally make an appearance. Of course, the Sunday newspaper was a treat for everyone as well. Evelyn preferred the comics, an enduring propensity since she was old enough to read the pictures.

Her father was in the living room with the news section, and her mother at the table with the sports page. The comics lay in front of Evelyn next to her syrup-covered pancakes, but so far, she had not given it more than a cursory glance.

"Mom?" she asked.

"Mmm?"

"Mom, I think there may be something wrong with me..." Evelyn tried to make it sound important without being life-threatening.

"Uh-huh..."

"I'm not ugly; I know that for sure. I mean, I have eyes, and I've seen many other girls that wouldn't hold a candle to me. I've got this great personality and a killer bod to go with it." She looked at her mother to see if she would get any response.

"Uh-huh," Luwanda said, turning to a follow-up of a sports article on page C-4.

Looking at her mom, she knew she had to get out the heavy artillery, "...and sex is great and all..."

"Uh-huh." Luwanda continued to read for a moment before freezing halfway down the article. She slowly lifted her eyes to Evelyn with one eyebrow lifted, giving her pretty face a look of complete incredulity.

Evelyn started giggling. "Mom! Why won't you listen? I'm serious. I need to have some advice here."

"About...?"

"No! Of course not; you know that's silly — but then again, if I could just get a date..." Evelyn looked at her mother a moment more before they both started laughing. They had a close relationship, and she felt she could ask her mother anything. Her father was a bit more distant, but she never doubted his love for her. They were more friends now than mother and daughter, but Evelyn never doubted where the lines were drawn. If push came to shove, she knew who held the power and authority.

"Okay, Mom, seriously, there is something really weird going on in my life. I used to think it was a personality issue, but I don't think so anymore. It's almost as if people have a tough time seeing me sometimes. I've been with my friends when we all decide to get something to eat; they all climb in a car and just leave without me as if I'm not even there. It's not natural!"

Luwanda closed the newspaper and set it down. She could see this was beginning to concern her daughter. It was true that Evelyn had not been on any dates yet, which was a bit of a mystery considering she was such a beautiful young woman. Nevertheless, she had plenty of friends and was on several of the school's sports teams. Luwanda naturally assumed that Evelyn was getting more than enough socializing. Perhaps, it was time for that mother-daughter talk she had been putting off for so long. Of course, she had covered all the be-wary-around-strangers talks, and the school had a sex education class. However, the other talk had been a bit more difficult to bring up. She had always tried to concentrate on chastity and watching out for all the wolves looking for Little Red Riding Hoods. She had never sat down and taught her about flirting and getting a young boy's attention if he was too blind to notice her. She had never covered romance. Maybe this was the time.

Before her mother could answer, the doorbell chimed.

"That must be Rita! She's supposed to drop off my new schedule this morning. Hold that thought! I'll be right back."

Luwanda half-ran to the front door and worked the lock to get it open. She always had difficulty with it. When Evelyn's father installed the deadbolt, he had either installed it incorrectly or bought the wrong one by mistake. Evelyn watched her mother pulling on the door a couple of times and thought she heard her mutter something about her father's "handyman" status before she finally got it open.

From Evelyn's vantage point in the kitchen, she could see a man dressed in a dark suit speaking to her mother. His voice was low, too low for Evelyn to understand, but she wasn't overly interested anyway. She figured he wasn't Rita and would have started reading her comics if she hadn't been so annoyed by the interruption.

Evelyn saw her mother knocked backward. It was so sudden that she had no time to understand. Her perception of time faltered as she watched her mother continue to fall in apparent slow motion. When Evelyn looked up, she saw the stranger enter their home and turn toward her father. Screaming, someone was screaming! Her mind continued in desperation to comprehend what was happening. Evelyn watched the pistol fire several more times, each slower than the last until the final flash of expanding gas ceased its outward movement. All was still. With that stillness, a horrible avalanche of understanding crushed Evelyn's world, and she stopped screaming.

Something snapped inside her. For the briefest instant, a demonic presence screamed in rage and agony before reaching outward toward the stranger. In that instant, a deadly tunnel vision focused every sense she possessed on the man standing over her mother—and just as suddenly, it vanished.

She was already moving out of his sight as two thuds struck the wall behind her, the impacts louder than the silenced handgun. Her mind was frozen in terror knowing she was about to die. She had no time to think or make plans; it was beyond her ability. Everything inside screamed for her to run, to hide, to survive.

Inside her bedroom, she saw the window and knew it was locked. Almost before understanding this, she was moving into her closet and slamming the door. Every feeling, every emotion, everything that was Evelyn, screamed hide! She knew he was coming; there was no hope. She had no time to think of her parents. She had no time to think at all. There was only terror.

Being inside the closet was insanity. It was like a child pulling the covers over its head. She could go nowhere, and he was coming. In the darkness, she pushed herself against the back wall and slumped to the floor. Completely overcome with fear, she was unable to prevent the scream that filled her sanctuary and tomb.

Click!

That single fatal sound locked Evelyn's diaphragm, shutting off any further ability to voice her terror. Silence filled the small closet as light began to enter. This was the end of everything, and she did not know why. She did not understand.

The door gradually opened until she could fully see him standing before her. He did not look like a monster. There was no horrible grimace on his face. There was no expression at all, and while this increased her fear a hundredfold, it also did something else — a surge of incredible anger seared her soul. He was pointing the gun at her face, but she saw nothing. There was only the incomprehensible rage that filled her with a terror more horrible than her imminent death.

As if awakening from a dream, she refocused on the gun, then his face. He appeared frozen except for the eyes; they were looking around the closet in confusion. He then rushed away, leaving the closet door partly ajar. Angry sounds filled the house, slamming doors, glass or porcelain objects shattering. Almost without realizing it, she stretched and pulled the door closed, leaving a small crack to see through.

Seconds turned into minutes and minutes to hours before she recognized the dead silence. Nevertheless, she remained frozen until a strange stillness enveloped her. There were no more thoughts or feelings, only emptiness. When her mind did begin to function again, she realized she was staring across the room at one of the dolls she had never given up. It was dressed in a puffy pleated princess's gown, like the one she had as a little girl.

As she watched, the doll stood and started running through fields of black weeds. The smell was terrible, like putrefying rot! Evelyn knew something was chasing it because the doll kept looking over its shoulder and running faster. No... it was not her doll; it was Evelyn. She was the one that was running! Something was chasing her!

There was a horrible crashing sound, and she looked up to see black and red clouds boiling in the sky. Lightning repeatedly flashed, hurting her ears with its thundering blasts. She ran in terror until she heard a low roar begin just below her ability to hear with her ears, but felt with her body, and it gained in volume until it was louder than even the thunder. It was a scream of torment, a scream so furious and angry that it seemed to suck all the hope and life from her. She fell to the rotting ground and looked behind her in terror.

There were no words to describe her feelings as fear transformed her blood into a frozen sludge. Standing before her was a demonic being so vicious and angry that Evelyn felt she could not continue to look and live. Its eyes were bright red, and its body was covered in what looked to be fresh blood. Its mouth was open in a continuous scream of rage that drowned out all the other sounds around her; its lips pulled back over sharp teeth in an unbelievably vicious snarl. Suddenly, a frozen bubble of complete silence filled her mind, ignoring everything else. Reality snapped closed like a steel trap as comprehension dawned and all hope ended. She realized what she was looking at — it was herself.

CHAPTER 02

THE SUN NO LONGER PIERCED the white lacy curtains of her pretty bedroom; the gradual darkening was a more suitable ambiance for what had occurred. Evelyn was sitting with her knees pulled tightly to her chest, a posture she had held for many hours. Dried tears stained her perfect complexion, lifeless green irises surrounded by bloodshot eyes that were normally the purest white.

Had she slept? She did not think so, but it was difficult to tell since her mind either seemed to be constantly in a dream state or not thinking at all. The small closet that was now her world had darkened faster than the bedroom. The door mostly shut except for a small crack, allowed her to see down the hall thanks to the position of the large dressing mirror.

Alternately, she observed an empty hallway, sometimes visions of a receding form dressed in dark clothing and carrying a handgun. Sometimes she saw the barrel of that gun pointed at her; the bore too large to be real, like a tunnel leading to eternity. Sometimes she saw dark eyes as she curled up, arms wrapped around legs, pulling as tightly as she could, trying to make herself a smaller target as if that were even possible. And, sometimes, she saw her mother falling, forever falling, the gun jerking as it emptied its deadly load in the direction of her father. The carousel of events repeatedly looping in her mind until dullness closed around her, its coldness a welcoming relief.

Other thoughts eventually began to occupy these spaces of emptiness that had once been the home of so much violence. She needed to relieve herself; she was hungry; she had to get ready for bed; tomorrow was a school day; there was a math test in the third period; and — she needed to find the stranger and utterly destroy him and everyone he loved or cared about.

Slowly placing her fingers against the door, she paused for the briefest moment before pushing gently. She listened as her heart pounded. She was afraid. It was not that she feared he was still waiting. It was the overwhelming certainty that she was alone, and except for her beating heart, the house was lifeless.

She found it frightening that she could think of her parents without grief. And yet, there was something, something untouchable, like an immense ocean straining to break through but being held back by a presence, dark and loathsome, ominously waiting just below the surface.

Evelyn tried to stand. At first, she wondered that she could not. She tried again, but with the same result. Concentrating more on her legs, she discovered them to be completely numb, and she had to push her knees down to let her feet stretch out. The feeling began to return – and pain. They ached terribly. She felt like crying, but again, no tears.

Holding to the doorknob, she struggled to her feet, standing there until her body reminded her of its needs. Stumbling, she caught herself again and slowly moved down the hallway to the bathroom. Before leaving, she splashed a bit of water on her face and dried it off gently. She looked at herself in the mirror. There had been a lot on her mind yesterday, things that no longer seemed important now.

There was no sense of time as she stood looking at her reflection. It may have been twenty minutes or several hours, but eventually, she found herself walking down the hall. She reached the kitchen and turned on the light. There was her plate, still full of pancakes. There was her mother's plate, now empty with the sticky syrup still shiny on its surface. Her mother's glass of milk was half-empty – or was it half-full? Evelyn's glass was full. Perhaps, she should finish her breakfast and drink her milk.

She stood facing the table with her back to the living room. She did not want to turn around – it was the final reality; it would make everything she already knew to be true – horribly final. She stood there for a long moment. When she finally turned, she noticed that the kitchen light did not extend completely into the living room. However, she could make out the slight lump on the floor that she knew would be her mother. Something forced her forward. She fought it desperately. She fought it with every ounce of strength she possessed – but she fought it uselessly. As her hand slowly reached for the light switch, she could feel the blood draining from her face, and with the final reality of the soft click, consciousness left her, and she fell to the floor next to the body of her mother.

The sun was up. It lit the living room as it had so many happy days in the past. It was Monday morning. Evelyn lay with her head against her mother's arm. It no longer felt like an arm, and she knew that her mother was no longer there. She stood.

Where were the tears? Where were the tortured sobs of a daughter that had lost the two most important people in her life? She felt nothing. The body of her father lay next to the couch. She turned from it and again looked down at the thing that was no longer her mother. Both sights were horrific, but she felt nothing. She heard the wall clock ticking slowly and listened to its regularity for several minutes before walking over to the phone.

Staring at it, she thought about what she would say, about what they would ask her. She thought about the stranger with the gun and watched him explode, his body parts cascading around her, covering her with his blood and gore. She again thought of finding everyone he ever loved or cared about and—and remembered a little boy named Adam. He had played with her on her fifth birthday. She had liked him and felt a special attraction for him. He seemed to be older than she was, but she felt that she wanted to protect him as if he belonged to her. Moreover, she thought of how he would now hate her because she was a monster.

Slowly reaching for the phone, she lifted the receiver and dialed 911.

"This is the 911 Operator. What is your emergency?"

Evelyn tried to say something, but words would not come out.

"Hello? What is your emergency? Help is on the way. Can you respond to my voice?"

Evelyn finally said, "My mother is dead."

"If you can hear me, but can't speak, try to tap the phone on a table, wall, or floor. Help is on the way."

Again, Evelyn said, "My mother and father are dead; someone killed them."

"Hello, hello? Can you hear me? Try to make a noise. A patrol officer will be at your door in a few minutes. Are you there?"

Evelyn looked at the phone for a moment before hearing the patrol car pull into the driveway. When she heard the knock, she could neither move nor say anything. A voice called several times. There was silence for a moment before the unlocked door opened, and two patrol officers carefully stepped inside. Evelyn stared at them. Upon seeing the two bodies, they immediately pulled their weapons and stepped back outside on either side of the doorway with one reporting what they had found. Within minutes, sirens could be heard, and five more police cars pulled up in front of the house with two others blocking traffic. Several patrol officers took up positions in the yards on either side of Evelyn's house and across the street to keep neighbors out of danger. The others took up positions next to the original officers at the door.

After reporting the status to their captain, they called for anyone still inside to drop any weapons they might have and to come out slowly with their hands visible above their heads. They did this several times with no response.

Evelyn slowly set the phone down on the floor and walked to the door. She did not have her hands up, nor did she say anything. She stopped and looked at the officers on each side, first one, and then the other. They did not react to her presence in the least.

Finally turning to the first officer she had seen enter the house, she said flatly and without emotion, "A man came here yesterday... he killed my mother and father..." With that, a floodgate opened inside, and she started crying, holding the officer by the front of his shirt with her head buried in his chest.

Oblivious to the crying girl, the captain initiated the search procedure and the officers pushed past her; the one she was holding onto almost stumbled in his attempt to step through her. The other officers stopped a moment to see what had happened before beginning their search of the house.

Evelyn had been thrown to the floor and now desperately crawled back to the phone. They were completely ignoring her, just like the 911 operator and the man yesterday with the gun.

Once they decided that the house was clear, they allowed emergency medics inside to check the bodies. They were obviously dead. Evelyn sat next to the wall with the phone receiver in her hand like a lifeline to sanity, staring at it.

"So, who made the call?" asked one of the investigators. Evelyn instantly looked up at him.

"Cherrie says the phone's still off the hook."

He walked over to Evelyn and saw it in her hand. She just stared at him in shock. The tearstains, the swollen red eyes, the look of horror on her face, she realized he saw none of this. He did not respond to her presence in the least, he just reached out and took the phone from her. "Cherrie? Yeah, this is Richard. The phone was lying on the floor. Whoever made the call has left the premises. Yes, and thanks, you did an excellent job. What? Oh yeah, it's pretty bad."

That is when she attacked, punching and slapping his face. Still, he did not acknowledge her, just standing there with a startled expression. Clutching the front of his uniform, she held on, crying great gasping sobs until he shook her off and began moving around the room looking for evidence. He appeared completely unaware of the blood dripping down his lips and chin.

The impossibility of what was happening, the dreadful horror of it was getting worse — nightmares inside nightmares, fear building to impossible heights, until she screamed and dropped to the floor, retching. After a few moments, she pulled herself into a ball. *With her eyes squeezed shut, she tried to stop existing, but all she could see was the face of the monster in her dream, a blood-covered face of terrible anger — and it was smiling at her.*

CHAPTER 03

EVELYN WAS SO EXCITED! Her mother was taking her to see her father at work. Today was her birthday, and she was five years old. It was because she was such a big girl that she was being allowed to go there.

"Mommy, will we have cake and ice cream too? I promise not to get anything on my new dress!" She looked down at the puffy pleats and patted them proudly. This was the prettiest dress she had ever had. She loved it.

Her mother, Luwanda Jefferson, looked to be a little distracted and had a worried frown on her face. "What did you say, sweetheart?"

"I love my new dress! I think I might be a princess." Evelyn patted her dress again. Looking out the window, she watched as a huge iron fence slowly passed. It was as high as a house and for some reason, made her feel sad. Beyond the fence, she could see what looked like a large park with beautiful green lawns.

"Evelyn, this is where Daddy works. Do you remember when we brought you here last year?" She drove up to the entrance gate, and her worried expression seemed to intensify.

Evelyn said no, but she did feel something, something that made her uncomfortable and maybe a little frightened. Her happy mood continued to deteriorate as she went through the process of entering the complex. When she had to leave her mother outside a series of white rooms, she finally remembered why she did not like being at her father's workplace. There were people, doctors and nurses she thought, because of their white clothing, asking her lots of questions that she could not answer and gave her shots and sometimes-rough examinations. Much of what they did hurt, and she cried for her mother, but they ignored her.

Finally, they placed her in a large white room with some toys and a large mirror on the wall. She was alone for just a few minutes before a boy, a little older than she, was brought in to join her. They said his name was Adam and that they should play together, after which the doctors left.

At first, the young boy did not appear interested in playing with her and with a brief look in her direction, quickly made his way to the assortment of toys. She watched him select a small model airplane before seating himself against the furthest wall. After a moment of indecision and shyness, she timidly walked over and stood a few feet away. When it did not appear that he was going to say anything or even acknowledge her, she asked him if he wanted to play. He gave no response and continued to ignore her. With all that had happened, Evelyn's feelings were quite tender, and she felt tears beginning to fill her eyes. She made one more attempt to join him and listened as he finally spoke.

"Go away. I don't play with girls."

For some reason she could not understand, she was crushed. He was just a mean boy, and she didn't like him either, but it was like having her mother or father say they didn't love her! She crouched down with her hands covering her face and began to cry in earnest. Evelyn wanted to go home. She wanted her mother.

Adam looked up with surprise at the sudden commotion. As he watched her, a not so seven-year-old expression touched his features, and he quickly arose and stepped to her side. He apologized, asking her what she wanted to do. In desperation, she said she wanted to fly away with him in the airplane he held in his hand. He laughed and said she was stupid. The airplane was obviously too small for both: after all, it only had one seat. When she started to cry again, he sighed in exaggerated frustration and agreed to let her fly with him if she would just stop crying.

As she wiped away the tears with her sleeve, she felt drowsy and wished for a moment that she could lie down and take a short nap. *However, when she opened her eyes, she found that she was sitting next to the little boy on a small bench-like couch and before her was a panel with switches and dials. He was putting on a brown helmet that covered his head and a pair of goggles over his eyes. He also wore brown pants and a brown coat, the collar lined with fur. Suddenly, looking at herself, she realized she was dressed similarly, and touching her forehead, she discovered her own set of goggles.*

She was speechless but excited as well. She realized they were inside his little airplane, and though she didn't remember entering, it all seemed perfectly normal. Outside the small cockpit, a long road stretched before them with trees and bushes covering the rolling hills on either side. The sky was blue and had bright puffy clouds that looked like great cotton balls.

Adam drew her attention back as he explained that he had finished his preflight checklist and they were ready to take off. She watched him flip small silver switches and turn little black dials before pressing a button. The sound made her start as the engine roared to life and the propeller in front of them began to turn. Smoke shot out the sides, and she trembled in fear as the spin-

ning blades picked up speed, disappearing into a blur. The sound terrified her, and with clenched teeth, she gripped the seat.

Suddenly, the sound became muffled as she felt something being placed over her ears. Looking toward Adam, she saw that he was adjusting something that looked like earmuffs over her head. When he spoke to her, she found she was now able to hear him clearly. He held her hand and told her everything was okay and to not be frightened. She didn't know why, but she found herself trusting him, and while his eyes held the look of an excited seven-year-old, there was something else there that steadied her and made her feel safe and secure.

Before long, the small craft was airborne and gaining altitude. Never having flown, Evelyn was stunned by the experience. When they neared and finally entered the clouds, she was amazed that the giant cotton balls were not more substantial. They appeared to be more like fog than soft fluffy blankets.

Looking down, Evelyn saw the tree-filled swamps change to forests and finally to rolling hills and prairies. Sometimes, roads and towns flew by, but they were now going so fast that she had difficulty distinguishing individual objects. Large bodies of water followed by more forests rushed past, mesmerizing her gaze until she saw the ground turn white with ice and snow

Soon, Adam slowed the craft and brought it closer to the ground, allowing Evelyn to see a beautiful wonderland. There were caribou and wolves, polar bears and seals, and as they passed over the ocean, whales rising out of the crystal blue. The amazing airplane was even able to fly underwater like a submarine, allowing her to have an aquarium-like view of the creatures below.

By the time they surfaced, Evelyn was so excited that she was barely able to control herself. This was, without doubt, the best adventure she had ever had, and she wanted to let the boy know it, but when she looked at him, he appeared to be worried. She watched as he scanned the dials and toggled a few up and down before finally looking at her and saying, "Houston, we have a problem..."

At that instant, the airplane began to shake and shudder, causing Evelyn to grip her seat in fear. He had said it would not hold two people – could he have been right? Were they going to crash?

Evelyn opened her eyes to see a doctor shaking Adam; he did not appear to be aware of it. The fact that she was also being shaken, combined with her fear of crashing, was just too much for her and she screamed.

Startled, everyone in the room stopped what they were doing and stared. Adam, now cognizant of his surroundings, turned to her, a comforting smile spreading across his face. As quickly as it had come, her fear dissipated. He was staring at her with an expression that said all would be fine and that she had nothing to fear. Adam was not a bad boy at all. He had let her fly in his little airplane and see all those wonderful things. She was sure that she liked him.

Without a word to either child, the doctors removed Adam from the room and began to ask Evelyn questions, most of which she had no idea how to answer and didn't want to anyway. These were bad people; she could feel it as certainly as she could feel that Adam was good. She would tell them nothing, no matter what they asked.

Eventually, the questions ended, and she was allowed to rejoin her mother who appeared to be upset. Evelyn was worried that her mother might be angry with her for not telling the doctors what they wanted to know. When she tried to ask about it, her mother squeezed her hand slightly, a signal that told Evelyn to keep quiet. Neither spoke as they proceeded out of the facility and walked to the parking lot. With all her heart, she wished never to return. It was a bad place filled with bad people. As their car drove away, Evelyn felt a surge of sorrow for her father and wondered if they were mean to him as well.

The trip home was a quiet one with neither Evelyn nor her mother speaking. Several times, she felt the urge to tell her about her dream, but on each occasion, something inside cautioned her not to. Perhaps her mother was angry or disappointed with her. Had she done something wrong?

After arriving home, Evelyn went immediately to her room and lay down on her bed. She loved dreams and had them often, but had never had one as vivid and real as the one at her father's workplace. She wished she could have dreamed longer. The doctors should not have woken her like that. She did not like them at all, and anyway, this was her birthday. They were just mean.

After a few moments, Evelyn's eyes closed. This day had been both exciting and frightening; she was exhausted, and it was not long before she entered a deep sleep.

The crystal blue sky was bitterly cold and bereft of moisture. There were no sounds or movements, not even the occasional sharp crack of shifting ice consistent with a more dynamic environment. The endless, frigid expanse was as flat and as hard as steel, broken by sporadic razor-sharp shards protruding outward at chaotic angles. What possible use could the universe have for such a hell-inspired creation as this?

Suddenly, a barely audible low-level hissing was heard somewhere in the distance. Two small dots appeared starkly against the ice, at first hardly perceivable, but progressively accelerating as they approached. Then, in a blur of speed, two small children streaked by on their bottoms, leaving the sound of laughter behind as they disappeared into the distance.

Evelyn's grin grew wider as she gained on Adam. He had passed her after she collided with one of the pretty things sticking out of the ground, but she was about to catch up. They were approaching a sharp turn with hundreds of protrusions, and she had developed a plan to force him to take the outside. He thought he was smart, but she knew she was faster. Following behind him by a fraction of a second, they entered the turn. Because he had to keep up at full speed to stay ahead of her, he was not prepared. In a sudden burst, Evelyn placed herself on the inside, forcing Adam into an unavoidable collision with the shards!

She shrieked with laughter as he collided into the razor-sharp steel-like shards, shattering them into countless sparkling specks of light, so pretty that she almost slowed down to watch. However, she had her lead back and wasn't about to give it up again. Looking over her shoulder, she watched him coming up like a freight train, and he had a look on his face that made her giggle.

Abruptly, he slowed, looking at something in the distance. Following his gaze, Evelyn beheld a beautiful light. They had been playing here for – well, forever, but she had never seen such a pretty thing as that. Moreover, it wasn't just pretty; it was warm and filled her with strange feelings. She almost wanted-ed to cry when she looked at it but wasn't sad at all.

Evelyn slowed down and returned to Adam. "What is it?" she asked in wonder. She noticed that his eyes were also a little wet when he looked at her.

"I don't know... isn't it beautiful?"

"I've never seen anything like it before... I want to see it. Can we?" Adam was always the boss because he was seven and she was five. She knew it made him feel better to be in charge. He had told her that boys are always in charge of girls and are always the boss. She had giggled about it and had agreed to play the boss-game though she wondered what a boss was.

Adam took her hand, and they started running toward it. They ran forever and ever, but no matter how far they ran, they never got any closer. They tried sliding, which was much faster than running, but it didn't make any differ-ence. Slowing to a stop, they sat looking at the beautiful radiance.

"I have an idea," said Adam as they stared mesmerized, "We should just sit here and wait for it to come to us."

After a moment, Evelyn turned her head and looked at him. "Do you think that will work?"

"Well, if we wait long enough, maybe it will." – and they waited.

At some point, Evelyn looked down and noticed that they no longer sat upon a frozen world. Grass and beautiful flowers covered the ground, and while she slowly moved her hand through it, she did not get up. The attention span of a five and seven-year-old cannot be underestimated and should have dictated that they eventually get up and play, but both sat for longer than Eve-lyn could remember. She had no desire to explore, or play, or make necklaces out of the flowers. She and Adam were content to gaze into the distance and watch the brilliance. Both were as comfortable and patient as the mountains on the horizon, and like them, they waited...

After an eternity, the light gradually approached. The brilliance softened into a gentle glow until it stood before them. Evelyn looked, but could not discern if something was inside.

Since Adam did not say anything for a few minutes, Evelyn whispered to the warm glow before them, "My name is Evelyn, and this is Adam." Then, after a pause. "Is anyone there?"

Without warning, images began to appear in her mind, slowly at first, and then in ever-increasing rapidity, until she had only a faint impression of the blurring sequences. This continued for an instant or forever; she could not tell. When it stopped, it did so abruptly, and she felt herself sway forward as the flow of pure intellect ceased. If a picture is worth a thousand words, what she had been given was more than all the words ever written.

Evelyn looked at Adam, who now stood with tears on his cheeks. Moving her hands to her face, she discovered her own. As his face turned to her, she felt her lips spread to match his wonderful smile. It was time to return.

CHAPTER 04

S ITTING ON A TINY branch outside the bedroom window, a sparrow investigated an empty bird feeder. It focused with one eye and then the other as if it might be missing something important. It was indeed a mystery. It came every day, and the tray was always filled with seeds. The variety was so much better than it could find in the trees or bushes. It also appeared to be safe, being so high above the ground and had become one of its favorite eating spots. However, this was the third morning it had come to find the feeder empty. Had it come late? Was another arriving first and eating everything? It was incomprehensible that the seeds were not there.

As it had done in the previous few days, the sparrow flew over to the windowsill and hopped over to the small tray. Again, it turned one eye and then the other to peer into the empty container. It was thus contemplating its misfortune when the window opened. Sparrows are very quick to react to danger, and this one was no exception. Even when investigating the mystery of an empty bird feeder, it was constantly watchful. But it did not move. In fact, it did not even notice the window open. It was not lifted quietly or slowly and should have startled the small bird to instant flight. However, the sparrow continued to hop around the container, fussing now that it was sure the tray was empty.

Two soft human hands reached down and wrapped themselves around the sparrow, but still, it felt no anxiety or fear. It remembered being covered by its mother's wing, snug and warm. It had been a wonderful time. Even now, it could feel the nest.

Evelyn stood near a window watching the sun silhouette the branches of a large tree. It had been the typical dreamless night, and she felt reasonably rested. Butterflies filled her stomach as she contemplated her plan, but her love for John was now a stronger driving force than her fear of the world. She had lived with this fear for over two years, and she was becoming convinced that if she did not change, something terrible was going to happen. She could not hide forever. She was headed down a dangerous path, one she knew she was not going to survive. For better or worse, she was leaving. She would find

27

John and — and what? She had no idea what she would do after that, except she was going to try and stay with him. John was her last hope; he was her last chance at sanity and maybe life itself.

As she contemplated the soft morning rays, she noticed a small sparrow settle lightly on the sill just outside the closed window. It hopped over to a small feeder and seemed to be upset at finding it empty. Evelyn had been staying in the house for just a few days. The owners were out of town. Perhaps they had forgotten to refill the bird feeder before leaving.

She opened the window and reached down for the fussing bird, softly cradling it in her hands. Holding it gently, she caressed it and made cooing noises. It was not important, but she felt she should do this one last thing before leaving. Finding a sack of birdseed, she filled the tray and set the tiny sparrow next to it. Though it would probably be unable to see the seeds, perhaps it would come back later. Closing the window, she watched the bird continue to fuss for a moment before flying away, leaving the full container.

Picking up her backpack, she gave the house one last look. Although it had not been very dirty or cluttered, to begin with, she had taken it upon herself to clean those places not normally cleaned, as payment for her time there. No one would ever know, of course. It was possible that they may see something out of place or different, but it was her experience that they would just decide it was something they had done themselves; they would never associate it with Evelyn — it wasn't possible.

All the doors and windows were locked. Even the front door's deadbolt was secure. Evelyn had become a master at breaking and entering over the past two years. She could spot where people hid keys with ease. She knew all the tricks. Finding this one under a fake rock next to the front door was not difficult. She filled her backpack with some sandwiches, a couple of bottles of water, a raincoat, and a single change of clothing. It was getting close to 8:00 a.m. and most people would be at work; she should be safe if she remained watchful.

Evelyn planned to meet John at Audubon Park, as she had often done over the last six weeks, and except for these last seven days, she had spent almost every lunch hour with him. She planned her trip carefully and timed it well enough that she knew she would miss most of the traffic, another lifesaving skill she had developed.

Her first rest spot was the playground. It was almost an afterthought, perhaps too small for anything else, but for Evelyn, it was a desert oasis. The small park was a strip of land 75-feet wide and 150-feet long. A short rusty fence with two entrances surrounded it, their gates long since removed. There was one playground swing, with missing chains and thus no actual swings to play on. The grass, long dead from neglect, was now little more than gray dirt. The best thing about the small park was a large oak tree with a bench set beneath it. But, even the once green bench was now gray and cracked from the weather, its legs buried in concrete, no doubt to discourage locals from removing it.

Evelyn stood next to the tree and surveyed the area, making sure she was alone. It was important. She remembered standing in another park last year believing she was safe, that she could rest for a few minutes. He had come up suddenly from behind and collided with her. He wasn't a big man, maybe 180 pounds, but he hit with enough force to throw her violently to the ground. Although he was just jogging, he was not able to see her standing there and had thrown her several yards. The jogger had merely picked himself up and briefly looked to see what he may have stumbled over before continuing on his way. For days Evelyn was terrified, convinced she had a broken leg. It was bad enough being in so much pain, but she knew she could not get help and that caused her days of fear that she might permanently lose the use of her leg or worse. As it turned out, it had been a bad sprain. She recovered and accepted it as a valuable lesson. Always be aware of what was going on around her!

No one was in the park, nor could she find any people in the surrounding streets or yards. Everything appeared secure. Evelyn removed her backpack and set it on the bench. She sat next to it with her arms stretched out over the backrest, lifting her head to the sun.

Closing her eyes to the early morning rays, she tried to decide how to spend the remaining hours before her appointment with John. Sometimes she would see a movie or read at the library, even though it was always dangerous to be around people. But, it was people she most wanted to be around. With all her heart, she wanted to be seen and heard and to be once again part of the world. However, most of all, she wanted to be with John.

Since finding out about his dreams, Evelyn had not seen him again. After almost a week, she had finally come to a decision. She desperately hoped that her choice to leave with him was the right one. His last visit had proved both wonderful and horrible. She spent a lot of time contemplating it before finally making her decision. Of course, the future was never certain, but John had shown her that her life was changing, and he was a part of it now. She had until his lunch to be there; until then, she had to find something else to do. Her recent depression was dragging her down, and she could not afford that, life was depressing enough as it was.

She thought of the library. She had spent many hours in several of the local ones, especially the one converted out of an old mansion. It wasn't far and would give her several hours to read and think safely.

The place she had stayed for the last few days had plenty of food; she had not needed to worry about shopping. Over the past two years, she had learned to look for places like that. Mostly she was able to eat and stay warm without going out to a supermarket or restaurant. Of course, in the beginning, she had spent a lot of time in restaurants; that was before she had been stabbed with a fork and splashed with hot coffee. Today, she avoided the "easy life" and usually cooked for herself. Being around people required her complete attention, but when she was resting or sleeping, she needed the protection of complete privacy.

Evelyn's parents had always encouraged her to have an active life. She had been a good student and was active in a variety of sports. Swimming and track were fun, but her true love was gymnastics. She loved the competition meets and the attention she received; it was one of the few places she was ever really noticed. But, compared to her life now, she was "Miss Popular" then. She occasionally wondered if there was a connection between her wallflower existence growing up and what had happened to her recently.

"Hello, young lady."

Evelyn jumped up, realizing she had been carelessly daydreaming. In front of her was an older gentleman with a cane.

He spoke to me. He's staring right at me, and he spoke to me!

His eyes were kind, and he looked to be about to say something more when Evelyn heard a small voice behind her say hello. Again, Evelyn was startled and moved away several paces, keeping both people in sight, her excitement waning as she realized her mistake. A small child holding a rag doll in her arms smiled up at him.

"What are you doing on this fine morning?"

"Playing."

"Is that your dolly friend?"

"Yes! And she likes to swing."

"Is that right? Well, I'll bet you like to swing too. It's too bad there broken."

"Uh-huh."

"Where's your mommy?" The man scanned the park area before returning his attention to the child.

"She's at work."

"Oh, does your mom work at home?"

"No."

"That's too bad; she'll probably be a while."

"Maggie is home."

"Is Maggie your mom's name?"

"No," she giggled. "That's my sister's name."

"Oh, so your sister's watching you?"

"Uh-huh."

Evelyn watched the man briefly look up and down the block and over his shoulders.

"I like cookies and milk. How about you?"

The little girl looked too young to be out by herself. If her sister was watching her, she wasn't doing a good job of it. In fact, it looked like someone should be getting her home before she got into trouble. Maybe the man would help her.

"Mama makes cookies. I like cookies."

"I make cookies too," he said. "I'll bet you'd like them."

"I like brown cookies," she said excitedly.

"Well, do you want to know a secret?"

The little girl's eyes opened wide.

"I make wonderful chocolate cookies. How about we just go to my place and try some?"

Once again, the man scanned the area with a concerned look. At one point, he looked straight through Evelyn before moving over to the young girl.

Something was beginning to worry Evelyn. Perhaps she was just nervous from being taken by surprise. She watched the man take the girl by the hand and walk her toward one of the park exits.

As they walked away, Evelyn noticed that he no longer appeared to need his cane, and he had not once asked the child where she lived. Comprehension washed over Evelyn like a bucket of ice water! She couldn't believe it.

He's taking the girl—he's stealing her!

Fear and anxiety filled her! What could she do? Someone had to stop him—they were leaving! She quickly scanned the surrounding homes, searching for anyone that might be coming to the child's rescue. There was no one to help, no one except Evelyn, and what could she do?

Her fear turned to helpless anger as they approached the exit. Without further thought, she ran forward and grabbed the man's cane, yanking it out of his grasp. For an instant, he stared at the cane before Evelyn threw it back toward the bench. He watched it bounce off and clatter against the cement. A look of bewildered astonishment filled his features before being replaced by a flurry of foul curses erupting from his mouth. Still holding onto the girl's hand, he quickly retrieved the cane and looked around to see if anyone was watching.

He was evil! Evelyn could feel it radiating from him now. Fear and anger filled her heart as she watched him once again pull the child toward the exit. It was now ominously clear that she was the child's only hope. If she helped the kid and was hurt — if she needed a doctor... In that instant, she realized that she had no choice and the child was out of time.

"No!" she screamed, running to the child, taking her under the arms, and pulling her away from him.

Evelyn stumbled backward as he fell to his knees, grunting in pain and astonishment. She turned with the child in her arms and fled across the playground to the opposite exit before looking back.

Vile exclamations vomited forth from him, but he must have begun to feel like the danger was too great to continue the abduction. Watching the child run away, he hissed, "Go home, you little brat!" He stood up and rubbed his knees a moment before grabbing his cane and quickly leaving the playground. As he hurried down the deserted street, he kept giving furtive looks to see if he was still unseen.

Evelyn breathlessly watched him go. She was frightened but filled with a strange sense of satisfaction. How could something like this happen? What if she hadn't come by when she did! He had meant to harm the child in some way; she was sure of it. She continued to watch until he disappeared around a corner.

Looking down at the child contentedly sitting in her arms, she realized she had no idea where the girl lived.

"What now?" she thought desperately. "I can't just leave her here on the playground."

"You can run fast, Manny! I can run fast too," she said excitedly to her doll.

Evelyn set her down on the sidewalk and, still holding her hand, went back to retrieve her backpack. How was she going to find out where she lived?

Leaving the playground, Evelyn made sure there was no traffic before releasing the girl's hand, hoping she would have the sense to return home.

The child, probably thinking of cookies, continued across the street to a fenced duplex. She went up the porch steps and through an open door with Evelyn cautiously following.

"Maggie!" the girl shouted, "Manny and me can run fast!"

Evelyn could hear some rock music playing in another room. The little girl ran to it and yelled, "Maggie, Maggie!"

Maggie, apparently, was busy talking to someone on her cell phone while a CD player blasted music over a set of small speakers. Maggie ignored her sister.

"Maggie, I want cookies. Manny wants some too. You want some too, don't you Manny?"

Maggie continued to ignore her.

"Maggie, Maggie, Maggie!" she yelled at the top of her little lungs.

Now Maggie turned to her and screamed, "Shut up!"

"Maggie, I can run fast, and I want cookies!"

"I said, shut up!"

Evelyn watched the exchange in disbelief. The teen was not a good babysitter or even a very good sister for that matter. Feeling her anger rising, she walked over to the CD player and threw it violently against the far wall, pieces flying in all directions.

Silence.

In a sudden realization of what she had done, Evelyn's anger abruptly ended, and her hands flew to her mouth in embarrassment.

Maggie looked over to where the CD player had been and then across the room to where it lay shattered. She looked at her sister and back to the busted CD player. "You little creep!" she yelled, "That was my player!" She jumped off the bed and grabbed the toddler by the arm, bringing her hand up to strike her.

Evelyn immediately grabbed the teen's arm and pushed her back down on the bed, her anger rising again.

Maggie looked briefly startled, but this time when she stood back up, she settled for screaming instead of hitting her sister. "Get out of my room, now!"

Evelyn took the child's hand and brought her to a small kitchen located at the back of the house. She could still hear Maggie yelling into her cell phone, telling someone what her sister had done. With tears running down her cheeks, the child clutched the small rag doll to her chest.

"Maggie is mad at us, Manny!" she cried.

Kneeling, Evelyn pulled her into a gentle embrace, trying to think of some way to console her. After a moment she put her hand on the doll's head and moved it around as if it was talking. If this didn't work, the child would probably run screaming in fear.

"Let's eat something! Do you want to eat something? Manny loves you!"

The little girl looked at the doll for a moment, obviously surprised, but pleasantly so. She didn't know her doll could talk!

After a moment, the child stopped crying and rubbed her eyes. "I love you too, Manny, do you want something to eat?"

Evelyn set the little girl at the table and looked through the cabinets, finally finding an open box of cookies. She placed a few on the table along with a small cup of milk.

She again moved the dolls head and said, "Look, Mommy. I made you some cookies and milk."

Again, the young girl looked at the table and smiled, seeing the treat now. The girl began to eat the cookies, occasionally offering a bite to her doll.

After another moment, the child said, "Thank you, Manny."

Evelyn said, "You're welcome, Mommy."

The child smiled happily and continued to eat.

Evelyn leaned back against the cabinets feeling a mixture of conflicting emotions. She knew this sort of thing happened in the real world, and she, of all people, wasn't likely to change anything. In a way, this little girl was very much like Evelyn. Her sister was treating her like she didn't exist, or maybe like she shouldn't exist. She knew that the teen would have suffered as much as everyone else in the family if the child had been kidnapped. Moreover, it was a shame that it would probably take some tragedy like that to change her. Watching the child, she hoped her mother would return soon; she could not stay much longer.

Soon, the teenager came into the kitchen and looked at her sister eating the cookies. She then put her arm around her and gave her a little apologizing hug.

"Do you want some more milk?" she asked.

Before leaving, Evelyn made sure the teen was in control. It looked as if she was regretting her earlier outburst and sat with her sister on the living room floor to watch some cartoons.

Thinking of the CD player, Evelyn wondered what the teen must have been thinking if she was giving it any thought at all. It was not possible that a little girl that young could have thrown the player so hard as to shatter it. Nevertheless, whatever she thought, it looked like she was comfortable with the explanation. For the past two years, Evelyn had witnessed this behavior repeatedly. She accepted it as something she could observe but never understand.

Opening the door to leave, she watched them for a moment longer. The teenager had her arm around her sister, and they were laughing about something not in the least bit funny on the television screen. Evelyn closed the door behind her and stood for a while looking at the empty neighborhood. After a moment, she unconsciously wiped a tear from her cheek. She was no stranger to loneliness, but sometimes it felt worse.

CHAPTER 05

E VELYN MADE HER WAY to her favorite library, not one of those modern ones designed with large expansive windows providing just the right lighting conditions or the sterile systematic layout of bookcases, and the dry, unimaginative seating that vaguely reminded her of a bus station. This one had originally been a large mansion. The rooms were papered with beautiful flower designs, each different from the rest, and framed by dark mahogany reaching upward to the twelve-foot ceilings. The spacious living and dining rooms, the many bedrooms, the sitting rooms, even the food preparation areas, were now all filled with words, with stories, lives lived, and lives imagined, a world now gone but permanently etched into the society left behind.

Although old and musty, Evelyn felt a sense of permanency as she walked the carpeted halls. She had been here many times before and knew where she should go to stay out of the way of any visiting patrons. As Evelyn passed through the front sitting room, now set up as the librarian's checkout desk, the woman never once looked up, being completely unaware she had her first visitor of the day.

In the hallway, she came to the stairs, leading to a second story. The banisters were richly polished, and the steps leading up were covered with worn, but thick carpet; she loved the feel of it. At the top of the stairs, a large hallway led to more rooms, each full of every assortment of books.

Finding her favorite room, she went to the back corner behind a large reading table. It was surrounded by chairs and took up the entire center, but still left plenty of room for the many bookcases lining the walls. An old steam heater, coated through the years with multiple layers of paint, was set against the wall next to her hiding place. It was just large enough to keep Evelyn out of the way, and she knew that most people did not come into the history room anyway.

Looking up, she found the book she had been reading on her last visit. It was The History of the Decline and Fall of the Roman Empire by Gibbon, Edward [1737 - 1794] 2nd edition. She did not know why she liked it. Maybe it was because it made her feel like part of the world if only its history. Maybe, like her, it was because it spoke of things no longer in the world.

She looked at the book's worn surface for a few moments. Holding it close, she breathed in the sweet musky scent. The library was quiet today, and she knew she was safe, but letting her mind wander — well, it might cause problems. Still, it was so quiet and warm; it reminded her of home, of safer times. As she looked at the cover, her mind wandered to the past, back to the days before the end of her life...

JUNIOR HIGH, JUNE 5, 2015

She had practiced for weeks, but just thinking about dancing with a boy at the sixth-grade graduation dance made her so nervous that she felt like crying. So many changes were occurring in her life; she was excited, confused, and frightened; her feelings were changing, her body was changing, and she was often left feeling insecure and confused. Her mom told her it was all very natural, which helped, but did not completely vanquish her concerns.

On the day of the dance, they had left a little early to pick up a friend. She was not a close friend, of course, because Evelyn did not seem to have close ones. However, she was as close a friend as Evelyn had ever had. Her mom was picking up Margaret because Margaret did not have a ride, and Margaret's mother had made her promise to stay with Evelyn at the dance. It was alright though because Evelyn was so nervous she wanted someone to be with her, and it could not be her mom — no way!

She convinced her mom to stay in the car instead of a chair in the dance hall, knowing that she would be taking pictures the whole time if she came in. She wore a white blouse, a black-and-white checkered flared skirt, and a scarf around her neck of the same material. She just knew she would be the prettiest girl there.

Her dad had to work that night, but before he left, he had a chance to see her dressed and said she would put Cinderella to shame. Mom told her that her dad was the wisest man she had ever met, and Evelyn did not doubt it.

Walking side by side, Margaret held her hand until they were out of sight inside the school building, at which point Margaret dropped it and said, "I can't believe my mother said I had to babysit you. Are you going to be okay by yourself? You're not a baby, are you?"

Evelyn froze. Would she be labeled a baby, something that would stay with her all through the upcoming junior high school years, or was she going to accept the almost assured solitude of the school dance?

"You go on; I'll be fine," she said, trying to be brave.

Margaret gave a quick insincere smile before leaving her standing alone in the hall.

Convincing herself that everything was going to be all right, she entered the room. Even though they had started early, her mom had still arrived a few minutes late. The other kids had seated already. She saw a few teachers looking through the music in anticipation of what to play first. Girls sat on one side, boys on the other. All the girls were talking to each other adamantly, being careful not to watch the boys. The boys, on the other hand, were completely silent, most staring down at the floor or studying their hands, probably wondering how they had ended up at the dance, to begin with, even though they must have tried so hard to avoid it. They did not look as much like students as condemned prisoners on death row.

As she walked to one of the chairs on the girls' side, the room fell silent. Glancing at Margaret, she felt her face burning with embarrassment. Before she could sit down, Mrs. Cahill started the introduction.

"Girls and boys, we, the faculty of Donald Elementary, want to congratulate each of you for completing your first six years of school. You have done well, and we know you will continue our proud tradition of excellence in junior high."

The other teachers and assisting parents in the room clapped excitedly.

She continued, "In appreciation of your hard work, we are giving you this wonderful school dance."

The adults began clapping again, even louder this time, which was a signal for the kids to clap also.

Mrs. Cahill raised her hands after a few seconds to quiet the clapping, and in a more ominous tone, one recognized by each child, she said, "Please remember the school rules. There will be no shouting or fighting. Only approved dances are permitted. There will be nothing vulgar or suggestive. If you have any questions about what this means, see me." She paused for effect, looking pointedly at each child in the room before continuing further. "Everyone has to stay in the gym unless you get a restroom pass from Mrs. Yeong; she will issue you one at the door. There will be restroom monitors as well." The serious, no-nonsense expression on Mrs. Cahill's face switched to a pasted smile as quickly as it had previously fallen from her more normal frown. "Now, have a wonderful time and enjoy yourselves." With that, she motioned to Mrs. Hawthorn with a nod.

Mrs. Hawthorn placed a CD into the player, and the dance began. A few of the boys with girlfriends came over and asked them to dance, but most of the guys sat frozen like statues. The girls continued to ignore them, but after the second song, groups of girls started dancing together. This made the guys even more embarrassed; not only were they not brave enough to ask the girls to dance, but the girls would rather dance with each other than them. You could almost hear a collective groan.

Evelyn continued to sit and busied herself by sorting through her purse, though her attention was elsewhere. Every time she saw a boy get up out of the corner of her eye, she thought, "No, no, no, not me!" When they did not ask her, she thought, "Well, what about me?" Eventually, a short red-haired boy with freckles named Ricky came over and stood next to her. She looked down and started concentrating on her shoes with great intensity. She thought her face was going to catch fire from embarrassment before he finally asked her if she would dance with him.

She looked up and smiled as if she had done this a thousand times before. He led her to the center of the room, and they began dancing to the beat.

"You must be in Mrs. Cahill's class," he said.

"Yes," she replied softly, trying not to look at him.

"I guessed as much. I'm in Mrs. Hawthorn's class."

Since there were only two sixth grade classes at Donald, she thought this was obvious, but did not tease him about it. Instead, she tried to compliment him. "You really dance well!"

"Yeah, I know. My sister is in junior high, and she's been teaching me for a long time. I guess I'm her test partner. I usually make her pay me though." He laughed at that.

Evelyn smiled also and started to warm up to him. "I've been practicing too."

He snickered. "Yeah? Well, I think you need a lot more practice. You look like a dancing turtle!" He laughed more loudly.

Evelyn was crushed. She stopped dancing and stared at him.

"Hey!" he said with an angry expression, "Don't stop now. The song isn't over yet."

She tried to start moving again, but he again showed his lack of tact by saying, "Come on! You're out of step with the music. You have got to be the worst dancer I've ever seen!"

She did not think she could have been more embarrassed. Several other kids dancing next to them laughed and appeared to agree.

She stopped dancing again as tears filled her eyes. She wanted to be anywhere else in the world but there in the middle of the dance floor. She was too humiliated to move and covered her face with her hands, to hide the tears.

Someone bumped into her and knocked her down. When she looked up, she saw the couple still dancing as if nothing had even happened. Ricky was walking away to ask another girl to dance.

Completely devastated, she ran out of the room, passing Mrs. Yeong, the teacher at the door with the passes. She did not stop to ask for one, and Mrs. Yeong did not attempt to force her to stay in the room. She figured Mrs. Yeong probably understood and felt sorry for her; she kept tapping her foot to the music and smiling as if everything was as normal as could be.

NEW ORLEANS, LIBRARY—PRESENT

...Evelyn slowly became aware that she had fallen asleep and had awoken to someone stacking books on the table. She had no memory of him entering. Raising her head, she watched as he collected the stack and left the room. The heavy book Evelyn had been holding was now on the floor beside her. While the library was probably one of the safest places to drop it, she chided herself for being so careless. She was getting sloppy. Being completely unaware of the approach of the man and girl this morning confirmed this all too well. She had not remained safe by being careless. Something was changing. Apathy was beginning to dull the urgency she had always felt, an urgency that kept her in a state of constant awareness of her surroundings. Of course, as with loneliness, Evelyn was not a stranger to depression either. Feelings of hopelessness, unworthiness, and even suicide were always there, though just below the surface of some churning obsidian sea of blood, a world of fear and fury. She often felt it staring intently back at her from that dark place like some predatory creature. But she had fought it and would continue to fight for as long as she had strength. She may have hope now, maybe a future.

Reaching for the book, she noticed tears on the back of her hands. These were not strangers either. They often appeared in her world, and she seldom remembered their arrival. Staring at them for a moment, she thought helplessly, how can I continue to do this? How can I continue to fight? She had long ago stopped trying to make sense of it, but there were times when she felt she just had to find out. Why were her parents dead? Why was she still alive? Why couldn't people see her? Or, for that matter, why couldn't anything see her? Even mosquitoes never bothered her anymore. It was as if she no longer existed. A car could roll over her. People could step on her or drop things on her. Someone could slam a door on her. No one would ever warn her of danger. No one would ever see her in front of them. And, no one would ever love her again. She was alone, so utterly, and completely, alone.

But, with John, perhaps there was hope. Evelyn finally picked up the large volume and returned it to the shelf; she no longer felt like reading. This day was turning out to be one of her bad ones. Sometimes they were okay, not often, but sometimes. She desperately wanted today to be the beginning of a new life. Of course, it could never be a normal one, perhaps a life with some happiness though — maybe just a little?

Adjusting the heavy book to align it with the others, she thought again of what would happen if someone were to see the book rise through the air with no supporting hands. Nothing would happen, nothing ever happened. If no acceptable reason offered itself, they would consistently refuse to believe it had even happened. And Evelyn was never an acceptable reason.

In the beginning, she had repeatedly tried to get people to recognize her, to see her, to acknowledge her. Nothing ever worked. If she was the one doing it, they always came up with some other excuse. Evelyn even experimented with ways to force people to see her. She tried to make sure there could be no other explanation than that someone unseen was doing it. Her attempts always failed. No matter how unlikely or illogical, they would always believe the cause was something else. She could not understand it then; she could not understand it now.

Moving from place to place was dangerous, though she had become talented at finding safe areas. Normally, they were places in public where she could remain stationary for long periods of time, or at least until most people were gone. However, sitting quietly in a safe place was boring. Perhaps her favorite spot was the one she had selected in Audubon Park where she had met John.

Since that first meeting with John, she had tried to arrive early, making sure she had as much time with him as possible. She had also spent those weeks talking to him, telling him everything about herself, though it was easier to do that when no one could hear or see you.

She thought about his journal. He always brought it along, and while at first, she had tried not to read it, an unbearable curiosity eventually overcame her respect for his privacy. He kept it inside his backpack. And, even if he didn't always remove it to read or write in, she often found herself sitting next to him with her heart beating rapidly, reading his personal feelings and thoughts. It was probably his diary as much as anything else that began strengthening the bond she was feeling for him. Thinking of him now, she desperately hoped he would return; he had to be there.

Audubon Park was about a mile from the library. With most people at work, the empty side streets provided a relatively safe route. The earlier incident at the playground had given Evelyn an effective wake-up call, and she quickly made her way without incident.

Beautiful mansions bordered the park on the east and west sides. Very old oak trees surrounded by well-kept lawns dotted the south and a par-62 golf course bordered the north. Many of the trees had thick branches that stretched outward for many feet, some almost touching the ground. With an easy jump, she could catch hold of her favorite bough and swing herself over it, safe from any dangers below. Occasionally, she would stand and balance on it, and if she bounced just right, could start it slowly oscillating a few inches up and down. This surprised her. Being small, she was amazed that she could move something so large.

The Park, with its ancient oak trees, had come to her rescue and she loved it. She loved the smell of the freshly cut lawns, the woody fragrance of the leaves and rough bark. She loved the smell of showers on hot summer days and the mist that sometimes lifted like translucent clouds from the grass. Since losing her family, she felt more at home here than at any of the houses she had stayed in. Sometimes, on warm rainy days, she would descend from her tree and splash through puddles like a little girl, sometimes laughing, sometimes crying.

Evelyn knew she was changing and that events had forced her to leave behind the frivolous world she had grown up in. She had tried unsuccessfully to revive the destroyed innocence. She wanted to go to dances and to have boyfriends. She wanted to giggle and laugh and be completely superficial. However, as much as she wanted to be like everyone else, she never would be. She also knew she had to do something about it, or eventually lose her mind.

She had come to recognize that being fit and limber was a survival skill, and thus, exercising had become a serious pastime. Too often, she needed her body to respond quickly. She recognized that this morning's daydreaming was an example of where she was headed and a danger signal that she was giving up. Depression was going to kill her. It had pursued her for months after the murders and had reasserted itself regularly ever since. She needed some purpose other than merely staying alive. She had hope now, but this depression only acted to forestall any of her plans, making her want to surrender.

Evelyn's plan to be with John was a radical one; it was a complete change in the philosophy that had kept her alive for so long. If he returned, it would mark the beginning of a completely different life for her, one where she was not that scared little girl anymore. Perhaps she was wrong in seeing herself as a victim. She had saved that little girl this morning, regardless of the consequences. The experience had been both, frightening and exhilarating, filling her with self-confidence and hope.

Of course, her darkest plan, the one held deep inside, she tried not to contemplate. She knew revenge was wrong. Her parents had always taught her to be a moral, chaste person. Nevertheless, there was a dark burning hovering just below her imagination. It wanted blood; it wanted revenge; and it wanted it with every fiber, every scream, every tear, and every hug, now forever unanswered. She knew it was there, but also knew she had to keep it from surfacing. She feared it would change her into something that she could not control, something that would viciously rule her and remove all goodness and virtue from her heart. She feared that if she ever let it lose, it would change her into something more horrible than even the dark stranger could ever have dreamed of being.

CHAPTER 06

ENTERING THE PARK, EVELYN surveyed the area for workers busy with park maintenance. The heavy-duty lawnmowers were one reason she had to stay off the ground. If she fell asleep, one could seriously injure or kill her, and the driver would never be the wiser. Also, having a 300-pound man step on her without the slightest hesitation was going to break something she wanted unbroken.

Her tree was not too far from the park's edge, close to a winding jogger's trail. Well-kept grassy picnicking areas were nearby. Being able to watch families eating and playing together was a bittersweet experience, for which she longed. She only had to cross one small road to reach the safety afforded by its branches. It was about thirty yards on the other side. She looked at her watch to make sure she was not too late for his visit. She didn't want him to be disappointed. She laughed at the thought. Perhaps he was as close to a boyfriend as she was ever going to get.

She approached the tree and easily sprang for the large oak branch above her head, reaching her legs around it and pulling herself into a sitting position. Brushing her hands off, she noticed the small black ants crawling over her upturned palms. Looking down at the branch, she observed a trail going in all directions, trying to find their chemical path again. Soon they continued their path over her legs as if she was not even there. Perhaps she was not. It was quite amusing. Those things she was once afraid of, no longer bothered her. She could even hold spiders, things that once horrified her. Insects never tried to bite or sting her. Nothing ever tried to hurt her on purpose because she supposed, nothing could be aware of her. Removing fear made the world a very beautiful place.

Evelyn stood, brushed off the ants, and moved along the branch toward the trunk. This tree was their tree, their home, hers and John's. That is how she was beginning to think of it. The old oak was a haven. It was the center of her life. It was the place where she could be with him, and once again believe in dreams. A week ago, she had thought those dreams had ended, but a mysterious yearning drove her forward. Any normal reactions or fears she may have had were too weak to resist its power—and it was exhilarating.

She pulled out a snack and placed the backpack behind her as a pillow. It was a trail bar and was supposed to be healthy. It had oats, nuts, and raisins; she hoped it was. Her mother had been health conscious and always made sure that Evelyn had the opportunity to eat the best foods. She wondered what the last two years had done to her. For a few moments, she stared at the snack and thought of her mother. She missed her so much. Luwanda had always been her best friend. Would she agree with the choice Evelyn was making? As a tear found its way downward, she knew she would. Her mother had given her the strength to make the necessary decisions, keeping her alive for the last two years. Regardless of the future, it would stay with her forever. She sat quietly and waited. This meeting with John was the beginning of her new life. She would not go back to her old one. Being with John had changed her. The horrible revelations of their last meeting had been as frightening as they were wonderful. The scary part was obvious; the wonderful and exciting part was that, somehow, he knew she existed, if only in his dreams.

It was after their last meeting when the best and worst of both worlds had collided, and depression had overcome her. However, with each hour that passed since then, not seeing John became more intolerable. She understood that she could not live without him. Her isolation, fear, and helplessness would end. For good or bad, she would face it. She did not know how these things worked, but she knew she loved him, and incredibly, he had said he thought he loved her too. She could not give that up.

The day after overhearing John's prayer, she had returned to their tree, but he never returned, not that day, nor any of the following. She had no idea what to do. She was beginning to feel desperate, like some caged animal. A crushing weight pressed down on her heart, creating a feeling of desperation that approached a life or death scenario. Her future was dissolving, leaving nothing but a frightening void in its place.

She climbed down from her security — their home — and stood next to the trunk. She watched for him in silence and thought about how they had met and how it had all begun...

SIX WEEKS EARLIER...

Like giant mushrooms, cumulus clouds had begun to build and promised a much rainier afternoon than expected. Earlier that morning, the situation had been different. A cloudless sky had encouraged her to venture out; even the summer's oppressive heat had lessened, inviting her to face the world again.

Staying in the empty house she occupied had become boring. Besides, it looked like someone would be moving in soon. It was not difficult to decide. Like countless times before, it was time to move on.

The first stop was the library to exchange a book. While the tree provided safety, she still needed something to fill the empty hours.

At the park, she climbed their favorite tree, the one with the ready-made back support. Two of the branches formed a depression wide enough for her to lean against without the danger of falling through. She positioned her backpack against the rough bark, creating a comfortable resting spot. Opening the borrowed book, Evelyn had not read many pages before the soft rustling of the surrounding oak leaves gradually lulled her into a light sleep.

Her dreams had ended with the murders, both figuratively and literally. She no longer dreamed — ever. However, hearing a commotion, her eyes opened, and for the briefest moment, she wondered if she might be having one. A young man stood before her. He was standing on the limb she normally climbed. Furthermore, as she sometimes did, he was gently bouncing, causing the thick bough to move up and down a few inches. The fear that accompanied having someone so near, especially when it was a surprise encounter, was completely absent.

Evelyn no longer tried talking to people — what was the use? When necessary, she watched them, she maneuvered around them, and occasionally yelled at them in frustration, but she never talked. This was different. In fact, it was unnerving; she felt excited. She wanted to run to him, as if to a long-lost friend. Embarrassed by these startling feelings, she resorted to humor, instead.

"Hey, buddy, this is my tree, and that's my limb you're bouncing on." No response... hum. More forcefully, "Can't you see the no trespassing sign?" She smiled at his non-responsiveness. "Look, I don't mean to be rude. Having a guy bounce on my tree doesn't upset me all that much, but we do have to pay attention to those privacy laws." Evelyn took a closer look at the young man's features. "Being handsome doesn't give you special privileges. I suppose I could charge you, but perhaps, I should be the one paying; you are quite entertaining."

He stopped bouncing and waited for a moment before descending. Evelyn watched him, nothing moving but her eyes. He walked to the trunk where he had dropped a backpack and removed what appeared to be a lunch bag. Suddenly, aware of the emptiness in her stomach, she contemplated if perhaps he might consider sharing. That would certainly be nice of him.

She continued to observe as he sat next to the trunk and opened his backpack again, this time to retrieve a book. The unusual bond continued to exert its pull. Why? She braced herself, scanning the area to make sure they were alone, before dropping down beside him. Opening the lunch bag, he took out a wrapped sandwich, which to Evelyn's delight turned out to be a hamburger! It had been a while since she had enjoyed one. The last two years had made it difficult for her to dine on her favorite prey; there were just too many people around. After all, even Count Dracula had to creep around in the dark to find his victims. It was tough being a monster.

Kneeling beside him, she watched as he took a large bite of the hamburger and opened the book in his lap. Evelyn swallowed as she watched him chew. It was difficult to decide which she wanted to watch more, his face or the hamburger. She eventually settled for his face. He was handsome in a rough sort of way. His eyes were grayish blue, his nose straight and his lips... Well, it was difficult to tell with his mouth stuffed with hamburger, but before that, they had appeared full and gentle. His hair was light brown with a conservative cut. She thought she might like to run her fingers through it, and even began to reach, but stopped short of touching him. Her face flushed.

Returning her gaze to the sandwich, she decided that a person this big must surely have purchased more than one. Leaning closer, she took one of the fries before investigating deeper into the sack. Yep, there was another. She removed the second hamburger and opened the paper wrapping. Almost lovingly, she brought it to her nose, inhaling softly. The smell brought a sigh of anticipation to her lips. With it still held close to her nose, she looked over the edge of the paper wrapping into his eyes for just a moment before finally taking a bite. It was incredible!

She collapsed back against the trunk and moved into a more comfortable position next to him. Casually, almost offhandedly, she said, "I appreciate the lunch, John." She chewed thoughtfully for another moment before continuing. "How did you know I wanted bacon on mine? You're always so thoughtful." Evelyn smiled.

Taking another fry, she looked up into his eyes again, fascinated by the situation. Here he sat reading, while no more than a foot away, she sat eating part of his lunch and having a make-believe conversation with him. The few times a boy had bothered to notice her in school and ask her out on a date invariably ended as no-shows. It had been more damaging to her self-esteem and pride than any real feelings for them. However, sitting next to John or whatever his name was, felt very comfortable, if somewhat weird. It was a good kind of weird.

For the past two years, she had stayed as far from people as possible, approaching only when necessary. She had no idea why she was behaving and feeling as she was with John, but as she sat watching him, she suddenly became aware of his cologne. Feeling embarrassingly wicked, she slowly moved her nose to his cheek. With the scent suddenly making her senses swim, she blushed again and quickly sat back against the tree. What was going on?

Finishing his first hamburger, he reached for the empty sack, still not taking his eyes off the book. This was the part she hated. Standing and stepping back, she watched. It was always interesting and depressing at the same time. What would he do? What would he think? What story would his mind make up to explain the missing sandwich? It took a moment before a look of confusion spread across his face. For the first time, he looked over to the empty sack, and not believing what his hand had already confirmed, he brought the bag up and peered inside. After a moment of perplexed thought, his eyes opened wider, and he gave a resigned sigh.

"You would think you could trust a guy to get a customer's order right. I guess I'll have to write myself up." He smiled as he placed it inside his backpack. Then, after another moment of thought. "Oh well, I'm getting too fat anyway."

As he stood, she noticed again that fat was not one of the adjectives she would have used to describe him. He looked quite fit, maybe not a gymnast, but fit nonetheless.

Looking at the remainder of the hamburger in her hand, she felt a tinge of guilt. Stealing food was the only way she could get it. Whenever possible, she tried to pay back by collecting shopping carts or helping to stock shelves, and if she ate from someone's home, she did what housework she could. No one ever noticed. In the rare instance where they did notice something strange or impossible, they would simply refuse to believe it.

She watched as he prepared to leave, and it occurred to her that she might never see him again. Incredibly, this filled her with a deep sense of desperation; she did not want him to leave! The surge of emotions frightened her, and she took a step backward. What was happening? Why did it feel like he was abandoning her? Looking again at the hamburger, she tried to think of a way to stop him. She watched as he shouldered his backpack and moved a few steps from the tree before stopping. She reached out a hand and desperately wanted to call to him, but recognized the futility of doing so. If she tried physically restraining him, he would probably experience some insane stress that would be worse than knocking him to the ground. He turned and looked at her. At that moment, she felt like a park statue. With her hand outstretched and her lips parted, desperate to say something, anything to stop him, she found herself frozen in place. It may have been her imagination, but she again felt every muscle in her body locked down as with steel cords. For a moment, he stood looking at the tree; she realized he could not see her. Of course, he could not see her — no one could see her. Tears filled her eyes as he turned and walked away. She felt the binding cords slowly relaxing, allowing her to sink into the grass, her emotions, a virtual storm. What — was — happening? Why was she so heartbroken? She felt as if she had awoken from a dream and was seeing and feeling for the first time in her life. Lifting the hamburger still held in her hand, she looked at it for a long time before realizing she had not given him anything in return. She had stolen from him and had not done anything to repay him.

Looking to where he had disappeared, she said softly, "I'm sorry, John. I'm sorry for stealing your food. I'm sorry for being invisible. I'm sorry for everything."

CHAPTER 07

ALTHOUGH SHE HAD NOT expected to see him again, he came back every day, and on each visit brought something to eat and a book to read. This was also when she discovered that he sometimes wrote in his journal. Although she still felt embarrassed about invading his privacy, it was the link that sealed her love for him.

She found that her tree seemed to be his favorite spot. He would casually walk around the tree, looking at this or that before finally seating himself against its trunk.

Occasionally, she brought a sandwich for him. She discovered that she could replace the one she took without causing her invisibility to kick in. The first time he discovered the switched sandwich, it only caused a moment of confusion before he smiled knowingly and started eating. He never said anything. She could only guess at what story he had made up to explain it. She did not care. She was just grateful to share something with him.

Her days with John were the happiest of her life. Notwithstanding she was only a ghostly apparition, she was able to make-believe, to dream, to talk, and to confide in him, as if he could hear her — as if he could love her.

However, the day finally arrived when the dream ended. He arrived late without lunch or even his backpack. She remained in the tree while he walked around looking at nothing in particular. It looked like his mind was preoccupied, as if something was deeply bothering him. Though he was still standing, she felt certain she knew his movements well enough to stay out of his way, and there was that strange feeling of trust she had when he was around. She dropped softly to the ground next to him as he gazed at the tree's bark, lightly running his hand over its roughness.

Evelyn felt she knew John and perhaps was closer to him than anyone she could think of besides her parents. She realized now that even before she knew anything about him, something drew her to him in a way she could not deny.

As she watched him intently, his uneasiness began to worry her. She had never seen him so upset. She watched him walk several paces away before returning and looking around as if he was concerned that someone might be watching. After a moment, he sat in his usual place, head tilted back against the trunk, eyes closed.

Evelyn remained standing, uncertain of what he was doing. Over time, she had begun to feel that he was becoming more than just a wonderful friend; she had never been in love but felt that if the strength of her emotions was any indicator, she might be now. They had spent many days together, and although communication was rather one-sided, she had told him quite a lot about herself. Of course, she realized it was not much of a relationship.

"I've been having dreams," he said quietly, so low that she was not sure she had heard correctly.

She stared at him for a moment before slowly kneeling next to him.

"I know it makes no sense. I may be going crazy." He was quiet for a moment. "But if I don't find out for sure, one way or the other... I probably will."

Evelyn was now as still as a rock, barely breathing, and if it were possible, her attention now became even more focused on him.

"It's the same dream every night, except different in some ways. It's not like the ones I normally have... these feel so real."

His voice was low, but she could hear each word crystal clear as they imprinted on her heart. Seeing his eyes still shut, she suddenly realized that this was a prayer, and she tried to stand, to move away from him. It was a very private moment, and she felt she should not be listening. However, once again, those strange unbreakable cords of steel bound her tightly. She knelt frozen and knew it was not her imagination. An icy fear began to fill her heart.

"I'm on a hill with only this ancient oak tree offering its cool shade. The sky is as blue as I can ever remember it being. I sit against the trunk reading... and it's the same thing each time. I look up and there she is — standing beside me."

A tear started down Evelyn's cheek as she listened to his impossible words.

"She is clothed in a white gown that gently moves with the breeze as if it has no substance, only light and texture. Her hair is dark and short but so light that it too does not appear to be a part of the world. Her eyes are like emerald oceans, full of life..."

Evelyn could not believe what she was hearing; she did not dare to believe. Her throat felt like it was closing, and she was having trouble breathing.

"I ask her to sit next to me, and she does. I ask her name, but she never speaks. She looks at me with those beautiful eyes, and her smile is like that of an angel, I've never seen such beauty. I talk to her about silly things, stuff about my work, my home. She never answers, but I can tell she is always listening and... I think we are in love."

Evelyn could no longer stand it. The cords that bound her vanished as suddenly as they had appeared, and she put her face into her hands and cried. Her breath racked with sobs, not of sadness, but elation greater than she has ever felt before!

"Heavenly Father," he said, "I don't know what it all means and why the dreams all end the same way. A storm comes. The sky turns dark, almost like a great and terrible bruise covering it. Howling winds begin tearing great limbs off the tree. I'm so afraid... there is lightning and thunder as I've never seen or heard before. Then I look at her — this angel that I thought I loved so much, this angel... has turned into a demon! Her face is full of fury; her eyes are blazing with so much hatred and anger — I can't stand it! I jump up and run. I must escape, but as I run, I hear her voice calling to me. I turn to look. The sky, the oak, and the wind are still in turmoil, and her eyes still blaze, but she is reaching out to me, and there is such sadness on her face. It's like she's asking me to forgive her for some unimaginable wrong she has done. And then I awake." Evelyn watched in horror as tears dropped from his closed eyes. "Please, Dear Father, help me understand this." With that, he bowed his head and cried softly.

The moment had been both tender and terrifying. Evelyn remembered staring at him with a feeling of horror and disbelief. He knew! In some subconscious way, he knew! Moreover, somehow, he knew about the other, that thing she had buried inside, refusing to let it out, fearing to let it out. She had jumped to her feet and started blindly running! In the past, she had always waited for him to leave first, but could not help herself. She was oblivious to the dangers around her. She had to escape; from him, from herself, and from the awful presence buried within her heart.

John never returned. Was she going to follow through with her decision? Could she? Slowly, as if with a mind of their own, her legs began to carry her away from the oak tree, through the grass, and to the small road that she hoped would lead her to John. She passed several groups of workers busy doing various maintenance jobs. Each step she took made her feel more confident than the previous, and soon her determination began to overcome her fear. She had to find him. She would find him!

John had always come from the direction of Saint Charles Avenue, a large boulevard where electric streetcars still operated. It did not take Evelyn long to reach it. Surprisingly, even though she had lived all her life in New Orleans, she had never traveled far from her neighborhood. She was not familiar with this section of town. There were a few businesses across the street that he might work at; she contemplated how she would cross the lanes of traffic to reach them. It should not be that difficult, but she always feared something was going to hit her. However, her excitement rose when she spied the restaurant sign in the next block. It had the same familiar picture that was printed on John's lunch bags.

When she arrived directly across from the restaurant, she waited for the traffic to clear. It wasn't difficult to choose a moment to cross safely, but once she made her decision and started forward, a sudden terror filled her mind, producing an uncontrollable fear that she was about to be hit! She rushed as quickly as she could to the other side, striking the rough brick exterior next to the entrance. Gasping, she placed her back against the brick wall and held onto her bruised hand, looking fearfully at the passing traffic.

Trying to calm herself, she took a few deep breaths. She was safe! Her reaction to such a simple act as crossing the street was completely wrong! She knew it but could not contain the fear. Somehow, she had to get control of herself. She could do this—she had to!

Verifying no one was near her, she turned to the restaurant and pressed her cupped hands to the window. It looked safe, but from experience, she knew that did not mean much. Checking again for anybody that might be headed her way, she made her decision.

Evelyn entered and quickly moved to the side of the entrance in case someone might be headed out. She stood there scanning the room. The place was mostly empty, two people at the counter and one at a small table along the front, no obvious danger. She moved to the farthest table next to a window and looked for a place to hide if anyone should come toward her. The table she chose was next to a soft drink machine with a small space next to it. She could squeeze into it if she needed to; it would do.

The hamburger shop had a dining area large enough for nine tables. There were two on either side of the entrance and one booth in front of each side window. Three larger tables were spaced out in the center of the room. These were normal old-time tables. The type you covered with tablecloths. She wondered that such a place still existed with all the fast food places around.

She had selected the booth closest to the serving counter. The serving counter had several stools where customers could order take-out or have a cup of coffee and maybe some pie or cake. The place was nothing like the large franchise restaurants. It had more of a home-style atmosphere. There were older black-and-white pictures on the back walls showing how the shop had changed in earlier years. Evelyn was impressed. Any place that could still be open after all that time had to be a wonderful place to eat. Even if she did not find him here, she might be able to get something nice to eat in the meantime.

For about thirty minutes, Evelyn sat in the booth watching the last of the customers finish up. No other people came in. She still felt this was the most likely place. It was where he came for lunch each day; the hamburger bags proved that. However, he may not be coming since it was past lunch. If necessary, she could wait here for the rest of the day and sleep here tonight. Hopefully, John would come for lunch tomorrow.

What then, was she just going to follow him home? Her plans were only half-baked, and the truth was that she had no idea how to proceed. What would she do if he came in with a girlfriend? The thought filled her with dread. There was every possibility that he had a girlfriend already. She closed her eyes and frowned. What was she thinking? This whole plan was crazy! Still, she was committed. She would just have to take it one step at a time. The one thing she was sure of was that she was not going back to living the way she had for the last two years! She sat and waited.

As time passed, the restaurant remained empty of customers. Evelyn wondered if this was normal or just because lunchtime was over. The server behind the counter appeared to be getting bored as well. Evelyn watched her wipe down the counter and the various machines several times, and she had already cleaned the table used by the last customer. There seemed to be little to do. Once, she had gone into the back and had talked to someone, but Evelyn had not been able to hear much. When she returned, she started the ritual of wiping down everything all over again. Still, there were no customers.

Evelyn watched the clock as the minutes slowly dragged by and became increasingly disappointed. The chances of John coming by today were dwindling. He had either already come by or was not coming at all. Perhaps, he did not even come here anymore. That thought depressed her even more. If that was the case, how was she ever going to find him?

Finally, after a long interval of no customers, the server came from behind the counter and headed toward Evelyn's table. She carried a cup of coffee, something that had special significance to Evelyn since being scalded last year. Evelyn quickly stood and stepped out of the way to see where the woman would sit. It was on the other side of the booth where she had been sitting. Keeping her eyes on the woman, she cautiously sat back down across from her.

"Hey, Adam!" she yelled. "Can you watch for customers? I'm going to take a break."

"Anything for you, Rose," he called, "You know I'm just your humble servant."

Evelyn's racing heart reacted to the voice before her mind did. Was this John? Could she be that fortunate?

"Yeah, right!" she laughed. "How about taking my shift for the rest of the day while you're at it?"

Adam came through the kitchen door wearing a white apron and a smile bigger than she had ever seen. "You know how much I'd love to do that, but... doctor's appointment, sorry." He continued over to their table.

It was John! He worked here. She could have come to see him anytime over the last couple of months. Moreover, it appeared that she was going to have to start thinking of him as Adam instead of John. That was all right though, calling him John had always felt odd; and now that she thought about it, Adam seemed a better fit anyway, and strangely familiar.

"Yeah, whatever; you still have thirty minutes. How about fixing me one of those great hamburger specials you're so proud of."

He laughed and pulled a hamburger on a saucer from behind his back, setting it in front of her. "Just so happens, I was hoping you would want one."

She gently tapped the table with the palm of her hand and said with a big smile, "You are such a darling! I'll love you forever; now, how about a drink to go with that?"

"Of course, my lady," said Adam, and giving a slight bow, he moved over to the drink machine and poured a Coke. "You want a Sprite, correct?"

"You know I don't."

Returning quickly back to the table, he said, "Okay, I guess it'll have to be Coke then."

"Teaser," she laughed.

Evelyn had listened to this exchange with mounting concern. Could Rose be Adam's romantic interest? She looked more closely at her and recognized Rose's maturity. While it was still possible, Evelyn found herself breathing again. John, or Adam rather, was quite a charmer. She would have to get used to the name after spending so much time thinking of him as John. Being a charmer might mean he had plenty of other romantic interests though. Wait a minute, she thought. What was she thinking? What did it matter? She was even less than a ghost to him. She would probably always have to be content with being his dream girl; that was the only place where he would ever see her.

Evelyn was startled as Adam began to sit down on her. She had become so comfortable around him that it took her completely by surprise. She desperately moved over against the window, trying to give him as much room as possible, but he scooted over some more as if the window seat was his favorite. As he bumped softly against her hip, he stopped for a moment, looking a little confused. Rose was still talking about how sweet he was, but Evelyn could see that Adam was concerned about something. He moved a little closer to Evelyn, pressing harder to her hip and stopped again, a strange look coming over his face.

Evelyn bit her lip softly and stared into his blue eyes as he looked through her.

"Hello? Hello? Are you there?" Rose patted his arm.

"Huh? What?" Looking back at Rose in confusion, he moved back a little, giving Evelyn a little more room.

"Customer," Rose whispered to him.

"Oh! Sorry, sir," Adam apologized as he jumped up and hurried to the counter. "Let's see if I can make my little indiscretion worthwhile for you. You will not be disappointed!"

The older man, a long-time friend of his father, laughed and said, "That's okay, son, your father was the same way." Both laughed as Adam went to fix his order.

"Ten minutes, Rose, and I'm out of here."

"I got it, pretty boy," Rose said as she continued to look out the window at nothing in particular.

Evelyn watched the customer and noticed that he appeared to be upset. When Adam finally came out of the kitchen for something under the serving counter, the older man said, "Hey, Adam, you know that I didn't mean any disrespect to your father, right? He was a good friend, and I would have done anything for him."

Adam said, with about as much kindness as Evelyn had ever heard, "Greg, you were my father's best friend. I know you loved him. I don't take any offense at anything you say, now or ever."

There were tears in the old man's eyes as he continued, "He was like a son to me, Adam. I just don't want to say anything disrespectful about him; I'll always miss him."

Adam patted him on the back. "I know you will. You'll always be my friend as well." They looked steadily at each other for a few seconds before Adam smiled and said, "Now get those rickety old bones over to that table so I can finish your burger!"

Greg turned and headed to the table mumbling something about "smart-aleck kids."

Adam laughed from the kitchen. "What's that you said?"

"Nothing," he said, as a smile spread across his face.

Adam laughed even louder.

Then Greg responded with, "I'll tell you what, just as soon as I get my burger," and he chuckled.

Looking like she was headed to the gallows for her hanging, Rose got up from the table and walked back to the serving counter. As she took up her post next to the register, another person came in and headed for the kitchen. He went past Rose and through the kitchen door without as much as a nod to her.

"Good afternoon to you too, Ralph," said Rose.

"Hey, Adam, you owe me, man!"

"Ralph, I'll owe you for the rest of my life," replied Adam.

"I don't want you to owe me for the rest of your life! I want you to pay up now, preferably before I die."

"Hey, Ralph, don't be so hard on me. Don't I let you date all my girlfriends?"

"Yeah, that reminds me!" said Ralph. "Stacy says she doesn't even know you and wanted to know where you got her phone number from!"

Adam laughed. "Did you enjoy yourself?"

Ralph gave a half-smile. "Well, sure, she was a real lady. I don't figure I've ever seen someone dance so well."

"There you go!" said Adam. "Account closed."

"Now wait a minute," said Ralph, his voice rising.

"Just kidding, buddy, don't get excited." Adam laughed, taking off his apron and hat. "Tomorrow's payday; I'll pay you first thing before your shift's finished." Adam opened the kitchen door and, turning back to Ralph, said with a suddenly serious look on his face, "I appreciate the help, Ralph; I need this."

"Yeah, sure, get on out of here." Ralph smiled. "I'm just riling you."

"Rose," said Adam in passing, "I'll be here to pick you up after work and take you home."

"That's alright, got a date tonight. Bernie will be over to do the honors."

"Are you sure? You know I don't mind coming back."

"No, really, he's picking me up in his new Toyota."

Adam stopped dead in his tracks at the door. "His new Toyota...

that piece of junk is twenty-five years old! I'd better be here to pick you up or at least take you both out on that date..."

Rose laughed. "Get out of here, silly!"

CHAPTER 08

ISTENING TO THE EXCHANGE between Adam, Rose, Ralph, and the older guy, Evelyn could not help being drawn into Adam's world. Everything she had learned about him in the park was real; there was no fakery.

During these exchanges, Evelyn had gradually worked her way around to stand next to the door. Even though she could have just opened it and walked out, she never felt comfortable having people make excuses for why she could not exist.

When Adam left, she followed closely behind him, and from habit, she quickly took inventory of the pedestrian traffic. They were alone. She had no idea where Adam was going except that it was an appointment with his doctor. She did not even know if he had to walk or ride the bus, or even if he owned a car. She was nervous and a little frightened but excited to be with him, and she was determined.

She did not have to follow him very far before he stepped into the street next to a small Dodge. It looked old and covered by a fair amount of rust. When he opened the driver's door and got in, she quickly entered the rear passenger side, closing it with a bit too much force. The resulting sound did not worry her because she knew he probably would not hear it anyway. However, as soon as it closed, he jerked his head around to look in the rear seat area, and then outside to see who might have slammed the door. Exiting the car again, he walked around and looked in both directions. No one was near enough to have jumped out and run away that fast. He ran his fingers through his hair and returned to the driver's seat. Evelyn sat quietly looking at him, wishing he could see her — if only he could see her.

After driving several blocks, he gave the back seat another quick look. Evelyn noticed he gave the rearview mirror much more attention than anyone she had ever seen and wondered if that was normal for him or if he was just nervous about something. He had said the appointment was to see a doctor. She hoped the reason was not serious. Her feelings for Adam had increased in intensity almost daily since she had met him. Her life was strange, even Twilight Zone strange, but with all that had happened, she still could not understand her almost desperate attraction to him — she was beginning to feel a possessiveness that frightened her. Was she stalking him? She had seen movies and read books of people doing that, and it was always bad, but was that what she was doing? He had no way of knowing she was there except for his dreams.

The trip lasted only about fifteen minutes before he turned into a medical center. Parking the car, he turned off the engine but did not immediately get out. He just sat still for a while, occasionally looking in the rearview mirror.

Then he said quietly, "You know I'm going nuts, right?" He was looking in the mirror again, and it seemed like he was staring directly at her.

She said nothing.

"I've got this theory; it's crazy, but it still feels right. Come to think of it; I must already be crazy if I'm talking to you." He rubbed his face with both hands and let them slide over his head. "The doc says I'm just having some neurosis caused by the death of my father. Of course, that's just the type of thing a psychiatrist would say. You tell them someone is haunting you, and they immediately think your mother beat you as a kid, or it's your father's death that has scrambled up your mind."

Evelyn felt the blood rush from her face as she realized what had happened. Adam was going to the doctor because of her. She was the one hurting him; she was the monster! She had become so comfortable with not being seen that she never imagined it would hurt him. Not only had she given him nightmares, but he believed he was being haunted, something stressful enough to drive him to a psychiatrist. I'm so sorry! I should never have started talking to you. I never knew you would be able to suspect somehow. It wasn't real. It was just a stupid dream. Please don't be hurt—please don't believe I'm real. She thought this, but her heart rebelled. Evelyn knew she did not want him to forget her—not now, not ever. She truly was a monster. It would be better if she were dead.

Like her entire life, this was turning into a mess, and it was becoming insane! What was she thinking? Was she going to cause him to become ill or lose his mind over some horrible nightmares? Nothing was going right. She did not want to hurt him, even if it meant she had to go away. This last thought caused a desperate sob to escape her lips.

"The way I figure it, if I'm crazy, the doc should be able to fix it. If not, you and I need to do some serious communicating before I completely lose it." He looked at his watch. "Okay, this is it. Let's see what the doc has to say." He opened the door and got out but stood there a few seconds before closing it. She then watched as he came around to her door and opened it.

Evelyn didn't move. How could this be happening? What was he doing?

"I just wanted you to know that I believe in being a gentleman for the ghost ladies too." With that, he closed it and said, "Okay, let's go.

She waited inside the car until he opened the front door to the clinic. Again, he paused for a moment as if waiting for someone to enter before allowing the door to close behind him.

She had not intended to go with him, but everything was becoming so strange that she couldn't prevent herself. Jumping out of the car, she ran to the front door and opened it. He was standing about ten feet inside the hall, just looking at the door. It slowly closed on the air cushion before clicking. She stared at him, not knowing what to think.

"You see? I figured you weren't with me. I'm starting to have this feeling when you're around. It's hard to explain. I should talk to the doctor about it. Well, perhaps not; he already thinks I'm nuts." He laughed. "I have to agree with him, of course, but being crazy is not nearly as interesting as being haunted. At first, I thought maybe it was just the oak tree that made me feel so good. But then, there were days that I didn't feel it and days I did. I started doing some experiments of my own, and once the dreams started, I knew either I was going crazy, or you were real. As it stands right now, the score is two to zero that I'm crazy. But..." He paused. "I hope I'm not." He said this last part almost in a whisper. Pressing the elevator button, he waited a moment for the door to open.

Evelyn did not know what to think or say. She only knew that her heart was on fire. She could not remember being so happy and frightened at the same time. As he stepped into the elevator, she quickly moved beside him before the door closed. She was afraid of doing anything that would cause him further stress. What would happen if she somehow scared him? She could not stand the thought of Adam being afraid of her. He seemed to be noticing her presence. Was it possible? Was she just imagining it? It was a dream too wonderful to contemplate, but somehow it must be true; she wanted to believe it so much!

The elevator only went up one floor before opening, and Adam walked out into a small lobby. She followed him to the receptionist, trembling slightly.

"Good afternoon, Miss Stewart. Am I late?"

Miss Stewart looked at the clock and said with a smile, "I thought I told you to call me Barbara, Mr. Yates."

"I'd be happy to, just as soon as you start calling me Adam," he said with a broad grin.

Miss Stewart, who was probably in her late fifties, said in a drawn-out southern accent, one she did not have a moment before, "Now, Mr.

Yates, you know a girl like me has tender feelings. If I start calling you by your first name, you might want to ask me out or something." She fluttered her eyelashes at him and then said in her normal voice, "As usual, you're right on time. Doctor Elliot said to send you in as soon as you arrived." Standing, the receptionist walked to a closed door across the room and opened it. "Doctor Elliot? Adam is here." She again fluttered her eyelashes at Adam and gave him a Cheshire grin before returning to her desk.

Adam thanked Miss Stewart and entered the office. The doctor was one of those men that at first sight, you thought appeared too young to have a practice of his own. As you took further notice, his age became more apparent. He was kind and personable, and in truth, he was probably about the age of Evelyn's father when he — No, she wasn't going to start traveling down that ugly path right now!

Doctor Elliot quickly came from behind his desk to shake Adam's hand. "I'm glad you could make it, Adam. I was afraid after our last visit that you might have decided to tackle this on your own. We have been making great progress these last few weeks. Please, sit and make yourself comfortable."

There were two couches and a chair in the office. Adam knew which was his. Evelyn watched him cross the room and take his seat on the couch. She noticed that Adam appeared a little nervous and decided to sit next to him. She had long since become very comfortable by his side; now that she also knew he was suffering, she was becoming protective as well, even if she was the reason for that suffering.

The doctor picked up a notepad off his desk and brought it over to sit in the chair next to Adam.

"How have you been doing this week, Adam? Has business improved any?"

Adam smiled. "It could be better. It could be a lot better. We still have some regulars, but that's it. Sales are too low to pay the bills, and I have to use the insurance money just to meet payroll."

"How about school, have you decided to quit until you get the restaurant going again?"

Adam was quiet for a moment before answering, "I've been trying to convince myself that there was hope, but I think I've been kidding myself. Nothing I do is increasing traffic enough to make it profitable. I'm not ready to quit yet. However, if this doesn't turn around soon, I may not be able to avoid it." Adam then looked the doctor in the eye and said, "Not to be rude or insensitive, but Doc, the amount I have to pay for these sessions is not making it any easier." A subtle expression of surprise briefly touched the doctor's face, and Adam smiled to soften his comment. "Naturally, they are important for me. Nothing is more important than one's mental health, right, Doc?"

"Adam, life is full of challenges. You have experienced some great tragedies in your relatively short one. That is not to say that others have not, but a person's trials are uniquely personal and should never be compared to the suffering of others. Sometimes it is difficult to see how these experiences can make us stronger, but they can. In the last couple of years, you have lost your entire family, you have a failing business, and you must decide on whether to quit your business or your education. That is a lot to cope with for anyone. On top of that, the strain has begun to affect your emotional stability. It is no small wonder that your condition isn't worse. You are a very strong young man, and while you are improving, you must address this developing emotional issue. You can be the most successful man in the world, but if you lose yourself in the process, you have failed." Doctor Elliot waited a moment for Adam to say something, but he remained quiet. "Do you understand what I'm saying?"

Adam looked up at him and said, "Yes, I understand, and I very much appreciate your help."

The doctor continued, "Good. There are a few things I want to touch on today, and as usual, I want you to try to be as honest about your feelings as possible. Okay?"

"Sure, Doc."

"Fine, to begin with, have you taken my advice about staying away from the park?"

Adam grinned. "Actually, yes, I have, and it has produced some pretty good results. I'm glad you suggested it."

"Excellent," Doctor Elliot said. "As I said last week, the park and that tree you stop at appear to instigate feelings and thoughts that worsen your depression. We are looking for environments that will stimulate and strengthen your self-image. I'm happy you followed the advice. How are the dreams now?"

Adam's countenance brightened. "Doctor, it's just amazing! After I stopped going there, they just stopped. However, the strange thing is that after they stopped, I had time to think about it, and they didn't seem as bad as when I had them every night. You know how I said that there was a bad part and this very good part? Well, thinking back to the dreams now, I can't remember the bad parts very well. I know it must have been bad enough for me to start coming here, but now that I stopped dreaming it, it's not as disturbing. The only part I remember is the first, where this girl is next to me. I've got to tell you; she's special."

Doctor Elliot looked at Adam a moment before scanning his notes.

Evelyn saw him turn back several pages before saying, "Adam, I would like you to recount what you have told me about the dreams? Can you do that? Would you mind repeating what you remember?"

"Certainly, Doc. In the dream, I'm sitting on this hill under a large oak tree. I mean it's huge, probably a thousand years old, who knows? It's much like the one I told you about at Audubon Park; only that one is not nearly as big or old of course. I'm sitting there looking at a stunningly beautiful sky and watching these clouds. I remember there was a breeze, and I feel like everything is precisely as it should be. Then, there she is standing next to me. Wow! She's wearing this white gown of some extremely delicate material; maybe it's pure light, I couldn't tell. And her face is like…incredible. She could have been an angel for all I know." Adam laughed.

The doctor smiled as he jotted down a few notes before urging Adam to continue.

"Right... well, as I said, there she is sitting beside me as if she would rather be there than anywhere else in the world. I tell her about everything, losing my mother and sisters last year in the crash, the death of my father this year, about my business, my school, even the dreams of what I want to do in life. She just sits there with this gentle smile, but never says a thing. Still, I know she's listening to every word. I can feel the love coming from her like... I don't know — it's like a radiance meant just for me. It's fantastic, Doc, it's the best dream I've ever had in my life. To be honest, I've considered going back to the tree to see if it would start the dreams going again. However, if the frightening part was extreme enough to send me here, it can't be a clever idea, right?"

Evelyn did not know what to think of his dreams. In some way, she might be the one causing them. If she could do that, perhaps she was also the one causing her invisibility! Was it possible? Since the murders, she had lived in a world where no one could see her. No, not just not see her, in most cases, they would not have even been able to recognize that she might have caused something. It was beyond insane! Moreover, it was never cut and dry; the severity of her invisibility seemed to be determined by how the person reacted to the incident as if it were under intelligent control.

Doctor Elliot finished writing on his pad and set it down on a small table between them. "Adam, so you say you originally came here because there was more to the dream than what you told me just now, and that it was so terrible that it caused you to seek professional help?"

Adam stared at him a moment. "I don't understand. Of course, that's what we have been talking about. What are you saying, Doc?" Adam was becoming frustrated.

"Well, Adam, we may have a few more sessions to complete before I can decide on your progress. I have all my notes here, and in none of them do you mention this. You spoke about your reoccurring dream. You said it was bothering you, but you never said anything about it being frightening."

Adam just stared at him a moment before asking, "There was nothing about a... a... I can't remember, but it was bad Doc; that, I do remember." He looked at the doctor for help, but he had nothing to say.

Doctor Elliot changed the subject, and they talked about his sisters and mother for a while. He wanted to know how Adam was getting along with his friends and if he had ever contacted any of the resources given to him. After about forty-five minutes, he looked at his watch again. "It's okay; I think you're making fine progress. Can we meet again next week? I believe Miss Stewart has you preset for twelve sessions."

Adam's mind kept going back to what the doctor had said about the dream and what he had originally told him in the beginning. "Doc, how could I have just imagined it? Can I be that sick?"

"Adam, it's alright. These things sometimes take a while to sort out. I will be here to help. I promise we will get it all taken care of." He laughed gently, "Believe me, I've been doing this for many years, and I haven't lost a patient yet."

Adam looked down with his head cradled in his hands.

"It's going to be fine." Doctor Elliot looked at his watch again. "Let's call it a day and take this up next week. I'll let Miss Stewart know." He stood up, which was Adam's signal that the session had ended.

Evelyn stood and quickly walked to the small table where the doctor laid his notes. As Doctor Elliot was escorting Adam out into the lobby, she opened the pad and scanned it. There it was—all of it. The entire dream, recorded in detail, and the doctor could not see it. Once again, she was preventing someone from seeing what was right in front of their eyes. She quickly dropped the pad and hurried out of the office.

Doctor Elliot was speaking to Miss Stewart about Adam's next appointment, and she could see the elevator just closing with Adam inside. Running to the stairs, she rushed quickly but carefully. Falling was not an option. If she broke something, she would not be able to get help.

She reached the entrance lobby as the elevator doors shut. Adam stood with his eyes closed, the fingers on his right hand slowly massaging his forehead. He looked disheartened. As Evelyn's mood began to mirror his, she watched as his hand stopped rubbing, but remained in place.

He opened his eyes and said, "Are you there? You must be; I felt nothing as I came down the elevator and stepped out, but now... I'm not sure what I'm feeling, but it feels the same as I've felt dozens of times in the park. For a moment — for a moment, I thought my delusions had left me for good, and that the doc was right." He stood quietly, his arm returning to his side. "Perhaps I am crazy, or depressed, or emotionally unstable, whatever Doc wants to call it, but I find myself not wanting to give this up — I want it to be real," and then, almost in a whisper, "Are you real? Are you there?"

From somewhere deep within her, an immense pressure began to build, and Evelyn felt her legs move her slowly forward, almost with a will of their own, carrying her to stand before him, so near that she could feel his breath. There was no thought of the possible danger she might be in should Adam choose to walk forward. It was both frightening... and something else — she was burning. Her head settled against his chest, her arms gently wrapping around his, pinning them to his sides. She was frozen. She could no more move than one of the statues at Audubon Park. However, the deep freeze that held her in place did nothing to quench the molten fire within her. She was horrified to feel so powerless, but at the same time, she knew there was no place she would rather be.

Time appeared to stand still for Evelyn, and she had no sense of how long they remained so, neither moving, both as still as statues. Certainly, someone would have come and witnessed the strange scene if it had been very long.

Gradually, she felt her surroundings melt and the fire within cool. As if awakening from a dream, she felt her will return, and her arms gradually release Adam. Stepping back, she looked into his eyes. His expression was unreadable; his tear-filled gaze looking somewhere only he could see. What was happening to him — what was happening to her?

CHAPTER 09

REMOVING HIS HANDKERCHIEF, Adam wiped his eyes and returned to his car. His previous words filled Evelyn with hope, but the intensity of her actions had frightened and confused her. She felt at war with herself, a condition she had grown familiar with over the past two years. However, the continuous battle was changing her in subtle ways; she worried whether the changes were good or evil.

As she joined him in the front seat, Adam continued his silence, showing no awareness of the passenger side door opening and closing. She knew she should be nervous; she was always nervous. She considered it a survival trait. Nevertheless, her commitment to Adam was complete, something of which she was positive. Still, it made no logical sense. Looking at the entire relationship made no sense. It even left her feeling as if she, herself, may be losing her sanity. The only thing clear in her mind, and it was clearer than anything she had ever known, was that if she left him, she had no reason to live.

Evelyn did not know their destination, but it was unimportant as long as she was with Adam. As he drove, she settled back against the soft interior of the seat and watched the city pass before her. Gradually, her thoughts returned to her past. It was ever with her and commanded her attention in so many ways. She tried to understand what the recent events might mean. She knew Adam suspected that someone was with him if only a ghost. She doubted his suspicions though; ghosts were not supposed to feel pain and discomfort, or were they? Since the very beginning, she had experienced both. However, this might not preclude the possibility that she was dead. In her mind, being dead and being a ghost could be mutually exclusive. Was it possible to be dead and not know it? Had anyone ever experienced this before it happened? She thought not. Who could know what it was like to be dead without being dead? What if the god everyone always talked about hated her for not believing in him? What if he had sent her to some hell and it was never going to end?

Evelyn felt a cold chill of panic slither up her spine and turned to look desperately at Adam. In that instant, the feeling died as quickly as it had begun. Only its memory remained, a memory shrouded in a comforting blanket of warmth. Even so, her eyes remained glued to his. What was happening? She felt a battle raging—one she was losing. Moreover, what was the sudden comforting warmth that gave her the strength to continue, but to continue what? Who was she fighting? With whom was she at war?

As she watched him, she tried to organize her thoughts. She believed that Adam Yates was the most wonderful thing that had ever happened to her, and she was completely in love with him. However, maybe it was more than that. He was her connection with the world. He was the only person that had responded to her in even the smallest way. He was everything to her, but how could he be in love with her? He had never seen or spoken to her except within his dreams. Could you love a dream? She knew she was ignorant about being in love, especially about how men felt about it. About her feelings, she was positive, but even that did not make a lot of sense. Did it make sense for anyone? She had spent many hours, days even, talking to him about herself and even listening to his prayers. Evelyn knew it was a terrible invasion of his privacy, but could never stop herself. The more time she spent with him, the more she felt like a moth drawn to a flame. It was not often that young people, or old ones for that matter, were able to know someone as privately as she felt she knew him. Okay, that might explain her feelings, but why was he in love with her?

As Adam parked next to what she assumed was his home, a sickening thought occurred to her, and she inhaled sharply! She immediately began to break out in sweat and felt cold and clammy. A singular thought filled and consumed her. She barely restrained a scream as the logic of her thoughts raced towards a precipice she desperately wanted to avoid. What if she was somehow controlling what people thought, and she was the cause of everyone not seeing her? Was it possible that she was forcing Adam to fall in love with her against his will? Tears filled her eyes, and she felt a crushing pain in her chest! If this were true, she was indeed a monster! Could it be that he had no choice? If she could stop him from seeing her, then why not force him to love her! What kind of a demon would do that? If this were true, then she was the worst kind!

Evelyn could only watch in horror as Adam left the car and made his way to the front door. He did not pause or go through any of the theatrics performed earlier outside the doctor's office. Instead, he walked immediately into his house and closed the door.

Evelyn sat in the car sobbing uncontrollably. She felt a pain building in her chest and felt as if she was dying, wanting to die, to stop existing! The fatal logic repeatedly looped in her head faster and faster. With no thought or reason, she cried out to the only one that might be listening, if he existed and if he cared! God – don't let this be true! Don't let me hurt him! Please, not him! As the inescapable trap of Evelyn's logic slammed shut, the conclusion solidified into blood red granite, and her mind fell like a house of cards.

"Kill me!" she screamed at the top of her lungs, anguish filling her soul! "Please, kill me... don't let me do this! Please... help me... I love him, I love... The burning pain in her chest spread outward through her arms and legs, and like molten steel, it charred everything it touched, until only blackness remained. Nothing of Evelyn survived except a single point of light and an intense feeling of gratitude that she had been allowed to protect him — she would no longer be his monster.

Evelyn opened her eyes and looked at the dashboard. For a moment, she watched dust particles suspended in the hot interior of the car. She had no idea where she was; maybe she had stopped to get a nap in an unlocked vehicle. She sat up and looked around. Sweat slowly dripped down her face and neck; she had been sweating for some time and felt her face pulsing from the heat. She looked in the rearview mirror to find her face a bright red and her hair wet with perspiration. As her eyes refocused beyond the mirror, she noticed Adam's house and with it, the memory of him disappearing through the front door, followed by the memory of everything else. However, she now felt different about it, like looking back on something that had occurred years before. There did not appear to be any rational reason not to believe she was a monster, but a strong conviction filled her heart that she did not have the power to make Adam love her. She could accept that. She desperately wanted to believe it. Being a monster was one thing she could accept, hurting Adam was another thing entirely. Of course, she couldn't make him love her; he was much too strong for that. Forcing a person not to see was easy compared to making him love you — right?

She swallowed hard and turned to look around the neighborhood before stepping out of the car. His house was not very large but well kept. Azalea bushes grew on both sides of the front steps with flowers lining the front of the neatly cut yard. A bench swing hung on one side of the entrance and a wooden rocking chair on the other. Though the house was not very big, Evelyn had the feeling it might feel that way to Adam, now that his family was gone, also taken by tragedy it would appear.

She walked onto the porch and stood before the entrance, wondering if he had locked it. The hanging bench swing was painted white, but the chains were rusty. It appeared unused and abandoned, and left her feeling strangely sad. She reached out her hand and gave it a gentle push. A family used to sit there. There were happy conversations with friends and neighbors. Where were they now?

Turning back to the front door, she took the brass doorknob in her hand and gently pressured it to turn. The door was unlocked. Pushing slowly, she opened it wide enough to allow her to enter. Would Adam be waiting for her? She stepped inside and found he was not. Of course, he would not be; he probably came inside a couple of hours ago. She closed the door and stood quietly.

The living room looked more like a reception area to entertain guests than a warm place used to congregate and do family things. It had a comfortable looking cloth couch and an easy chair next to a coffee table. Except for a small assortment of figurines and a few books in the bookcase, he did not appear to use it. A narrow carpet covered the living room's beautiful wood-planked floor from the front entrance to the next room, which was the dining area.

Evelyn listened for any sounds that might indicate Adam's presence. There were none. Nothing broke the silence except for the rhythmic beat of an old grandfather clock. She was no stranger to entering unfamiliar houses, whether they housed people or not, though she preferred empty ones. However, this was Adam's home, and that made it the most special place in the world. Everything she looked at belonged to him.

Evelyn had supposed she was going to stay with Adam forever. However, with her recent doubts and fears, she was confused. Instead of thinking of his house as her new home, she was feeling like an intruder. It felt like she should stay in the living room for the present; going into the rest of the house would be too much of an invasion of his privacy. She thought about that for a moment and concluded that even being in the living room was an invasion. Still, she could not bring herself to venture farther into the house, at least not yet. Sitting on the couch with her backpack and not knowing what else to do, she waited.

The evening dragged on, but the house remained quiet. Adam had not come into the living room, nor had Evelyn heard any movement yet. Perhaps he had already gone to bed.

She reached into her bag and pulled out a sandwich from the thermal pouch. So much had occurred today, and she was feeling like an emotional wreck. It did not take long to discover she was much hungrier than she had supposed, and one item followed the next until her backpack was empty.

Having a full stomach improved her disposition, and the negativity of her earlier mood seemed out of place now. Things were not as dreadful as she had felt earlier, but what was she going to do? She believed that he would want her here, and she felt confident that if he was in love with her, like he said, it was his idea and not from some power she might have over him, other than the magic that any girlfriend might have. She smiled at the thought of being his girlfriend. If it was that sort of power, well, that was okay.

She recalled some of the techniques she had used when attempting to get people to see her. Of course, they had all ended in dismal failures. One of her early attempts, especially upsetting, had happened at an all-night grocery store. Most of the customers were gone and the night crew was restocking the shelves. Approaching a young man arranging soup cans, she tried to get him to notice her. As he pulled a can to the front, she pushed it back. The first time he watched a can move to the rear, he simply pulled it back. She tried it again, and he stared a moment before shaking his head and repeated his actions. When Evelyn pushed it a third time, he pulled out a cell phone and began texting a message to a friend. He texted a few lines about missing her and wanting to go to the movies with her on Friday. Putting his cell away, he again pulled the can forward. In frustration, Evelyn took the can and held it right in front of his eyes. He looked at it a few seconds before continuing to straighten the others. Angrily, she pushed the can up against his forehead, causing a temporary dent above his eyebrow, but to no avail; he continued to work as if everything was normal.

Ultimately, if she did something that someone saw, heard, felt, smelled, or tasted, and they could not explain it in a manner that did not include her existence, they ignored it. She was worse than invisible; she was unperceivable to an impossible degree. Her junior and senior high school experiences seem mild by comparison.

Evelyn yawned and sunk more deeply into the couch, attempting a more comfortable position. She listened to the wall clock as it slowly ticked away the seconds, unusually loud in the quiet house. It was not long before she fell into a restless sleep.

She slammed the door behind her, hoping she would not be discovered. She waited and waited, gasping for air with her head against the icy black surface, her hand clenched at the knob, desperately trying to keep the door from opening. Eventually, she was able to catch her breath but slowly sank to the ground from exhaustion – and time passed.

She had run an infinite number of times and each time she had been returned. But she was determined and knew that even if it took until the end of time itself, she would never give him up.

Lifting her head, she looked around and saw that the ground was covered with grasses and flowers of every possible hue, from the warmth of radio waves to the exciting sharpness of gamma. The sky was a deep blue, and as she stood, she saw that the world was covered in a blanket of them for as far as she could see. She felt a breeze blow gently across her face, carrying the most delicious scents — especially a very familiar one. Suddenly, she realized that this was his world! She had found him; it was his! He was here! She started running through the fields, searching — and time passed.

She had been searching forever without finding him, but his scent remained in the air; she knew she would not fail this time. Her feet passed over the flowers leaving neither footprint nor broken stem. Her passage was quick and seemingly endless until she came upon a hill. The entire world had been flat until then, and she realized with excitement that this one small hill was the center of everything.

Growing on top was a very large oak tree, with branches that stretched out over the ground as well as the sky. She climbed until she stood under it and placed her face to the trunk, breathing in deeply. It was his! Did he place it here for her? She sat back against the trunk and looked off into the distance closing her eyes — and an eternity passed.

Opening them again, she observed something wrong with the leaves; they looked stiff and dry. He would not come if it died or became sick! She had to water it!

At the base of the hill, she observed a clear stream and sitting on a stone beside it was a water pitcher. She would keep his tree alive. He would know that she was not bad. She would water it, and when he came, he would know that she loved him and would never hurt him.

She filled the pitcher and watered the oak each day, watching and waiting for him — and time passed.

And then one day — he was there. Running as quickly as she could to the top, she looked at him sitting with his back pressed against the trunk. He turned to look at her, a smile spreading across his lips, and asked her to sit with him.

"I've been waiting for you," he said.

She tried to speak, but nothing would come forth. She tried to tell him she loved him and that she was not like her sister. She wanted him to know she was not bad and that she would never hurt him or let her sister harm him, but nothing would come out of her mouth.

Adam reached for her hand and said, "I want to tell you that I love you. I love you more than I ever thought I could love anyone. And, I feel like I have known you forever." He turned and pointed to the tree. "Maybe we can live here. I can make us a home at the top. Would you like that?"

And with that one simple question, she was able to speak. "I would love that, Adam; it's a wonderful place for a home. But, how can you love me? I'm

*not a nice person. I have horrible feelings inside, so terrible that they frighten
me. I think I'm going to hurt someone." And then, looking up at the tree, she
said, "Of course, I would love to live here with you, but could you forgive me
for being a monster?"*

*Adam brushed the back of his hand softly against her cheek and said, "Can
you trust me?"*

Evelyn opened her eyes and saw that the sun had set. The living
room was dark except for the light from a street lamp, its glow dimly
entering the front curtains. She reached up to her cheek and felt lingering tears. Had she had a dream? Was it even possible for her to dream
anymore, and if so, why could she not remember them?

She stood and went to the dining room entrance, standing there for
a moment. Adam must be asleep by now. It would do her no good to
stay in the living room. If she was going to stay at all, she needed to
settle in. She knew she would never leave him if there were even a
chance that he loved her.

She discovered that there were four bedrooms, a bath, a living room,
a dining room, and a kitchen. Each bedroom had its own neatly made
bed, three singles and a king-sized one in the master bedroom.

She found Adam asleep in one of the singles. To her relief,
he wore pajamas. She was relieved to know that she was not going to
have to be embarrassed every time he went to bed or walked around
the house. Even though he was the only one here, he was modest. Maybe it was a habit of growing up with sisters. His journal mentioned at
least two. From the decorations, she guessed one was young enough to
play with dolls. The thought of his family also being taken made her
feel even more compassion for him. Because of that, she felt she knew
his pain and could not bring herself to break the solemnity of the family
bedrooms. Even though he would probably never see them as being
disturbed, if he had not done so for all these months, she was not going
to disturb them either.

Evelyn considered sleeping on the couch. She found a sheet and
blanket but stood indecisively in the hallway. For the last two years, she
had been alone. She had nothing anymore, especially family or friends.
She had been lonely for a very long time. Living with Adam was a new
life for her, and although it would present problems, she was committed. She could not go back.

Walking to his room, she found a sofa bench beside his bed. Next to
it sat a small table with a lamp. Finally, he had a small desk in the corner. In the past, she had always found ways to be alone, even when
sharing a house with someone else. She was not always able to find one
that was accessible as well as empty, but she always kept some distance

between herself and the owners. With Adam, she felt different, and she trusted him in a way she could not fully explain. And yet, this whole experience was about as strange as any she could imagine. Here she was in a young man's room — not just any young man, but one she loved. She was going to have to be delicate about this. The fact that he did not see, hear, or smell her made no difference. Her mother and father had taught her about chastity, modesty, and a whole lot of other things that made this situation borderline — no, not borderline, it busted the border all to pieces! She knew she was going to have to be more creative than ever before.

She covered the sofa with a sheet and stretched a blanket over it. She listened to the sounds of Adam's soft breathing for a moment. She knew there was no way he could see her, but she continued to watch him, trying to make up her mind. What to do? This wasn't a problem, so why couldn't she decide?

She went back to the living room and opened her backpack. She was wearing a light jumpsuit made from polyester and a pair of footies and tennis shoes. Living on the run, she had learned to keep everything with her always, not knowing if, or when, she would have to move again. Material possessions had to be at a bare minimum. She had to carry everything she owned, either on her or in her backpack. It was a Spartan life to be sure.

Reaching into her backpack, she withdrew a loose fitting sleeping gown. With the weather as hot as it was in New Orleans, she had to sleep either in her underwear or in something that was light and cool. After the wintry weather settled in, she would exchange it for something warmer, but for now, it would have to do. Living with Adam made the underwear idea DOA. She had very few things left that allowed her to feel like a person of virtue. Her world required hard choices if she was to survive. Nevertheless, she had decided to keep virtue as close to her heart as possible.

Taking the sleeping gown to the bathroom, she set the shower as hot as she could stand it to loosen her tense muscles. After shampooing her hair, she let the hot stream beat against the back of her head and neck until she could feel the temperature finally beginning to cool off. She had not realized she had stood there for so long. She quickly dried off and dressed before cleaning up the mess she had made. It was not much considering the way it had looked before she arrived.

Evelyn looked at her reflection and pulled her brush through her hair a few times. Her reflection looked a lot more confident than she felt but ready or not, she had made her decision. The past was over. She turned off the light and opened the door. There were no sounds. Quickly going to the living room, she put her shoes and socks into her back-pack along with the jumpsuit and underwear. She would wash every-thing tomorrow and maybe "purchase" a few things from the store.

Back in Adam's room, she placed her backpack next to the bench sofa and pulled back the blanket to sit down. One dim nightlight al-lowed Evelyn to see him and a smile touched her lips without her being consciously aware of it. She wondered again if this was right.

After a few minutes, her head dropped suddenly, and she realized she was falling asleep sitting up. Sighing, she ran her fingers through her hair to make sure it was dry before lying down and pulling the blanket over her shoulders. Facing Adam's sleeping form, Evelyn closed her eyes and contemplated what she would do tomorrow.

The light blazed in her eyes! Pulling up the blanket, she squinted to see what was happening. For a moment, she had forgotten where she was. He was pulling off his pajama top when she finally realized where she was, exactly where, and got a glimpse of his bare chest before quickly turning over and facing the window. She had the blanket pulled over her head and her face was beet red. Yep! She thought I am going to have to get a lot more creative.

She heard him moving around a bit more before leaving the bed-room. A minute later, she heard the shower start. Evelyn tried to imag-ine what her mother would say if she were standing here now. She could not think of anything right off, but she hoped her mother would see the humor in it.

After a while, Evelyn partially removed her head from under the blanket. The first thing she noticed was the scent of cologne. The next was that she was feeling faint. It smelled delicious to her. This was so stupid! There was one side of Evelyn that was frightened at being in this situation, but there was another side that felt completely different. Fear almost overwhelmed her as she fought impulses she could not begin to understand. These feelings were not normal, at least not for humans. She was fighting desperately against a force that appeared to be laughing at her pitiful struggles, and she quickly realized she was being played with. Nothing she could do was going to prevent — but she never had time to discover what that was. The struggle abrupt-ly ended, leaving Evelyn gasping for breath. The only thing she under-stood was that the ending had nothing to do with her resistance. Then, without warning, the blanket held tightly in her clenched fist, was sud-denly jerked off her body. This, along with the previously unnatural battle, caused her to do the only thing she could think of. She closed her eyes tightly and curled into a ball.

"...must be getting sloppy," Adam muttered. "Don't remember putting this here last night." She felt the blanket drop back on top of her and heard him say under his breath, "Got to go, no time for house cleaning."

She heard coins being placed in his pockets and later, the front door closing. Except for his lingering scent, she was now alone. She laid there a moment more in silence. What had just happened? What was it that had practically frightened her to death? As she reached for hints at what it might have been, the memory of it dissolved into puffs of smoky vapor. Evelyn was left with nothing more than a feeling that there was something she should remember, but could not.

Adam's bed was still unmade, and his pajamas were in a pile on the floor. He might have just been in a hurry, but then, there was the bathroom last night. She concluded that tidy, he was not. She hadn't had time to investigate the rest of the house thoroughly but suspected her cleaning skills might come in handy to pay for her keep.

Evelyn never needed to worry about having clothing and food, except for the danger required in obtaining them. She understood the necessity of having to steal everything; she didn't like it, but it was part of her world now. She had the clothing on her back and some stuff in her backpack. As she was going to be staying, she needed to get some things. She had looked in the girls' closets, and the older girl seemed to be about her size, but she knew she could not disturb them for the same reason she could not sleep in their beds. Adam would, of course, be supplying the food.

She hoped she could find a way to prepare something for him to eat in such a way that it would not indicate her existence. This did not appear to be an easy thing to do; she had tried it before, and if there was even the slightest chance that she might be suspected — However, with Adam, things might be easier. He already appeared to be having an awareness of her. He explained it as a feeling. Perhaps she wanted him to see her so badly that he was sensing her.

With Adam gone, Evelyn had time to wash, not only her clothes but his as well. She quickly cleaned the kitchen, the bathroom, and made his bed. By the time the dryer beeped, she had made the place look presentable. It was time to go shopping.

Turning briefly at the front door, she looked back into the house and realized that she was happy and feeling very comfortable. She smiled. Yes, she was home.

CHAPTER 10

S INCE HIS FATHER'S DEATH, his subsequent time off, and trying to decide how to proceed with his life, Adam had lost a lot of his customer base. Business was so poor that he had to cut back. He did most of the cooking himself now, though he had Ralph as a backup and evening cook. His strong arm was Rose. She did everything and then some. When the restaurant began to fail, they had both taken a cut in pay instead of looking for other work. Ralph had even taken the time to work in his place so that he could make those doctor appointments. They were more like family now than employees.

Rose was serving some young cub scouts who appeared to be having a good time. Although the den mother looked like she had her hands full, the young boys were well behaved, considering. As Rose returned to the register, Adam went over to have a chat and make sure everyone was satisfied.

"I hope everything's alright." He smiled. "Those are the best hamburgers this side of Magazine Street!"

Several of the boys spoke up at once. "Thanks, Sir! These are great!"

"Yes, thank you very much... what was your name, Mr.?" the den mother asked.

"Please, just Adam. This was my father's place. I'm trying to do as good a job as he did. If you have any suggestions, let me know!"

"I like the milkshakes!" one of the scouts said, "You can actually drink it! Most places just give you ice cream and call it a milkshake."

"Well, we have ice cream also if you would like some," Adam replied.

"Well, Adam, we think you're doing a fantastic job, don't we guys? Everyone tell Mr. Adam, thank you!"

The group replied with a roughly coordinated, "Thank you, Mr. Adam!"

Adam laughed and thanked them. He then returned to the counter and stood next to Rose. "Looks like the lunch rush might be over."

Rose smiled. "I'm not sure we can call it a rush and still go to church on Sunday."

"Now, Rose, you can always go to church on Sunday. It's not for the honest anyway," he smiled. "The Good Book says honest people don't need to go to church, just the sick, or something like that."

Rose said, "Matthew chapter 12, verse 9. But when Jesus heard that, he said unto them, they that be whole need not a physician, but they that are sick."

Adam stared at Rose a moment and blinked. "Why, Rose, I didn't know you were a Bible thumper."

"I'm not. That's the only verse I know."

Adam raised one skeptical eyebrow. "And that one verse just happens to be the one you know?"

Rose had started cleaning off the milkshake machine when she noticed Adam still watching her.

"I'm sorry, did you say something?"

Adam just smiled and walked back to the kitchen. In a little while and after a few more customers, the scout group left. Adam noticed the den mother kept trying to catch his eye as they walked out. When he did look, she gave him a big smile and a silent "Thank You!" Adam smiled and waved. Knowing Ralph would be in shortly, he tried to get the evening shift setup. He had done a lot for Adam, and he wanted to do what he could to let him know how much he appreciated his help. Both Ralph and Rose were the reason the restaurant had not closed yet, but it was not their work and dedication that he was as thankful for as much as their friendship. They had stayed with him when he needed it most. Finishing the setup, he walked over to Rose who was still standing by the register. He didn't say anything for a minute. "Rose, I want to tell you... well, you know how much I appreciate you staying on, right?"

Looking up, she said almost sarcastically, "Adam, you know how much I like you and all, but it's not you, it's all the money you pay me."

Adam laughed. "Yeah, well I'd like to talk to you about that. It seems we need to cut it back a bit more." Adam had stopped smiling.

"Don't push it, buster!" Rose said and started cleaning the milkshake machine again.

Adam laughed. "Rose, I don't know what I would have done without you and Ralph. Moreover, I'm not just talking about the restaurant. Both of you have helped me in ways I can never repay."

"Wait a minute!" Rose said, acting shocked, "What did Ralph ever do for you?!" Then she got serious, and her eyes moistened a bit. "Adam, you're a good boy, and I've seen quite a few bad ones. When the Good Lord made you, he broke the mold. If I'm able to help, I'll be here. You're more than a friend; I think of you as the son I've never had. If you ever, I mean ever, need anything, you just come to Rose. I'll give you everything I have if you need it. I'll always be here for you." She turned around and started cleaning the milkshake machine that was practically sterilized now.

Adam put his hand on her shoulder and gave it a gentle squeeze.

Without turning around, she asked, "I was wondering. How did the appointment with your doctor go yesterday?"

Adam tried to keep the worry out of his voice. "The doctor says I'm doing fine, but still wants to see me again next Friday. I'm not sure I need to keep going. It seems like a waste of time and money."

Reaching into a small pocket, Rose removed a small crumpled napkin and dabbed her eyes. Turning to him, she said, "Adam, you better be giving that doctor your time! He didn't go to school for fifty years for nothing. Yeah, it cost a bit, but they know what they're doing. He can help you."

"I know, but I'm feeling better now. Doc said I was almost finished anyway. He just wants to keep an eye on me for a while, I think, and see how much more of my fortune he can get." He said the last under his breath, but loud enough for her to hear.

She just stared at him, not smiling.

"No, seriously, he said he was pretty much finished, and that I was doing fine. Anyway, if I need some more counseling, I'll sit down and talk to you. I can't believe he gets paid for doing what you do for free, and do so much better."

The last part got her smiling again. "Well, you just take care of yourself, and remember, I'm always here."

Ralph came in wearing a huge grin. He gave them a big smile and said, "Good evening, guys. Wonderful day, isn't it?" Then, he stepped into the kitchen. Both Adam and Rose just stared at him through the kitchen-serving window. They could hear Ralph quietly singing something.

Rose looked at Adam suspiciously. "You didn't give him a raise, did you?"

Adam just raised his hands to his chest; palms out in surrender. "I have no idea what this is about, honest!"

Rose continued to look at him doubtfully.

"Anyway, I have to head home. I have some things to pick up at the cleaners before it closes." Then he moved closer to her ear and whispered, "Keep an eye on him, and let me know what you find out."

She smiled and nodded slightly. As Adam walked out, he smiled to himself and thought, What would the world be without workplace politics and intrigue?

In the car, he had time to think. The visit to the doctor yesterday had made him rethink what was going on in his life. Just when he thought he was getting his head straight, he found out that he couldn't trust his memories. Maybe he couldn't trust his feelings either. If he was losing his mind, and it was starting to look more possible, trying to communicate with a would-be ghost could be leading nowhere. Of course, there was no such thing as ghosts, at least he had never believed in them before. Why start now? Moreover, it was just a bad dream that had gone on too long. It probably was caused by the loss of his family. Still, and he had to smile at this, she was a beautiful woman; the feelings he had for her, whether she was real or not, were real. Because of these feelings, he wanted it to be true. There was no other reason. This morning when he got ready for work, he had felt that same comforting feeling as from the dream. Yesterday, when he had exited the elevator, he had felt it again, only much stronger. He had been positive at the time that something real was going on. Did she exist or was she only in his mind — and his heart?

Adam drove his car into the driveway and sat for a moment. A decision had to be made. Was he going to continue this or accept that he needed more help from the doc?

He had another dream last night, and this time, she had talked to him. He wasn't sure what it meant. He wondered if it was just another dream that didn't mean anything at all, or was she real and trying to talk to him while he slept? How could he be sure? He couldn't control what he said in his dreams, it just happened. What could he do to take this to the next level, if there was one?

Taking a deep breath, he turned off the engine. The house looked no different. He felt no different from when he was at work. When would he feel it? Would he feel anything at all? He walked up the walkway and onto the porch. He still felt nothing different. Putting the key in the door, he turned it, trying hard to know when and if the feelings started. He stood there not opening the door yet. Maybe he was trying too hard. He took a moment to think about the stuff he had to do this evening like wash up his clothes and clean the house. Tomorrow was Sunday, and the restaurant would be closed. He gripped the doorknob and opened it a crack, still nothing. He felt disappointment starting to surround him. He opened the door and looked inside. He still felt nothing different.

With no warning, he was engulfed by a feeling of love and caring, so much so that he was overwhelmed. Unable to move, he felt tears fill his eyes. This had to be real! He didn't know how he could be so sure, but he was.

After the feeling subsided, he closed the front door and said, "Okay, I know you're here. You have to be." He wiped the tears from his eyes before continuing. "You've made that crystal clear. I don't know what you are or why you're here, but I know you are, and I hope you know that... well, although I might be crazy; I've never felt this way about anyone or anything. I guess the fact that I can't see you makes it a lot easier to say. We need to talk. I don't know exactly how we can do that. I suppose if you could talk to me, that you would have done so by now. You either won't, can't, or don't know how. I'm sure you have your reasons though. I had a dream where you spoke to me for the first time. You asked something, and I answered, but I don't remember what it was. Perhaps, that's how we can communicate. You might be able to answer my questions when I'm asleep and dreaming..." Adam took a deep breath. "Or maybe... we can just take this a bit slower, especially if you're feeling threatened."

He chuckled softly for a moment. "That's pretty funny. People are supposed to be afraid of ghosts, not the other way around. Right? Of course, you may not even be a ghost; you may be an alien or demon, but I don't care. I know how I feel. We can make this work." He took a breath. "For now, I think I need time to get used to the idea that you're real. I guess we could go into the kitchen and sit for a while. That's normal, right? I've never been comfortable in here, never really use it." He started walking to the kitchen feeling a little strange but also feeling the warmth that suggested she was near.

He sat down at a chair and then jumped up, pulling another one out before returning to his. "I guess I need to remember my manners." He smiled broadly. Sitting there for a few minutes, he chuckled. "Now that I believe it, all I want to do is sit here with you! I don't know what to say."

Starting to feel a little shy, he looked at the table a moment before saying, "Maybe you would like a bite to eat? I do cook for myself, and I think it's good. Um, do you eat though? I guess if you're a ghost, you don't, but if you're an alien, you might. I wonder what you eat." Suddenly he had a chill up his spine. "I've seen my share of alien movies." He laughed nervously. "I hope you're not here to eat me." His laugh was a bit forced.

Again, he felt that warm feeling envelop him, and he knew that if she wanted to eat him, he would have been dinner a long time ago. "Yeah, well... sure; that's a kind of dumb thing for me to say, stupid actually! Look, I'm sorry I even said it! I've embarrassed myself and probably you too."

The warmth lessened, but he could tell she was still near. Looking down at his plate, he picked up the fork and looked at the food sitting there. He didn't move for a moment, just staring at it.

"As I said, I'm a pretty decent cook. I think you will find that this dinner is great... I..." He felt confused again. "It's not something I normally cook... but you have to admit, it smells good." And with that, he realized his mouth was starting to water. "I hope you enjoy yours too... I see I gave you a smaller helping than my own. I hope you like it."

He took a bite and couldn't help closing his eyes a moment as he chewed. "You know, I am a great cook, but I didn't know I was this good!" He was halfway finished when he looked at the other plate. The food was still there. Nothing had been eaten.

"Well, I guess you might not eat food after all. That means you're probably a ghost. That's okay though! A ghost is fine; I can live with that if you can." After thinking about what he had just said, he started laughing, then choked. Clearing his throat, he started laughing hysterically again.

"I'm sorry, but this is all very funny, wonderful, but funny too!" Every time he thought he had calmed down, he would start laughing again. "I don't think I've laughed that much for a long time. It feels good, really good."

He finished his meal and used a roll to wipe the plate. "I don't think I ever made anything this good before." He looked over at the kitchen counter and stove. "And I don't remember being such a clean cook either. Cleaning up before I eat was never something I use to do. I must have known I was going to have guests when I..." Again, he felt confusion start to enter his mind. He knew something wasn't right but couldn't put his finger on what it was. He looked over at her plate, but the food was still uneaten. "Maybe you don't like that kind of stuff. That's fine. We can try something different later. If you don't like it, I won't get my feelings hurt." He smiled. "Of course, if you feel shy about eating with me watching, then I could just go into the other room. I need to do some house cleaning this evening anyway. I always like to take it easy on Sunday." He sat there a moment like he might be waiting for an answer. "Yeah, well, I guess I better get started. I'll be right back. You just go right ahead and eat."

Adam quickly went to his bedroom and started to do a fast pick-up of his stuff. It might be a female ghost, but he didn't want her to see his messy room. Stopping, he looked around and saw that his bed was made, and the room looked cleaner and more orderly than he could remember. The bed was made; the room was picked up. He tried to remember picking it up this morning, something he never did. Maybe he did and just didn't remember. Lately, his memory was getting terrible.

"Well, I guess that's finished!" he said as he headed for the bathroom. Again, he found it spotless. "Man! I'm good!"

Crossing the hall to the laundry room, looked down at the dirty clothes basket, which was always full on Saturdays, now empty. He leaned back slightly against the washer and tried to remember this morning. It was difficult since his life was so routine, every morning was nearly the same. He just couldn't remember doing it, but evidently, he had. Perhaps he suspected she would come to his house. Yeah, that must be it.

Again, he smiled and thought, And what a guest! Maybe I'm being too forward about this eating thing. Being a ghost, she most likely doesn't eat. After a moment of contemplation, he thought, Whew, talk about a couple having communication issues!

When he returned to the kitchen, he saw her food still on the plate. "Look, it's okay that you don't eat. I'll just dump it, and we'll do something else. He picked up their plates and placed his in the sink. Hers, he scraped into the garbage disposal and turned on the water to wash it down. "You know, not eating must be a real drag. I mean, eating is one of the most enjoyable things that we humans do! If not for that, my restaurant would surely go out of business. Besides, it can sometimes be a dream experience, kind of like what we had here tonight. Too bad you didn't get to enjoy it."

Adam finished loading the dishwasher and said, "Would you follow me? I have something I want to try."

In his bedroom, he set up a folding table and a couple of chairs. "Please, you sit there, and I'll sit here. I have some questions I want to write down for you to think about. Maybe you can answer them for me, or if you can't, then maybe we can figure a way to overcome this communications thing. Okay? Okay then!"

He got a piece of paper and a pencil and sat down, putting the paper in the center of the small table. "Let's see if you can write first. I'll just wait. If you can do it, try to lift the pencil and make a mark on the paper." He waited.

He concentrated on the pencil with as much intensity as he could, willing it to move. He waited. After a few minutes, he let out his breath and sighed; it had stayed stubbornly still, not even a quiver of movement.

"Okay, let's try this then. I'll hold the pencil, and you try to possess me or something to make it move." Taking the pencil in his hand, he put the point on the paper, closing his eyes and clearing his mind. The feeling of love surrounding him increased, and he felt reassured that it had to work this time. He waited for what seemed like ten minutes. When he looked down, there was nothing but a blank piece of paper.

"Strike two," he said. "Now don't get worried; we can do this." He put the pencil back on the paper and said, "I saw this on a movie once. I'll start moving the pencil on the paper, and you see if you can make it give me a message." He moved the pencil as unconsciously as he could. The tip swirled this way and that. Sometimes it made loops, sometimes just sharp lines, but nothing that looked like a message. After a few minutes, he stopped and looked down.

"Okay, this may not be as easy as I'd hoped." After another moment's thought, he said, "I'm going to take a pad of paper to sleep with me. When I'm asleep, I want you to write something on it. Maybe you can't get past my conscious mind. Maybe I'm keeping you from doing it." He silently didn't believe this, but he was running out of options.

EARLIER ....

Evelyn nervously watched the streetcar progressively getting closer. Though she waited alone, she felt suppressed fear. This was not her first trip since the death of her parents. In the beginning, she had used streetcars regularly. However, her last trip had almost caused her severe injury. The exit door had pinned her arm, and if not for the observant conductor, would have dragged her down the tracks. Fortunately, he had noticed it partially ajar and opened it to try again. She had suffered little more than a bruised elbow, but it made her realize how easily she could get hurt. After the incident, she became more and more reclusive, until she rarely went out at all except to visit the library or park.

This was one of those instances when her invisibility seemed to have a mind of its own. Normally, because she was the one causing the problem, the driver should not have been able to see it. On the other hand, perhaps he just thought of it as a mechanical problem, and it had nothing to do with her. Regardless, she promised herself that she would never ride one again.

As the streetcar finally approached her stop — without slowing, she understood the problem. She was the only passenger. Unless a rider was going to get off, the streetcar would continue without stopping. She watched in frustration and a little bit of relief, as it passed. "Well, what did you expect?" she said aloud.

As Evelyn watched the third streetcar pass without stopping, she understood that this wasn't a popular exit point. Frustrated somewhat by the lost time, she jogged several blocks to the next one. She still had plenty of time though. Today was Saturday; the trolleys were on a tighter schedule to accommodate the increased shoppers and sightseers. Besides, another rider was waiting at this stop. She would stay close to him when he boarded.

He was an older man, perhaps forty or fifty, somewhat overweight, and dressed in khaki pants and a flowery short-sleeved shirt. As she watched him, she thought about how most people had a sense of being alone, even in public places. Shoplifters thought that no one was watching, even though there were plenty of cameras around for just that purpose. Even if they were not actively monitored, a recording could be made. Also, other customers often saw what was going on, even if they didn't report it. Evelyn felt a rush of shame as she considered what she was about to do.

Abruptly, she changed her train of thought. It was considered bad manners to stare at people unless you wanted to get their attention. However, she never seemed to have had a problem with people watching her or "staring" at her in the way her friends said the guys did — especially not now, of course. That was fine with her; it seemed creepy anyway. However, observing others over the last couple of years, she recognized that someone was always watching. If a person believed they could watch in secret, they usually did so, trying not to be obvious about it. Evelyn knew she was able to watch others with complete abandon, but chose not to because it made her even more aware of the thing she had become. Still, standing there watching this man waiting for the streetcar, she wondered if perhaps there might not be other things watching her, things unseen. The chill that had begun to go up her spine was replaced by apprehension as the next streetcar approached the stop.

After boarding, she found several empty seats, but she would not be sitting; that was just asking for trouble. Instead, she positioned herself next to the rear control station. Once the streetcar reached its final stop, the conductor would change the connecting poles running against the lines above, and take a position where Evelyn stood. By then, she would be gone.

Exiting the streetcar could be a problem. If no one else was getting off, the conductor might keep on going. He might never even hear the bell in the first place. It depended on whether he thought someone else had pulled the cord, but with so many passengers, there would be nothing to indicate it was Evelyn. However, the real problem was being the only one getting off. If the driver saw no one, he might assume it was a false bell and never open the door to begin with, or worst yet, close it prematurely. Fortunately, Evelyn heard several other bells as people indicated their intentions and followed them off without incident.

Her next problem was getting to the shopping mall across the street.

Several of the others waited for the pedestrian light to change, and it was vital that she cross with them. Traffic was heavy. It would be extremely dangerous for her to cross alone. Traffic turning right could proceed if no one was on the walkway. Obviously, no one would see her. Even after crossing the street, she would have to navigate the huge parking area. It was full of Saturday shoppers coming and going. This would be even more dangerous. Walking behind a car backing up was bad enough if the driver could see you — they would not see Evelyn.

The light changed, and everyone crossed quickly. Evelyn stayed close to a young woman dressed up in a work outfit, hoping she was headed to the mall. This would be her safety shield. Together, they crossed the walkway without incident and entered the congested parking area. Even so, before reaching the mall entrance, a driver began backing up without looking. Stomping on his brakes, the car jerked to a stop as he blasted his horn in irritation. The woman, in turn, greeted him with a plethora of insults that would have done a drunken sailor proud. Once inside, Evelyn left her shield and quickly moved to an empty area to catch her breath and calm her nerves. This was exactly why she didn't do this kind of thing anymore. The world was crazy; how did anyone stay alive?

She had been here before. In the beginning, guilt and fear had filled her heart as she nervously watched surveillance cameras looking for shoplifters. Once, she had tried an experiment by taking a movie camera and recording herself with a sign telling whom she was and asking for help. She took the camera to a police station and placed it on the counter at the front desk. As long as she waited, no interest was given to it. She finally left and came back a week later to find the camera lying on the floor against a far wall; someone had probably elbowed it off the counter without realizing it, and it was eventually kicked across the floor. In a week's time, not even the cleanup people had seen it sitting there. Did this mean that if someone ran the video, she wouldn't be seen? Evelyn was sure that it meant exactly that.

Being very careful to avoid other people, she found the store she had last visited. At first, she couldn't believe she was at the proper place. She went past the store and looked at the surrounding ones before being certain that the boarded-up front windows belonged to it. Why had it gone out of business? She thought about it for a moment before the thought came that it could be because she had taken so much stuff! Did they go broke because of her?

Evelyn's mouth dropped open before she finally nixed the idea. She had not taken more than a couple of pairs of jeans and a shirt or two.

Surely, that wouldn't have made them go broke — could it? Maybe they had not closed because of only her, but if others were also taking stuff...

Evelyn walked farther down the mall to a different store, her face burning red with shame and embarrassment. What was she going to do? She tried several times to take something she thought she would need, but each time, shame overcame her. For about fifteen minutes, she sat against a wall behind a clothing rack, crying. Everything was so wrong. How could she live without doing this? Her clothes had holes wearing in them, and while that may have been the fad in some places, she needed warm clothing for the upcoming winter. She tried again to pick out some things, and at one point, had several in her arms, but when she left the store, she had nothing. She had seen homeless people wearing worn-out clothing and felt even guiltier. Where did they get their stuff? She thought of going through dumpsters as she had seen others do. Was she any better than those people? She knew she was not. She was a thief.

Dejected, Evelyn left the mall and made her way home. She had decided to come up with a different solution than stealing, but when she thought of Adam, tears filled her eyes again. Was she going to steal from him also? No, she could work for what she took from him. While not completely honest, what else could she do?

Returning to Adam's house, her mood gradually improved. She was becoming excited about the prospects before her, and even the danger of being in public did not detract from it. It was as if her life was starting over again, and there was a deep joy building inside as well as a growing urgency to be with Adam again.

Back at his house, her first job was to go through his double sliding door closet looking for a place for her things. His winter coats and sweaters were on the far side, something he wouldn't be using for a while. She hoped if she placed her few items there, it would cause him the least amount of trouble. She could only guess at the problems that she had caused other people's minds as they tried to work around her presence. Evelyn did not want to cause Adam any more trouble than necessary.

His house was not excessively disorganized or dirty but could use some of what her mother had always called deep cleaning. She found his utility closet and used the available cleaning items and disinfectants to make sure the bathroom and kitchen were spotless. She straightened the rest of the house, vacuumed the bedroom carpets, and mopped the floors. By the time she finished cleaning the windows, it was late, and she still wanted to make something for Adam to eat when he returned. How he was going to see it, she hadn't figured out yet.

Entering Adam's bedroom, she sat on the edge of his bed, thinking of her mother. Evelyn had helped in the kitchen for as long as she could remember. Even as a little girl, her mother had played with her, allowing her to help with the meals. There were even times when her mother allowed her to fix some rather unconventional delicacies for her father's dinner, like chocolate-syrup-covered spinach and jelly bean soup. She was never told that it was silly or tasted strange; this was something she had quickly figured out for herself. Her father and mother would make a big deal of enjoying it and complimented her on her creativity. These were usually nights when the family ordered pizza for dessert afterward. She smiled at the memory and began crying softly.

As she grieved, her memory returned to that day, and the crying became a wail, before quickly igniting a deep, unquenchable fire. With her fingers gripping the bedspread, turning white with the effort, she let out a deep, uncontrollable scream of anger and fury. She wanted to kill it, to tear it to shreds! She wanted to find and destroy the monster, and everyone connected to it! She wanted to take away its family and those it cared for and loved, as it had taken away hers! She wanted to make it not exist anymore—she wanted her mother back; she wanted her father back!

Evelyn slowly became aware that she was lying on Adam's bed and had been staring at a picture on the wall for a very long time without really seeing it. In the picture, she saw Adam and two beautiful young girls. A man and woman stood behind them. They must be his family, the ones he no longer had. They were both alone now. Adam had suffered as well. Something had taken his family, just as surely as something had taken hers. Were their deaths as senseless? How was he able to cope and stay a good person, or was he also holding some dark secret inside his heart? Did he want revenge? She did not believe so. Somehow, he had come to grips with his loss. She knew there was only one way she would come to grips with hers.

Pushing herself up into a sitting position, she let her gaze slowly take in the room. When it passed the clock, she realized with a start that she only had a short while before Adam's return. Standing, she straightened the bed and walked to the kitchen. As she prepared dinner, she was amazed at how much she loved Adam and how much she wanted to be with him forever. This is where she wanted to be. This was her home now. She desperately hoped he wanted her also.

She had just removed two tumblers from the cabinet when every muscle and tendon in her body froze. Her eyes rolled back, and she felt an incredibly intense certainty as a voice in her head said, there is nothing we will not do to love and protect him. Evelyn audibly gasped. There was no pain, but the intensity astounded her. Her muscles immediately returned to normal, and she held on to the counter to keep her balance. The tumblers lay on the floor, and it took a few moments before she could pick them up. She tried to understand what had happened, but the memory was quickly fading. After a few minutes more, she was again preparing dinner.

Everything was completed. The table was set, and she had just removed the tuna casserole from the oven. The only thing remaining was the question of how to get Adam to see it. She knew she was pushing things, but wanted it so much that reason and logic were taking a back seat. Breathing deeply to calm herself, she headed for the living room to wait for Adam's arrival.

Entering the room, she discovered Adam standing in the doorway, a worried look on his face. Evelyn's heart melted as she ran to him and hugged him, placing her head against his chest.

"I missed you so much," she whispered. After a moment, she released him and stepped away, her face flushed.

"Okay, I know you're here. You have to be." He wiped his eyes before continuing. "You've made that crystal clear. I don't know what you are or why you're here, but I know you are, and I hope you know that... well, although I might be crazy, I've never felt this way about anyone or anything."

Evelyn's heart was burning. It was almost too much for her to accept. After having been ignored for so long here was someone that not only knew she was there but was actually talking to her. She listened as he tried to describe what he had been experiencing in his dreams. When he said that he didn't care if she were an alien monster or demon, she grimaced. She was certain she was not a space alien but not so sure about the demon thing. He told her he believed that they might find a way to communicate.

"Yes!" she said excitedly, "I've been trying to figure that one out myself!"

Finally, he took a deep breath and closed the front door before inviting her into the kitchen. As they entered, she remembered the dinner and prayed that he would be able to see it.

"You made it. You made the dinner!" Evelyn desperately repeated. "Please see it."

In the kitchen, he stood for a moment looking around before sitting. He quickly stood again and pulled out a chair for Evelyn. He was definitely a gentleman.

It didn't take long for her to realize he did not see the meal before him. He had just made some comment about her, or what she may be used to eating when an unusual look came over his face. He appeared uncomfortable or perhaps frightened. He said something about her eating him and tried to laugh about it, but not very convincingly. She smiled at his silliness and placed her hand on his for a moment.

"Adam, even though you look delicious, I'm not going to eat the only person in the world that even knows I exist, and especially not someone that loves me... and especially not you," she whispered.

Adam then looked at the table and appeared to see everything before him, but he didn't say anything at first. He just stared, confused.

Evelyn waited for him to come to grips with what was in front of him if he could. She was just starting to feel defeated when he began to talk about how he was a good cook, and that perhaps she would like to eat. That's when she noticed the confusion starting to dawn on him. He started saying things and then correcting himself as if he were not sure what he wanted to say. He referred to the meal as if he had been the one to prepare it, but obviously was having a hard time with that explanation.

She began to realize he was getting better at accepting things done by her, comparatively speaking. Another person probably would not have even seen the food on the table at all. He suggested that they eat. She picked up her fork and waited for him to try his. When he took the first bite, she watched the look of delight on his face and again felt everything would somehow work out between them.

She was almost through when Adam suggested that she eat hers as well. She looked at him and then down to her plate. She closed her eyes and sighed, knowing that he simply could not see or accept what was happening. They would have to take this one step at a time. Eventually, perhaps, they might be able to communicate in some way other than him just feeling her presence.

She continued to listen as he talked about the great dinner he had prepared. As he spoke, he kept running into logical roadblocks. Some of what he said didn't, and couldn't, make sense. She could see his subconscious desperately trying to come to grips with what she was doing to him. It was both depressing and frightening. She could do nothing but watch him stumble around the truth.

"Well, I guess you might not eat food after all. That means you're probably a ghost. That's okay though! A ghost is fine; I can live with that if you can." This sent him into a laughing fit, followed by a coughing bout, followed by another laughing fit.

Evelyn stared at him with sincere concern. Was he going to be able to handle this? She had to do something, but what?

"I'm sorry, but this is all very funny, wonderful, but funny too! I don't think I've laughed that much for a long time. It feels good, really good." He finished his meal and used a roll to wipe the plate. "I don't think I ever made anything this good before." He looked over at the kitchen counter and stove. "And I don't remember being such a clean cook either. Cleaning up before eating was never my strong suit. I must have known I was going to have guests when I..."

He looked over at her plate but still could not see that she had eaten it. "Maybe you don't like this kind of stuff. That's fine. We can try something different later. If you don't like it, I won't get my feelings hurt." He smiled. "Of course, if you feel shy about eating with me watching, then I could just go into the other room. I need to do some cleaning this evening anyway. I always like to take it easy on Sunday." He sat there a moment like he might be waiting for an answer. "Yeah, well, I guess I better get started. I'll be right back. You just go right ahead and eat."

Evelyn breathed a little easier. He seemed to be taking it well. He wasn't going to go crazy on her, and she found herself feeling a lot of pride over this. It was as if he was stronger than she was. He was stronger than the monster that had entered his life, and he would subdue it.

When he returned to the kitchen, he looked at her empty plate. "Look, it's alright that you don't eat. I'll just dump it, and we'll do something else. You know, not eating must be a real drag. I mean, eating is one of the most enjoyable things that we humans do. If not for that, the restaurant would surely go out of business. Besides, it can sometimes be a dream experience, kind of like what we had here tonight. Too bad you didn't get to enjoy it."

After scraping her empty plate into the garbage disposal, Adam finished loading the dishwasher and asked Evelyn if she would follow him. "I have something I want to try."

In his bedroom, he set up a folding table and a couple of chairs. Taking a pencil and piece of paper, he said she might be able to write on it and sat there for a few moments waiting. She picked up the pencil and wrote her name.

EVELYN

He stared at the page for a minute before suggesting, "Okay, let's try this then. I'll hold the pencil, and you try to possess me or something to make it move."

Evelyn laughed. "You want me to possess you?!" She knew he had this idea fixed too deeply that she was a ghost. They would have to work on that one. But then again, even a ghost would be better than whatever she was.

She placed her hand over his and guided the pencil to write her name, but again he just looked at it and saw nothing. Evelyn covered her face in frustration for a moment.

The next test was pretty much like this one, but now he was going to move his hand on the paper, and she was supposed to guide it. She watched him start moving the tip lightly over the sheet. Her name was on it twice already, and she didn't feel like this was going to work, but tried again anyway. This too failed. He was simply not able to see what she wrote, no matter how much she wanted him to.

Evelyn could see that Adam was getting as frustrated as she was, though he tried to be positive about it. When he suggested she try to write on the paper with his hand during his sleep, she thought it was doomed to failure. He had no idea that the problem was in his head and not on the paper. She thought that perhaps he might be able to convince himself that he could have been the one that wrote it in his sleep instead of her. However, if he did that, it defeated the whole purpose of trying to communicate. If he thought the message was coming from her, his mind, or maybe it was hers, would not allow him to accept it. There just had to be another way of doing this. She sat back and watched him.

CHAPTER 11

A S SHE HAD DONE COUNTLESS times before, Evelyn looked at his features. She loved his hair, his strong nose, his eyes... his lips. She could kiss him now, and he would probably never know it. Sure, he felt something when she was near and maybe something more when she touched him, but would a kiss be any different? She continued to look at him for a moment longer before she covered her face with her hands and made a sound of frustration!

"As I said, I've never believed in ghosts. Are you a ghost? If so, then you would be able to make yourself known; at least that's what all the ghost stories say. Then again, what is a ghost? If they do exist, does anyone understand them? But if you aren't a ghost, what are you? Demons would come under the same heading as ghosts, I suppose, but how about aliens? Forgive me, I'm a bit of a science fiction fan, and I've given these things more than a little thought."

"No, no, and... let me see, *no!*" Evelyn said half-joking with him. "I'm just me. And I want to be seen again. In particular, I want to be seen by you."

Adam thought for a moment. "Okay, what do we know about the situation, and what do we suspect? First, I have these dreams where I meet a beautiful woman... that would be you."

"At *last*," Evelyn said, "You say something true for a change! Beautiful is good."

"Next, the dream always ends badly, evidently, *very* badly. To make matters worse, after I decide not to return to our tree, the bad ending not only stops, but I can no longer remember it anymore, the first part, great, and the second part gone. Now, what's that all about?!"

Evelyn had contemplated this some. "I'm thinking that if I'm the one causing all this, perhaps after I heard your prayer about the dream, I somehow stopped you from remembering some details, in particular, the ending. Confidentially, I wish I didn't know about it either."

"Anyway," he continued, "The next thing I know, I'm becoming aware that the same wonderful feelings in my dream come back every time I'm at the park, specifically the oak tree. That could be because it reminds me of the tree in my dream. Again, the tree in my dreams is probably inspired by the one in the park."

He took the paper with Evelyn's name written all over it and started writing the points he was covering.

"At the restaurant and on my last visit to the doc, I find that those feelings are following me. They are no longer just in my dreams or at the tree. I try a few experiments, and it appears they grow much stronger sometimes than at other times." Adam's eyes widened, and he said excitedly, "I've got it! Listen, this is very important, and it should work, I think."

He went to bed to lie down with his hands interlaced over his stomach. "Now I want you to come near me when I ask you to. I've found that the closer you are, the stronger the feeling."

Evelyn stood, excited again. It might work! Whatever was happening to stop him from being able to see her, or anything else for that matter seemed to have a hole in it—not a very big hole, but one that allowed her feelings for him to come through. And because he was so sensitive in that way, he must be able to feel it. Or, she thought, maybe it was just her subconscious mind that was allowing him to feel certain things about her because she loved him so much. It didn't matter, she thought breathlessly. The experiment might work!

Getting as comfortable and relaxing as much as possible, he said almost in a whisper, "Approach the bed and stand next to me."

Evelyn immediately ran to his side, searching his eyes for some sign he had felt something.

A smile spread across his face, and he sat up and yelled out, "Yes, yes, I felt it! I felt it as sure as anything."

Looking down at Adam, Evelyn wanted to hug him but didn't want to mess up the experiment. "What next?" She could barely wait to continue.

Stretching out on the bed again, he asked her to return to the table. She returned quickly, and again he jumped up into a sitting position. "I feel it, it's true. You are there! Wait!" he said, lying back down. "Come back again!"

Laughing uncontrollably, they performed the test a few more times until he was positively satisfied it was true. They were both deliriously happy now that they were finally communicating!

"Oh man, this is unbelievable!" Adam exclaimed.

She sat on the floor next to the bed, talking excitedly! At this point, it didn't matter in the least that he couldn't hear her! In a confusing and constantly darkening world, they had found each other, and neither stopped to consider the significance of what was happening. The joy they both felt was overwhelming.

Eventually, he lay there with his eyes closed with a look of wonder on his face. Evelyn repositioned herself against the wall; her head tilted slightly to one side so that it just touched his bedspread. With the release of excitement, her tears began to flow. She hugged her knees and cried like a baby. She had thought she couldn't be happier than when he had said he loved her, but she was wrong.

"I love you," he said softly. "I don't know how this can be. I don't even know what you are, but I love you... I can't say it enough." He was whispering now and appeared to be drifting off to sleep.

She sat with her head inches from his, listening as his breathing became regular. After a few moments, she stood and looked down at him. It was strange how she could feel so much anger and fury and yet at the same time, so much love. She moved toward him, lowering her lips to within a hair's breadth of his. She paused. The warmth of his breath gently caressed her lips. She inhaled deeply, holding it prisoner, wanting to keep it safe forever before gently pressing her lips against his.

After an eternity, she stood, not noticing the tear that dropped to his cheek from hers. As if in a dream, she undressed and pulled on her sleeping gown. She could barely think as she was surrounded by a sea of emotions, completely alien to her. Her feelings for him were so intense that it was almost frightening. Turning from him, she went over to the window couch where she had slept the night before. She lay facing him and pulled the blanket up to her chin. With tear-filled eyes, Evelyn continued to watch, until sinking into a deep sleep.

Adam, barely awake, lifted a finger to his cheek and felt Evelyn's lingering tear. Somehow, he knew. Somewhere within his heart, knowledge filled him, and he knew; as certain as he knew he loved her, he knew it was hers.

CHAPTER 12

ADAM SAT ON THE HILL with his back against the oak; its branches spread out providing shade from the heat of the day. He felt he could sit there forever.

Looking over, he found her kneeling beside him. She was dressed differently this time. She had sneakers on, some blue jeans, and a soft white blouse, its collar up and the top button undone. She was wearing a beautiful pearl necklace, each sphere shining brightly, and spoke to him.

"Adam, my name is Evelyn. I'm with you now, but I don't have time to tell you everything." He saw her look around like she was searching for some impending danger. She looked worried. "I want to tell you that I do trust you but... she doesn't."

Adam looked up and noticed the sky started darkening with swirling black clouds.

"You have to know I love you. I will always be with you as long as you want me." Thunder rolled across the blackening sky, and Adam began to become fearful.

"I don't understand!" he said as lightning flashed wickedly, striking several branches of the great oak tree. The thunder was ear shattering.

"Adam, you have to go now! She hates everything and everyone! She wants you to leave and never return. But not me, Adam, I love you, with all my heart and soul, I love you!" She had to yell over the intensity of the brewing storm.

Lightning bolts flashed viciously down on the tree tearing branches off with each bolt, leaving fire and smoking stumps in their wake. The sound was deafening, and Adam stood to run, grabbing Evelyn's hand, but when he looked at her face, he saw fury so full of hate that he jerked away. Her eyes were blood red; her lips pulled back in a horrible grimace! She reached for him.

Waking with a start, Adam looked around the room in terror. Realizing it was the dream, he ran his hands over his face and through his hair, shivering as he tried to remove the memory. After a moment, he sat up and looked at the clock. It was only 4:25 am. The dream had become worse, something he had not thought possible, and he remembered it now — every detail crystal clear.

As he sat there, he recalled the breakthrough with Evelyn. Her name was Evelyn! She had told him her name. Could it be true? Anyway, he was sure she was real, and he was not losing his mind.

Reluctantly recalling the dream, he wondered what it meant. Although convinced about their shared feelings, what was this thing she became? It was horrible! Adam briefly wished he could confide in the doctor about it, but that would no doubt get him committed. There she was, one moment, an angel from heaven, and the next, a demon from hell! "It's just a dream though," he whispered in the dark. As the doctor said, dreams are only representations of thoughts. He mused that Evelyn appeared to be as much representation as the dreams. He did not have a clue about what was going on, or why. However, he knew he wanted her with him. Something inside told him they were vital to each other. The progress last night gave him confidence that he was going in the right direction. Perhaps he could use it to communicate with her.

Stepping over to the switch, he started to turn on the light before pausing. Something came back to him. Last night when he was drifting off to sleep — what was it? Yes! He was positive he had felt a tear on his cheek, and he was positive it wasn't his. He remembered rubbing it between his fingertips. Unless he was crazier than he thought, it could only mean one thing. Evelyn was not a ghost after all. She was as real and solid as he was!

With that thought, Adam left the light off and slid open his closet. He took out his pajamas and laid them on the bed before self-consciously looking around the room. He still felt her presence but didn't know if she was asleep. Removing his clothing a bit nervously, he quickly put on his pajamas and sat back down on the corner of the bed.

Something was going on much stranger than ghosts and demons, or even aliens. He was unable to put his finger on it yet, but maybe that was exactly the idea. This thing about his memory becoming worse was not true either. He had never had a poor memory and always tested high on intelligence tests. The doctor had not found any physical ailments. He said Adam was as physically healthy as a horse; And was it normal that he started making tuna fish casserole taste so good? And how about cleaning up the house so well? Hardly!

It could have something to do with perceptions. What was seeing and hearing? What did it mean to smell or taste something or even touch, for that matter? All of these senses were realized only in the brain. The eyes didn't see. They only allowed light to stimulate nerves on the retina and this stimulated a signal sent to the brain. It was the brain that was seeing, not the eyes; it was the brain that was hearing, and the brain interpreted everything. Everything his senses told him was an interpretation of those signals.

Thinking of this for a bit more, he came to a startling conclusion. If someone or something were somehow manipulating someone's thoughts, they could create an illusion, even the illusion that someone was not there!

"Evelyn!" Adam shouted. He felt the strength of her presence increase. "I've figured it out!"

Evelyn awoke from her sleep to hear Adam's shout. "What?!" she shouted, before realizing he could not possibly hear her.

"Listen to this! I don't think you're a ghost or anything else except a beautiful and wonderful woman." He started laughing.

Evelyn unconsciously pulled up her blanket to her neck and stared at him. What was he saying?

"I think I've figured it out, or at least part of it. You can see and hear me, but I can't see or hear you because you won't let me. Well, I think you would if you could, but somehow your brain is doing something to mine and preventing it!" He stopped a moment to think over this theory. Of course, it has holes in it, lots of them. Like how can this happen anyway? "And, assuming it could happen, how could you have survived from birth? I mean, if you were born like that, how would the doctors or your parents have taken care of you when you were young? So that couldn't be right. Maybe it happened later. People have been known to have strange psychic abilities, why not something like this? Maybe something happened, and you developed this thing, and it won't turn off. Presto! You're left invisible!" He sat there in the dark, smiling like a monkey and feeling quite satisfied. "So, what do you think of my theory? Oh! Sorry. Adam thought for a moment. "If you understand what I'm saying, get closer to me."

Evelyn jumped off the couch and ran to his side of the bed. Then, for good measure, she gave him a big hug.

"Whoa!" He laughed. "That's answer enough."

Evelyn suddenly realized he had shouted out her name! Her eyes opened wide, and her mouth fell open. How could he possibly know? And, what happened to the ghost theory, or more likely, demon theory; what happened to those? Adam didn't look like he was finished doing his dissertation yet, so she sat down excitedly on the edge of the bed next to him, before looking down and realizing she was only in her gown! Her face turning red, she quickly jumped off the bed and ran over to her clothing on the rack. She finished dressing as she listened to him attempting to improve his theory. So far, it all made great sense.

He told her about the dream. In it, she had said her name was Evelyn. But then, the scary part started. Evelyn, from what she knew about her feelings, guessed that she had some split personality thing. Would she be strong enough to keep the other part from taking over? Pausing for a moment, she wondered which one was she?

"So, that's pretty much my theory as it stands so far," Adam gloat-ed. "It's rough, of course, but we can add to it later. In my dream, you were trying to tell me something but said you didn't have time. Per-haps it would work if I asked you some questions on a piece of paper; you could answer me in my dreams. I know it sounds crazy, but this whole thing is crazy."

Evelyn realized that he didn't understand that she had no recollec-tion of her dreams since the murder of her family. If she did dream now, she was never aware of it, and that was odd because when she was younger, she always dreamed. She remembered dreaming in color. Then, there was the time she was able to be aware she was in a dream. That one was the best! She remembered creating stuff out of thin air like magic. However, since the murders, no dreams. If she was in his dreams, it must be her subconscious mind doing it, perhaps in the same way it was stopping the world from seeing her.

Adam looked at the clock. "You know, Evelyn, I'm not sleepy any-more. How about we try one of my great breakfasts? I love pancakes on Sunday morning! Give me a chance to get ready, and I'll make you a batch you would die for."

Evelyn had a momentary flashback but held it in check. She had not had pancakes since that morning, but there was no way that Adam could know the significance of it.

"Um, I guess I should get dressed now..." He looked a bit uneasy. When Evelyn realized what he wanted, she laughed and left the room, heading for the kitchen. It had been a couple of years, but she was go-ing to make him the best pancakes he had ever tasted, and no alternate personality was going to stand in the way.

After his shower, Adam dressed in some comfortable jeans and a T-shirt and headed for the kitchen. He had been yelling from the bed-room that he was going to make her the Adam Yates Special Pancakes. No one could touch them. If he ever entered a cooking contest, he would win easily.

Entering the kitchen, he found the table set and a tall stack of steam-ing pancakes on a hotplate in the center of the table. There were two settings with large glasses of milk and what looked like homemade syr-up.

It was an odd experience. Adam's first thought was that a neighbor or a friend must have come over and prepared it. But when he realized no one was in the house except himself and Evelyn, he went over to the refrigerator to check on the ingredients he would need for making breakfast. Not finding the milk and eggs, he closed the refrigerator and looked at the table again. This time there were two breakfast settings, but no pancakes or milk. He walked to the counter where he kept the griddle and noticed it was on the other side of the stove. He turned around and looked at the table again. It was completely clear of everything. Stopping for a moment, he closed his eyes and waited. He knew something was wrong but wasn't sure what it was.

"Evelyn, something is wrong. I can't say what it is but... I think I saw the table set with the pancakes I was going to make. In fact, I'm pretty sure I made them, but don't think I had time to do it — or did I?"

Evelyn, seeing Adam was having a very hard time, went over to him and held him in her arms. As odd as it sounded, making close contact with him might make it possible for him to see her. Maybe the other one was fighting it.

He felt her near him and closed his eyes for a moment. "I think I may be having an issue here," he said, keeping his eyes closed. "I know I want to make you some pancakes. We both know that you may be doing something to my mind, and I may not be able to trust what I'm seeing or doing. But, with that in mind, I'm going to try and accept anything I see when I open my eyes, regardless of its impossibility."

He continued to keep his eyes closed for a few more moments as if afraid to see. When he did, the table contained the breakfast in full!

"Okay, I see it. Regardless of why it's there, I'm going to sit down and enjoy it with you." He said this with a certain amount of determination. He went over to one of the plates and pulled out the chair next to it. Standing there for a few moments until he figured she was sitting down, he pushed the chair in a little as if she were actually in it. The chair did not seem heavy to push, so he could not tell if she was there.

Evelyn looked up from the chair and smiled at him. He was trying so hard! She could not imagine how she could love him more.

He sat and put plenty of butter and syrup on the three pancakes he had placed on his plate. They were delicious! Being very cautious about making any judgments, he ate until they were all gone. It was not until he looked over at her plate that he froze, afraid to even think. Sitting on her plate, he saw some partially eaten pancakes and syrup. Closing his mind to the possibility of what this meant, he looked over, picked up his glass of milk, and finished it. When he looked back, he saw that the pancakes were gone. Not like they had never been there, but that they had been eaten, leaving some syrup behind on the plate. He looked up to where he suspected her face would be and said, "Evelyn, the breakfast was delicious and... and I..... know that I... didn't make them." He said this last part with some uncertainty. "And, I was able... to see your plate as well." He continued to watch, hoping that maybe he would see her also.

Evelyn sat staring at him. She had finished hers and was waiting to see what he would do. What he had told her filled her with such hope. She wanted to reach out to him, to somehow help him to see her, but she didn't know how to do it. "I'm right here. Please, see me. I want you to. I trust you with all my heart!" Tears again clouded her vision. He was probably never going to see her, but perhaps just knowing she was here would have to be enough for both of them. She pushed her chair back and walked over to stand behind his. Putting her arms around him, she kissed the top of his head and hugged him. Then, putting her lips to his ear, she whispered, "Adam, I'm here. I love you. I trust you. I will always be with you...please.

She still had her eyes closed when she heard him say, "Evelyn, I can feel you holding me... I can feel it! I can't see you, but I can feel you. It feels like you are behind me and you have your arms around my shoulders. Is it true?"

Without opening her eyes, Evelyn squeezed him tighter. He must see her. He must!

She heard him gasp. "Evelyn, I can see your chair, it's where you moved it before going to stand behind me. And, I can feel you squeezing me! I... this is wonderful!" And then he said, "No, wait! Don't go yet!"

Evelyn had not moved. She still stood, holding him tightly. "Evelyn, come back!" She heard the growing desperation. What was happening? She moved back as he pushed his chair to stand.

"Evelyn!" he gasped out. "I'm sorry! Where are you? I..." Adam looked desperate. "Please, I'm sorry! What did I do wrong?! I don't feel you anymore! I can't..." He began running through the house, trying to regain the warmth but was greeted by a cold resolute silence.

Evelyn was speechless. What was happening! Why couldn't he feel her? Blackness began settling around her also as she too became desperate. She followed as he searched the house over and over eventually ending in his bedroom. He stood with a look of anguish, his heart broken, and calling out her name repeatedly. She grabbed him by the shoulders, holding him as tightly as she could, but there was no indication that he felt her.

Eventually, Adam became quiet and settled on the edge of his bed, his face blank, a dead expression in his eyes so painful that it brought tears to Evelyn.

She slowly slid to the floor and began to cry, her soul wracked with the overwhelming loss. How could life be so cruel? Why had she been allowed to live instead of dying with her parents? Is this what she could expect for the rest of her life? What had gone wrong?

She tearfully looked up at Adam for a moment before the painful knowledge began to settle around her. She understood; with total clarity, she understood completely and with utter finality. She had moved too quickly. She had foolishly challenged it. Why couldn't she have been content with what she had? The other had stepped in and ended everything, had ended it completely and totally. She had won.

CHAPTER 13

EVELYN LISTENED TO HIS slow breathing; Adam had finally fallen asleep from sheer exhaustion. She had never seen such deep sorrow in another person. It had been different with her parents. She had desperately swallowed her grief until it changed into something monstrous; something buried within her, and she suspected, something that now haunted his dreams — the thing that had come irrevocably between them. But, for Adam, it was different. His grief was that of an innocent, flowing, unrestricted, and perhaps cleansing as it went. What had left her in an almost catatonic state was instead healing Adam.

She left the bedroom and slowly walked to the front room — the living room, the place where visitors should wait. That is where she should be, not in the rest of the house, and especially not in his bedroom. The future she had longed for could never be. The other would never allow it. No, Evelyn would never allow it, for she was the monster. They were one in the same.

Evelyn sat for a long while staring at the curtains. She had no desire to get up or do anything else for that matter. She felt that if she were to stop breathing, it would not have mattered in the least.

She was thinking of the futility of her life when Adam walked in and stood by one of the windows. He looked out the thin white curtain at nothing in particular. Everything was quiet. Evelyn stared at the back of his head for a moment before looking down at her hands again. She knew, as far as he was concerned, she was gone. For her, nothing mattered. Was he even grieving now? Perhaps he thought it was for the best. After all, what could have come of it, a relationship doomed from the beginning? It was a hopeless garden she had planted, one now covered by the snows of an everlasting winter. The hope and love she had thought possible in this life were gone.

When he turned, she looked into his eyes and again saw the pain. She was wrong. He was not overcoming anything; he looked completely lost. She quickly lowered her own eyes, not being able to stand his sorrow. He sank to the floor with his back to the window, his moist eyes staring at the couch where Evelyn sat, but through her at the wall beyond. She was gone.

They sat across from each other for a long time before she became aware of the rain. She stood and slowly walked to the door without looking at Adam and opened it. It appeared to be a hard rain, but she hardly noticed. She walked through the door leaving it open and stepped off the porch. The smell of evaporating moisture from the pavement and grass filled her senses. There was a time when she would have taken delight in this simple pleasure. Now, she felt nothing. As she stood there, her hair and clothing quickly became soaked. It did not matter; nothing mattered. She looked at the passing traffic and thought of all the busy people, people living with people, socializing, loving, caring for each other. She walked slowly to the curb, watching the traffic so unaware of her existence. It would be so easy. And...it would not be a bad thing at all.

CHAPTER 14

ADAM OPENED HIS EYES and tried to feel her presence; there was nothing. She was truly gone. For a moment, he thought maybe she had never been there, but his heart told him otherwise. Whatever had happened, whatever he had done, had frightened her off, maybe for good. Perhaps he had pushed her too fast, too hard. Still, he could not stand the thought that she might be gone forever. I can get her back. Somehow, somehow, I can get her back. He could not bring himself to accept what he knew in his heart.

He left his bedroom and walked to the front window. Was Evelyn out there? Would she ever come back? He watched the traffic for a while before turning around and sliding to the floor. What could he do?

After a while, he became aware that the front door was open and reached to close it. Looking into the rain, he saw a young woman standing by the curb. She didn't have a raincoat or umbrella and was getting drenched in the downpour. Standing, he stepped onto the porch and hollered, "Hey, Miss, you can use my porch until the rain stops."

She did not seem to hear him and in fact, looked like she was going to walk across the street, seemingly unaware of a large truck coming.

"Hey!" he yelled, "Wait!" Before realizing what he was doing, he was running and yelling for her to stop.

At the last moment, she turned to look at him; the truck splashing water against her already soaked clothing. She stood there watching him with a look of astonishment, rain dripping down her face.

"Hey, lady, I'm sorry! It looked like you were going to cross in front of that truck."

She said nothing as they both stood there in the rain.

"Look, you're wet! Why don't you come up to my porch, and I'll get you some towels to dry off with?" He put his hand out to her and pointed back to the house.

When she did not move or say anything, he thought that maybe she might be wary of his forwardness. He was a stranger after all. The neighborhood was normally pretty safe, but you couldn't be too careful these days. "I'm sorry if I startled you; I thought you were in trouble. I've got plenty of dry towels; it won't take a moment to get them. It looks like this storm might take a little longer to pass." He looked up and around, then back to her face. For the first time, he realized how beautiful she was, even soaked. He smiled. "Hey, really I'm not dangerous. I live right here," he said, pointing again to his house, "And all the neighbors love me. I'm harmless."

A smile touched her lips, and for the first time, she looked down. "Yes, I guess I am soaked! I don't know what I was thinking!" She laughed. "Thank you! I'd love to dry off."

They ran back to the porch and stood a moment looking at each other. The young lady did not appear to be embarrassed, but Adam suddenly felt awkward.

"Um, let me go get those towels; I'll be right back." He went inside, leaving the door open, and headed for the linen closet. When he returned, he found her standing inside the room, a small puddle of water forming at her feet. Realizing this, she quickly stepped back out the door. "I'm sorry! I didn't mean to get your floor wet!"

"It's fine." He laughed and dropped a couple of towels over it before inviting her back inside. She was obviously freezing, with her arms held tightly to her chest and shivering.

Self-consciously, he wrapped one of his large beach towels over her shoulders and gave her another to dry off. "Do you want to come in a minute? I can turn on a heater for you." He was feeling increasingly uncomfortable having her stand there with the door open. A cool breeze was blowing through it. He wanted to close it but was afraid of the implications of doing so.

"Would you mind if I used your bathroom to dry off?" she said unexpectedly.

Adam was struck dumb for about two seconds before he said, "Oh! Yeah, please. That's fine. It's right down the hall to your..." He noticed she was already inside before he had a chance to finish. Standing outside the door, he said, "There's a heater in the closet, just plug it in. I've got some hot chocolate. Would you care for some?" Putting his ear closer to the door, he thought he could hear her crying softly behind it, but wasn't sure. "Look, it's okay. I promise you're safe here." There was no reply. "I'll have that hot chocolate ready by the time you get out." He waited a moment more in awkward silence before another thought occurred to him. "Wait a minute!" he said suddenly, "I had a sister with some clothes that look like they might fit you. I'll just hang some things on the doorknob in case you need to use them while your stuff dries. I have a dryer you can use also. It wouldn't take very long..." He realized he was rambling. "Okay, I'll just go take care of that now." He thought that he was probably scaring her now. What an idiot he was!

Going to his sister's room, he paused for a moment before thinking, This is an emergency, Sis. He gathered a pair of jeans, a long-sleeved plaid camping shirt, and some thick socks. Then as he started to leave the room, he thought about the other stuff that women usually wear, and his cheeks blushed. He did not think she would want to wear someone else's underwear, so he just grabbed a hunting vest and brought that instead.

Stopping at the door, he waited a moment before saying, "I'm hanging the stuff on the doorknob. I'll have that hot chocolate for you in about five minutes."

Inside the bathroom, Evelyn still stood looking at herself in the mirror. She could not believe what was happening and was afraid of doing or saying anything that might end it.

Taking the towel, she dried her hair and removed her clothing. On the other side of the door, she heard Adam say he was hanging his sister's clothes on the doorknob and would get the hot chocolate made. She said nothing, still afraid of ending the miracle. Opening the door to get the clothing, she suddenly realized that if she wasn't invisible to him any longer, he could see her and she would be...! She quickly jumped behind the door and reached around with her arm to pull the clothes in.

Soon, she was dressed and had combed her short hair using one of his combs. Outside the door, she heard Adam say softly, "Are you okay in there? I've got the chocolate ready. You take as long as you need though, I'll be in the kitchen. It's right down the hall."

She waited until she was sure he was gone before, once again, looking at herself in the mirror. How long would she let this continue, and why was she allowing it anyway? Closing her eyes and taking a deep breath to calm herself, she finally left the bathroom.

Adam stood by the stove when she entered, and she half-expected that he would not see her.

"Please, have a seat. That's your cup."

He pointed to the one at the end of the table, the one furthest from his. Evelyn noticed the chair was already pulled out.

She didn't know what to say. Here they were drinking hot chocolate as if nothing had ever happened between them.

"Do they fit okay?" Adam asked.

"Yes, they're fine."

After some silence, Adam commented, "It looks like it's letting up some."

"Yes, it sure came on suddenly,"

More silence.

Adam was beginning to feel increasingly awkward. "There's plenty more chocolate; just help yourself. I'm going to take your clothes and put them in the dryer."

"No!" Evelyn said, suddenly embarrassed. "No, I'll do it." She jumped up and quickly moved to get her clothing out of the bathroom.

"It's just across..." Once again, Adam didn't get the chance to finish before he saw her enter the room just across the hall from the bathroom. He heard the dryer start, and after a moment, she returned.

Adam was beginning to feel he may have met her before and finally asked, "We've never met before, have we? You seem familiar."

She picked up her cup and put it to her lips, giving her time to think. If she told Adam who she was, would the demon punish her by ending this? Should she keep it a secret? What was she supposed to do? Evelyn felt terror build at the prospect of losing Adam again. When it seemed like she had waited too long with the cup to her lips, she set it down and looked at him. She had to say something, but what? Her eyes filled with tears as she tried to think of something.

Seeing how upset she was, Adam said, "Say... Um, I'm sorry! I never introduced myself. I'm Adam Yates. Please forgive my lack of manners."

Evelyn didn't say anything. She just continued to look at him, too frightened to move.

"Look, if I'm frightening you, I'm sorry! I'm not dangerous. At least that's what everyone says, and I believe it." Adam laughed half-heartedly. "Is there something wrong? Are you feeling alright?" Adam was starting to get an uneasy feeling about the entire situation and was wondering if he had done right by inviting her into his house. Of course, he had! He reprimanded himself. Something else was bothering her. "Would you like some more chocolate?"

Evelyn lowered her eyes to the cup again, several tears dropping to the tabletop.

"If you're hungry, I can fix you something." Adam was beginning to feel strange. Why? "I've got some milk in the fridge or some soda if you'd like that instead."

Suddenly, as if it had never ended, he felt Evelyn's presence again! He immediately rose to his feet, knocking the chair against the wall.

The young lady continued to stare at her cup as if nothing was happening. He wanted to call out to Evelyn but was afraid of frightening the lady more than he already had. He turned around and picked up his chair. "I'm so sorry for that! That was clumsy of me. I have a good friend that I heard at the door... I mean I thought I heard her, I'd better check. Uh, I'll be right back. Just give me a moment." As he left the kitchen and entered the living room, he felt her presence dimming. No, he thought desperately. She had to be in the kitchen.

The young lady was still sitting there with her eyes glued to the cup of chocolate.

"Uh, can I get you another? I think I was mistaken; she's not at the door." Adam felt like a fool. He was just making things worse. "Here, let me get you another cup." As he moved towards her with the pan, Evelyn's presence increased until he stood over her. He froze, staring at the top of her head, trying to understand what was happening. She had still not moved. Slowly, he moved his hand lightly across her soft hair.

With that single touch, his emotions exploded! He stumbled backward, and the pot fell from his hand, splashing hot chocolate across the floor.

"Evelyn!"

It was all he could say. Tears ran unashamedly down his face.

Evelyn lifted her head and stood, looking up at him. Words no longer mattered. They came into a tight embrace, both crying, and both terrified that the moment would be taken from them.

CHAPTER 15

WHEN ADAM COULD FINALLY trust his voice again, he asked, "How?"

With her head pushed tightly against his chest, Evelyn said, "I don't know, I just don't know."

"I thought I had lost you!" he choked. They stood for a long while, each holding desperately to the other, neither saying anything.

After what seemed too short a time, he slowly pulled back and gently took her hands in his. He looked into her beautiful almond-shaped eyes and suddenly realized that he recognized her. This was the angel from his dreams. From her startling green eyes to the cut of her silky brown hair, it was the same. Her lips, her nose, her flawless skin, everything was the same. "You're so beautiful!" he whispered, "I can't believe you're real. How? What happened?"

Evelyn looked down, blushing from his compliments, but fear filled her mind again. "I'm afraid. I don't know how long this will last. I think she thought we were getting too close. She can control how much I can be seen, and she's angry, she's a monster!" Evelyn was quiet for a moment before continuing. How could she explain any of it? "And she is afraid of something. I'm not sure I understand what, but she is very, very afraid of it."

Adam looked at her with a confused look. "So, I was right then? Have you somehow been controlling my mind? But, what is this about someone controlling you?"

"It's not me that's controlling you. Well, I guess it is me, but it's more like something inside me." Evelyn was suddenly confused. She had not thought this through well enough to explain it to someone else. Most of what she understood was in the form of feelings or emotions. She felt herself starting to cry again. "I don't want to lose you—not again. I don't. I don't," she whispered desperately.

He pulled her to him and tried consoling her. "It's okay! Everything is going to be fine. Don't worry; we'll figure this out."

Evelyn looked down at the spilled chocolate and said, "Oh! I'm so sorry. I didn't know how to tell you, or even if I could. I didn't know if she would let me."

"We need to talk about this as much as we can before something else does happen." Adam pulled his chair over to her, and they both sat back down. He took her hands in his and said, "Okay, Evelyn, I want you to tell me as much as you can about what has happened to you. Help me understand what's been going on."

She briefly told Adam about her childhood and who she was before the murders. As far as her parent's death, she skipped over it, only saying that a terrible thing had happened, and they had died. He did not push her on it. The rest, she told him in as much detail as possible, especially, the interpretation she had on his dreams. She explained that she did not think she dreamed, but if she did, maybe the other was not letting her remember them. But she also believed another part of her mind, a good part, was managing to talk to him in his dreams, but she had no recollection or awareness of it. The other presence he was seeing was some alternate personality of hers, maybe something she had created to protect herself. Whatever it was, it was truly horrible.

They spoke through much of the day, with Adam taking time to tell her about his life as well. He would have preferred not to have wasted it, but she insisted. He told her of the death of his mother and two sisters in a terrible auto accident and his father's just six months later. He also didn't elaborate on what had happened in his father's death. He had no direct living relatives as far as he knew, but he told her he had some friends, and they had helped him through much of it. Without trying to make her talk about whatever had occurred, he wanted to understand how she had survived afterward. The loneliness she must have felt, and the fact that there had been no one to comfort her saddened him deeply.

When he asked her about her extended family, she told him that she thought she had some aunts and uncles, but didn't know where they lived. Her parents always told her that her father's work kept them from visiting. She assumed that it was because they lived so far away. She remembered pushing it several times, trying to get them to set up a family reunion, but something always came up to prevent it. Also, there were few family picture albums. She knew it was somewhat strange.

Evelyn also told him about the way she was practically ignored as a teenager. Looking back, she said it was almost a precursor of her present condition. They both agreed that if it were not for his dreams, they most likely would never have been able to meet officially. It looked like one part of her was trying to hide and another was trying to reach out, especially to him. He was grateful for that part.

It was late before he finally asked her if she wanted to get something to eat. He said he was famished and Evelyn agreed. She was excited about finally being able to get out in public without worrying about being kicked, pushed, or run over.

"Let me get cleaned up; I know a place we can go," he said as he went back to change his clothing.

Evelyn also needed to get into something more fitting. When he asked her if his sister's clothes would be okay, she told him she had something in his closet. She smiled at the look of surprise on his face and told him she had placed hers behind his sweaters.

It didn't take more than an instant for Adam to connect the dots. Looking a bit shy, he asked where she had been sleeping.

Evelyn quickly looked away.

He laughed. "I guess that's why I saw the blanket there. Were you using it?"

She blushed and said, "Yes, and you yanked it off me! I think that was the only time I was ever thankful for being invisible." They both laughed, though Adam somewhat nervously.

Evelyn took her one change of clothing to the bathroom. Adam used the bedroom.

When he finished, he went to the kitchen and noticed immediately that the chocolate had been cleaned up. Evelyn was sitting at the table waiting for him in a pair of jeans and a pretty blouse.

"Well, it looks like I can still see you. Maybe your alter ego is satisfied that I'm not a danger. What do you think?"

Evelyn thought for a second. "I'm not sure. Something is going on, and I don't know what it is. I don't trust her though. She scares me."

Adam considered this and concluded that Evelyn might be more in need of Doctor Elliot than he was. But if she was right about this alter ego thing, he didn't think it would allow her to go to the doctor. They should not do anything that might provoke it to intervene again. He was surprised that they were able to talk so much with Evelyn remaining visible. She may be right about something having changed. It could also mean that her problem had ended. However, the thought came to him that Evelyn was very messed up. Even though he was absolutely in love with her, he wondered if she might not be a little dangerous. The entire idea was something right out of a psycho murder mystery. As long as she was invisible, it never mattered to him. But now that he could see her, he could not ignore the possibility that these things she had been through may have scarred her in some ugly ways, ways that may be psychotic.

CHAPTER 16

THE NEW ORLEANS SUMMER evening temperatures never dipped much below seventy degrees except for thunderstorms, which were always a welcome relief.

As they went out to have dinner, their conversations continued, especially about how they had come to meet. Adam found it humorous, but a bit embarrassing when she told him about the time she had first seen him jumping up and down on her branch.

Adam was the perfect gentleman. He was thoughtful and kind and always looking for some way to be helpful. His personality was genuine, unlike some of the guys in high school. Of course, she did not have much experience on the subject, but she had heard enough about it from the other girls. As she watched Adam driving, she could barely believe her good fortune, a strange thought considering her past.

She recalled the unusual event that had occurred on Friday, before entering his house. Her family had never been religious. She had never gone to church, but her mother had given her more rules to follow than most of her friends. She had never prayed—not until then. Evelyn did not know what to think about it. The event was so strange that she was almost tempted to disregard it as imaginary. However, taking a quick look at Adam, she wondered if it might not be wise to say a quick one now to keep her demon from ruining their date.

Even though they had spent lots of time talking, they did not know each other all that well. Except for the intensity of their unexplainable love, they were almost strangers. She had not told Adam her nightmare theory that perhaps he was in love with her because she was messing with his mind, somehow forcing him to feel that way. She felt strongly that this was not the case, but she was too frightened of its possibility to mention it. It had also occurred to Evelyn this evening that she had to find a way to rid her of this alternate personality—if possible. Perhaps, she was gone now. Maybe that is why the world was back to normal again. A smile touched her lips.

As Adam parked the car, Evelyn's eyes widened in surprise. She thought they were going to a hamburger or pizza place. Instead, it looked like a fancy restaurant. She looked at her jeans before again gazing at the obviously expensive building. Her concerns increased as they walked through the front door and she observed finely dressed customers being asked for their names and reservations.

Adam looked at her before saying with confidence, "Don't worry about it, I know the people here. I'll be able to get us in, no problem."

When their time came, Adam said, "Hey Mike! How's it going?"

"Adam! Where have you been? I was starting to think you had skipped town."

"Nope, I had some personal business to take care of." Then, more subdued, he said, "My father passed away."

Mike's countenance fell. "I'm sorry to hear it. Wow! Honest, this is the first I've heard. Is there anything I can do for you? Are you okay?"

"Sure, you know how it is. These things happen." Then Adam gave a half-smile. "Hey, I hope you know you're not getting out of this alive either?"

A look of confusion crossed Mike's features.

"Sorry," Adam said, "Bad pun on my part. I appreciate your concern! It's just that things have been so weird for me lately."

"Sure, I can understand."

Adam took a quick glance at Evelyn before thinking; you have no idea.

Mike continued, "But seriously if you need anything..."

"Well, Mike, I don't have a reservation, can you make an exception for my lady friend and me, just for tonight?"

Mike looked at him startled before putting on a stern expression. "Sorry, Adam, you know we can't do that. If we do it for you, we have to do it for everyone." Mike looked straight-faced at Adam for a moment; both just stared at each other. Then Mike started laughing and said, "Gotcha!"

They both laughed.

"By the way, did you forget your date in the car, or is she coming later?" Mike looked straight through Evelyn like she wasn't even there.

Adam turned with a sick feeling in his heart to find that Evelyn was still standing beside him, a frightened look on her face. When she realized Adam could still see her, she closed her eyes and began breathing again.

Adam quickly turned around and looked at Mike who was still looking expectantly at the door. "Come on, Mike," he said playfully, "You know my dates are always imaginary."

"Yeah," Mike chuckled, "But I thought this time you would have a real one." They both laughed, and Mike told him to get inside before he decided to make Adam wash dishes or something.

Then, as he began to follow the maître d', Mike added with sincerity, "Hey, Adam, I truly am sorry about your father. I'm serious; if you need anything, let me know."

The maître d' escorted him to a table in the back, something more private and not too bright. A pretty waitress, who appeared to know Adam, judging from her expression, followed them. After a friendly, but quick, conversation, the host left.

Watching Adam sit, the waitress had briefly looked over at Evelyn's chair as it was pulled out from the table. Returning her attention to him, she smiled. He looked nervously at Evelyn and then at the waitress.

"Hello, sweetheart," the waitress said. "When are you going to finally bring a real woman in here?"

Adam laughed as he looked over at Evelyn, surprised to see her giving the waitress a look that would have dropped a bull elephant in its tracks. "Come on, Naomi, you know you're the only woman for me."

"And you're the only man for me, sweetie. So why do we always have to meet like this? I'm serving you, instead of both of us sitting together?" She stood there as if waiting for an answer.

"Well, Naomi, if I were to marry you, you would still be serving me at home..."

"Over your dead body, honey," she said softly, "Naomi doesn't serve any man, except he pays her those big bucks first." She smiled at him.

Looking over at Evelyn staring at him oddly, Adam blushed and said, "Well, anyway, how about my usual. And you know what, I'm hungry tonight. Can I have two dinners?"

Naomi sighed. "Okay, so you want two rib-eyes on the same plate."

"Um, no, actually, I'd like them on separate plates. Oh, and we'll have two Sprites." He smiled before realizing what he had just said. "Uh, I mean I'll have two Sprites."

Naomi looked at him a moment, before saying, "You're a strange one, Adam! Instead of acting like you have a date, why don't you just ask me out and make it the real thing?"

Looking over at Evelyn, he was startled to see that she was now standing with a look of fury on her face. He quickly turned and said, "Naomi, you know I love you like a sister, but I have to have my fantasy girls too. Now, please, can I have those meals?" He looked over at Evelyn whose face looked flushed even in the dim lighting; she did not look happy.

"Okay, sweetie," Naomi sighed. "Two rib-eyes: one for you, and one for the fantasy girl. I hope, for your sake, she's more substantial when you get her home tonight."

Adam's eyes widened as he saw Evelyn grab Naomi by the shoulders and push her away from the table.

She stumbled backward, landing on the floor in a sitting position. Naomi quickly looked around to see what had happened, but finding no one near, looked back at Adam who was now standing and looking just as confused.

He asked with honest concern, "Are you okay?"

Bewildered and somewhat embarrassed, she smiled at him. "Yes, um, sure..." She stood up again and momentarily straightened her out-fit, before walking away as if nothing unusual had occurred.

Adam watched Evelyn sit. He believed Naomi would be fine, and he felt like the whole incident was somewhat humorous, but he was much too concerned about Evelyn to express this humor; she appeared very upset.

She did not look at him for a moment. When she did briefly lift her eyes, her face was blood red, and she glared at him accusingly. "Well, she was such an abhorrent jerk!" She again lowered her face to her lap, her eyes filling with tears.

Adam was silent for a while, but took the cloth napkin next to his silverware and handed it to her. Then he said, "She was rude... I'm sure she deserved it." He tried to laugh.

She looked up but didn't join him in the humor of the moment. What had just happened had frightened her—a lot! She had not been able to control it. She was here.

He let her have some space for a few minutes before commenting, "It appears you're still broadcasting. Just when you think this can't get any weirder, it does. So, now I'm the only one that gets in. That's not the best thing for you, but for us, it's still far better than what we had."

Their dinner arrived, and they ate, mostly in silence. Any talking that Adam did, he made sure the napkin was covering his mouth; it would not do for someone to see him having a conversation with him-self. It already appeared that Naomi thought he was running on three cylinders.

On the way home, Evelyn kept mentally kicking herself. Her first real date and she had ruined it. She just had to get a grip on this anger thing. No normal person would have acted like that. Then again, thought Evelyn, she was not even close to being normal. She must learn to control it, for Adam's sake.

As Evelyn sat listening to him, a darker thought surfaced. What if she was capable of worse—much worse! She knew she was. She turned her head to the window, to the city lights. With Adam, she had more than she could ever have hoped for, but something was wrong. It al-most felt like she was being manipulated or not in control as if she was not whole or—not even real.

CHAPTER 17

ETURNING HOME, ADAM AND Evelyn continued to talk about the past and the experiences she had growing up. The one thing they didn't talk about was the future. It had become a taboo subject that neither wanted to discuss. Evelyn knew she wanted to spend the rest of her life with him. But, didn't that mean marriage? Did Adam love her enough for something like that and was he willing to take on the weight of a schizophrenic wife?

The weight of all the emotions of the day eventually brought on exhaustion, and they both agreed they should get some sleep. Adam had to be at work in the morning, but he had asked Evelyn if she would stay with him. He said he never wanted to be apart from her again.

Now that she was visible, at least to him, they needed to make other sleeping arrangements. It just would not do for them to be sharing the same bedroom. But the house was big, and he suggested she take his older sister's room. He told her that if she were still alive, she would have loved Evelyn. In fact, he said, she probably did know about her.

Evelyn knew he was a religious person because of all the times she had heard him pray, but didn't know which religion. It didn't matter to her; she had never given the idea of an afterlife much thought. She had just taken it for granted that her parents were dead, and she would never see them again. She thought it would be great if people did live on after death, but she didn't believe it. Nevertheless, she was happy that it gave Adam comfort because she understood his terrible loss. He needed something to hold onto. Of course, she still loved her family, but she knew they were gone, and she didn't really need anything...

Evelyn laid herself on the bed in his sister's room and ran her hand softly over the clean sheets. A small night light allowed her to see the room dimly. She thought about how she did not need to believe in an afterlife and about how she was strong enough to handle the death of her mother and father. For a while, she watched as an unseen air-conditioning breeze gently moved a window curtain, and she lay there wondering how much longer it would be before she finally drifted off to sleep. So much had happened today. In a few moments, her eyes closed, and her hand slid slowly down onto the damp sheet beneath her cheek.

The surface stretched outward toward the horizon in each direction, eventually joining the crystal blue sky above. The scent of flowers and cologne per-

meated everything. A continual breeze, flowing from all directions across a perfectly flat world, passed over and through the infinite expanse until encountering the only resistance to its gentle flow — a hill. Upon that hill grew a great oak tree with branches that stretched outward and upward seeking to touch the very sky above.

Evelyn watched and waited. He had been gone for so long. She needed him now, as death needed life. Each day she brought her watering pitcher to feed the tree, hoping to entice him to return. She knew he loved playing on its branches; she had to keep it healthy. Every day, she would circle the hill and watch for him, and each day, when she returned to the beginning, another would begin, and she would continue and continue and continue...

She had spoken to her sister, her storm with its lightning and thunder. She had spoken to her anger and fury and now knew what she wanted. He was to find the destroyer of worlds and tell her where it was. If he did this, she would grant him paradise. If he did not... she would remove his very breath and add it to the breeze sweeping the plains forever and ever.

CHAPTER 18

A S TIRED AS HE WAS, Adam was too restless to sleep. When his mother and sisters had died, he thought his life could never be the same, and it wasn't, but he believed he and his father would be able to make it somehow. Then, with his father's murder, he almost lost all hope. If not for his friends, and, of course, God, he could never have gotten through it.

Now, there was Evelyn. How could he love her so much? It was as if she was the center of his world, and he had only known her for a short while. Actually, he had only known her in the flesh for about a day. So, why was he even thinking about marriage so soon?

He had always believed that a man and a woman were only half of what they could be without each other. Evelyn was part of his life now--no, she was his life. So where did that leave him? There was only one answer. Regardless of whether she was sick, he could not imagine a future without her.

He sat against the trunk, feeling the familiar gnarled surface against his back. The sky was clear except for a few wisps of white drifting against the blue sky above.

Turning, he saw her sitting next to him, and he smiled. She was dressed in a flowing white gown that sparkled with points of light too numerous to count. Her hair looked like soft silk, gently floating on the breeze, her eyes as deep as an emerald sea. Her lips seemed to draw him into a world of incredible mysteries beyond anything he could imagine.

She did not say anything. Instead, she turned slightly and rested her back against the great oak, and looked out over the world. After an eternity, she whispered, "Adam, she won't drive you away anymore."

With those words, Adam quickly remembered the demon and looked around in fear.

"No, please don't be afraid! We're safe now. This is our time." She looked at him anxiously.

Suddenly, Adam understood that he was in a dream! He slowly stood up, afraid to break the spell and put his hand on the trunk behind him. It felt real! He could only remember one other time in his life having such an experience, and it was nothing compared to this!

The world was beautiful beyond belief, but as he looked at Evelyn, he realized that it paled beside her. How could anyone or anything be so lovely? She was standing next to him now, looking up into his eyes with so much feeling that he could hardly bear it. Reaching to her, he let the tips of his fingers caress her cheek and the gentle curve of her chin.

She said nothing further, allowing Adam to become more comfortable with her and his surroundings.

Briefly pulling his attention from her, he stepped away to look out upon the world. He could see the flowers at his feet, but he could see those on the horizon just as clearly. The fragrances and visions were too wonderful to describe. The colors blended from one to another, and another and still another until he was looking at colors for which he had no names. He was no stranger to elaborate dreams, but this was like none he had ever experienced before.

Turning again to Evelyn, he saw that she was no longer next to him. In a sudden panic, he looked around and found her sitting at the bottom of the hill on a small rock next to a stream, one he had not noticed before.

Then, he was standing near her and watched as she allowed the flowing stream to pass between her fingers, creating ebbing swirls as it lovingly caressed her. It was so clear that he was able to see the bottom as easily as the surface.

Continuing to look at the intricate patterns created by the gentle current, Evelyn whispered, "She's allowing us to be together now."

Adam saw a stone next to hers and suddenly found himself sitting there as if he had been there all along, his face not six inches from hers. He waited, content, thinking he could watch her do this one simple thing forever and never grow tired of it.

After an immeasurable span of time, she turned her head to look at him, her eyes full of shyness, but maybe some mischief as well. She looked back down again and smiled. Adam, this is where I live now. It is where I wait for you, forever. Does it please you?"

Adam looked at her and said, "Evelyn, I don't understand what this all means. I know I must be dreaming, and yet it doesn't feel like it. And yes, it does please me. What is it though? Can it really be a dream?"

"This is actually your world, not mine. I came searching for you, but I have been here forever. My world is a dark place." She shivered. "I want to stay here and never have to go back!" She was silent for a time, her eyes wandering off towards the horizon, her face solemn, her lovely, pale brow furrowed with anxiety." In my world, I have a sister, and she... has issues. At the beginning of time, when I found a way to yours, she found out and came for me. I returned repeatedly, but she always found me. Oh, Adam, I don't want to return, but she will come and take me if you do not help."

Adam thought he understood some of what she was saying, but much of it seemed symbolic and enigmatic. "How can I help? Tell me. I'll do what I can."

Evelyn turned her head toward his, their lips almost touching. Putting her

hand on the side of his cheek, she moved her lips to his ear and whispered,
"Adam, you must ask me what happened to my parents."

Adam opened his eyes and looked around the room. With the dream fresh in his mind, it looked bland and lonely, empty of feeling. He sat up and thought about the dream. It was quickly evaporating from his mind like moisture from a hot cement surface.

Jumping to his feet, he switched on the lamp and located a pencil. He attempted to record the dream but could remember little more than her whispered message. Ask me what happened to my parents.

How am I going to do this? If she wanted to tell him about such a personal thing, she would have already done it. The dream had faded away completely. Only a feeling of warmth remained, probably from Evelyn's subconscious mind. His world was becoming progressively stranger by the day. What was he getting himself into?

It was still early, but he felt refreshed. This was a good time to beat Evelyn to the kitchen and fix her some breakfast. Smiling and being as quiet as possible, he cleaned up and dressed. In the kitchen, he pre-pared a couple of Spanish omelets, fresh squeezed orange juice, apple slices, grits, sausage, and two cold glasses of milk. As he finished set-ting the table, he heard a door close in the hallway.

"Hey, sleepyhead, are you going to stay in the sack all day?! We have a lot of stuff to do, places to go, people to see, hamburgers to make! Hurry up; it'll be great!" He looked up and found her standing there all dressed and looking like a triple-decker-super-duper Adam Yates Wonder Burger, with all the trimmings! "Wow!" he said, "You look great!"

Evelyn smiled shyly and said, "Aw, it's just some old thing I threw on. You probably say that to all the invisible girls you meet."

"Hm, I don't believe I've given any of them that particular line." He looked like he was trying hard to remember. "Nope, I'm sure of it, you're the first!"

"Adam, are you positive it's alright if I wear your sister's clothes? Please be truthful with me. If you have any misgivings..."

Adam blushed. "If I ever did, they're gone now."

Evelyn looked down at her clasped hands and said nothing.

"Please sit down. I've made a great breakfast for us." Adam pulled out her chair and slipped it forward as she sat. It seemed a little strange, but he had placed a single flower in a tall clear vase next to her break-fast.

Evelyn looked at Adam and grinned. "I can't believe you went through all this trouble. You shouldn't have. Perhaps, I can fix something here for you this evening. You may be surprised to know that I have quite a bit of cooking experience as well."

"It wasn't any trouble," he said, "I've been cooking since I was a kid."

As Adam sat down, she picked up her fork and tasted the eggs. With the fork in her mouth, she noticed from the corner of her eye, Adam's bowed head. Quietly placing the fork back on the table, she looked down nervously.

Adam looked up like nothing had happened and saw her concern. "Hey! No, I'm sorry. I didn't mean to embarrass you. It's okay if you start eating. This is just something I do. I don't mean to make you uncomfortable or anything like that."

Blushing, Evelyn said apologetically, "Adam, this is your house, and I need to go by your rules."

"No, really, I'm serious. Unless it's something you want to do, I don't want you to feel you have to join me."

Evelyn continued to blush. She did not know what to say.

"Look at it like this. I don't have any rules when it comes to you," he said, smiling, and began to eat. Then he stopped smiling and said matter-of-factly, "Except the one where you try to eat me. We have to draw the line there."

That did it. Evelyn burst out laughing. "I remember when you said that! You actually seemed serious about it. The fact that you thought it might be a possibility and yet still wanted me... well, it went a long way to convince me not to."

Again, they both burst into laughter. Any remaining feelings of awkwardness dissolved, leaving a warm blanket of intimacy behind.

Evelyn was honestly impressed by how delightful everything tasted. "What kind of seasoning do you use on these eggs? They're wonderful!"

"Sorry, family secret. Maybe I'll be able to tell you someday..." His sentence trailed off into the void as she looked to see him blushing and looking very intently into his milk.

Realizing what he may be referring to, she decided this was indeed the very best breakfast she had ever eaten.

CHAPTER 19

ADAM OPENED THE RESTAURANT by himself this morning; Rose, his waitress/cashier/wonder woman, would not be in until 10:00 a.m. He had asked Evelyn along because he could not bear the thought of being separated from her. They might even find a way to work together, but all he wanted now was to be near her. There was so much to talk about; he was sure he would never get bored again.

He was still in awe of the reality of their situation, strange as it was. But mostly, he was astonished that here he was, Adam Yates, bachelor for life, not only in love with a beautiful woman but in love with a beautiful woman that loved him as well. Sure, she had some issues... everyone had issues! Hers were just more technical than most. Just a little. He smiled. "You can sit over there, that's the one Rose normally uses for breaks. Unless it gets busy, that table is usually empty."

She followed him as he went to the kitchen and fired up the grill, switched on the kitchen lights, and prepared the coffee machine. As he worked, he talked to her about some of the things he thought might improve the business.

"Do you remember Friday evening before you left?" Evelyn asked.

"Hey! Were you in here then? Something happened at Rose's table that seemed odd. Was that you?"

She laughed. "Yep, that was me. I thought you were going to try to sit on my lap. I arrived earlier and chose that booth because it seemed out of the way. If anyone came in, I was going to hide next to the drink machine."

Evelyn was quiet for a while as Adam continued to do the setup. "I've noticed how everyone seems to like you so much. Someday, you have to tell me your secret."

"You know," he said, "There are so many angry people today. If you just give them a smile and a kind word and assuming they don't punch you out for it, it goes a long way to brighten their day."

Evelyn thought about this for a moment. "Is that what you do? I mean, do you always look for ways to make people feel better?"

"Not always." He grinned. "Sometimes I just try to make myself happy by saving invisible girls."

She blushed. "You do excel at that."

Opening the walk-in refrigerator, he asked if she would help bring some pies out to the counter display. "I have a few that didn't sell Saturday; just put those at the back so we can sell them first. I'll cut some more for the front."

Evelyn felt good about doing these strangely mundane things. It seemed so unusual for her to be doing this now when just last week she was hiding from everyone. How were they ever going to live a normal life with her still invisible? After a moment, she decided, normal or not, it was going to be wonderful.

Adam had completed the setup and was placing the money into the cash register when the thought came to him that someone with her abilities could be quite the thief. They would steal from you, and you would never know it. Coming around the counter, he said, "Let's sit for a bit. We have some time before Rose comes in."

Sitting at the table where Rose normally took her breaks, Adam said, "I was wondering something. It must have been very difficult for you these last couple of years. I know you had to hide and were frightened a lot, but you also had to do things that must have made you feel pretty awful."

Seeing the serious look on his face and the direction the conversation was taking, she became embarrassed and looked out the window to avoid his eyes.

"What I'm getting at is this. Just because you had to do some things that may have been dishonest, you had no choice if you wanted to stay alive. You've been through an impossible situation. And, I want you to know, I will never judge you on anything... ever!" He reached over and put his hand on hers, causing her to look into his eyes at last. He saw the tear threatening to betray her and squeezed her hand, briefly looking out the window. "Anyway, I hope you will grant me the same courtesy. I don't want you finding out about my rowdy days."

Evelyn smiled, thinking she could not even begin to imagine what he would ever have done wrong.

They both sat for a few minutes in silence, feeling perfectly comfortable with it. Adam finally said, "Evelyn, I had a dream again last night."

She looked up at him in alarm, wondering if it had depressed him.

He saw her concern and told her he was fine and that it was a real breakthrough of sorts. "I know you're going to find this very interesting. It seems that whether you remember it or not, you are speaking to me in those dreams. After I awoke, I couldn't remember a lot of the conversation, but I know it was you talking to me. Last night you gave me a message, something I'm supposed to ask you."

Evelyn didn't say anything.

"Look, I want you to know that I would never intrude on your privacy like this if it weren't you that was asking me to do it. I know it's crazy. Most of this just doesn't make sense to me.

"It's alright, Adam, you can ask me. This whole mess is my fault anyway. But are you sure it was me and not her?"

"Oh yeah, it was you. Believe me; I can tell the difference a mile away!" Adam laughed nervously.

Then Evelyn said, "But if she can cause you to see things that aren't true here... then why not in your dreams?" This thought had just occurred to Adam as well. What if she were manipulating him to do this?

Adam suddenly felt the blood rush from his face. Was he being used? Would it hurt Evelyn to ask her about the death of her parents? He just didn't know. "Evelyn, if you want, I can ask this later, or even not at all. It's up to you."

She put her face in her hands and tried to decide. After a moment, she looked at Adam and said, "Maybe we should wait until tonight when we are at your house. I can't imagine how a question could be that bad, but it might be better if we waited."

"Great! We wait then," he said. "Can I get you a soda or juice?"

"Yes," she said, "How about a small orange juice? Would that be okay?"

"Your slightest wish is my command," he said in mock reverence. Then, turning to the door, he saw Rose standing there with a very worried look on her face.

CHAPTER 20

ROSE!" ADAM JUMPED AS if he had seen a ghost, which was quite funny, considering. But given the circumstances, he had to say something meaningful. "You're here... on time!"

"Yes, I am." She just stood there looking at him.

"I guess it must be time to open?" He stumbled on, trying to make some intelligent statement, but not making any headway.

Rose didn't say anything.

"Oh heck, Rose, I'm sorry. I guess that looked pretty strange?"

"You could say that, dear, but I was thinking of something more in the line of a padded cell." She walked to the kitchen to put her purse away. Adam looked over at Evelyn, who had her hands covering her eyes, shaking her head gently back and forth with a grin on her lips.

"Yeah, okay! Well, I'm just going to go ahead and open us up now. It looks like we have a long line trying to batter the door down."

Evelyn looked at the door and saw no one there. "It's alright, Adam," she said. "Rose will be okay. Don't try to explain it."

Rose came back in and turned on the main restaurant lights. Taking out her pad, she plopped it down on the counter and called out, "Okay, who's first?"

It was now Adam's turn to stare at Rose.

"Excuse me, Adam, would you let that gentleman through; I believe you're in his way. How about you, little lady?" Rose had turned around and was facing the table where Evelyn was sitting. "Can I get you something?"

Suddenly, Adam realized what was happening and walked over to Rose, reaching for her hand. "Rose, I'm okay."

There were tears in her eyes.

"I was just silly," he tried to explain, "I saw you coming and decided to play a little trick on you. It was not a nice thing for me to do and I apologize."

She pulled out a crumpled napkin from her pocket and wiped her eyes. "I knew that!" she said, laughing, "But I just worry about you so much since that terrible thing with your father and your mother and sisters before that. How much can a young man take?"

Adam put his hand on her shoulder and patted it softly as she got herself under control. "Do you want to sit down for a bit? Obviously, I can handle the high customer load." He smiled. "Look, I was just going to get myself an orange juice, join me?"

"Well, I guess it's not too busy yet, just a small one." She walked over to the table where Evelyn had risen, allowing Rose to sit in her normal spot.

Evelyn said, "Adam, I'll just sit here next to you if that's okay. Just bring the other one and set it on your side of the table. She won't be able to see me drinking it."

He stared at her a few seconds before saying, "Amazing! I wonder if we couldn't use you for something useful, like maybe a superspy."

"No, Adam!" Evelyn said. "You can't talk to me with someone around." Then, looking at the expression on Rose's face, she said, "Now look what you've done."

Rose sat at the table with the crumpled napkin dabbing her eyes again. Evelyn was starting to feel a real attachment to this sensitive lady. She obviously had a lot of compassion.

Adam closed his eyes and dropped his head, arms at his side. "I'll get those orange juices," he said, defeated.

Evelyn moved over to Rose and knelt by her side. She patted her shoulder saying, "It's okay, Rose. I know you can't see or hear me, but I want you to know that Adam is doing just fine. He might be a little dense sometimes, as I'm sure you know, but he's not going crazy."

As Adam came out from behind the counter with the two orange juices, Evelyn asked him, "Adam, do you have an extra pencil and piece of paper? You can write me notes when you need to say something."

He turned around in mid-stride and went back into the kitchen bringing the juices with him. In a moment, he came back out and set one juice in front of Rose and the other, along with the pad of paper and pencil, he set in front of himself.

Rose thanked him and took a sip. Across from her and in the window seat, Evelyn took hers and drank some also before setting it back down in front of Adam's spot. He looked at Rose who did not appear to have seen anything unusual.

"Rose, that is just amazing," Adam said, without looking at Evelyn.

"Yes," Evelyn said, "But also pretty depressing when it's part of your life twenty-four-seven. I still can't understand how it works and I've lived with it for two years."

Rose looked at Adam. "What's amazing?"

"I find it amazing that you can have a heart as compassionate as you do, considering what you have been through."

Evelyn looked at him, understanding that he was still talking to her. She smiled and picked up her juice again, taking another swallow.

Rose said, "My poor Adam, my life has not been anything like yours. I'm just amazed that you can survive so much grief."

Adam took Rose's hand and patted it. He then looked out the window, which was just an excuse to look at Evelyn.

Evelyn finished her orange juice and said, "I think we can learn to do this with a little practice. Maybe for now though, you might not want to be talking to me in front of people." She reached over and put her hand on his, which still covered Rose's, and gave it a little squeeze. "I love you," she whispered.

Adam smiled and said nothing, but she could see his eyes brighten in a silent response.

Monday was not normally a big day, but it seemed like this Monday was even slower. He started writing notes to Evelyn, so as not to upset Rose.

Later, Adam thought of an idea. He wondered if they could talk over a cell phone. Surely, this ability was not so developed as to be able to affect radio signals. And he wondered if she were caught on video, would someone in a different location be able to see her? The idea excited him, and he wrote Evelyn a message about it. She smiled doubtfully but said it was worth a try. She had long since stopped trying anything new, convinced that there was no hope.

Rose had taken up her place behind the counter to serve a young man some pie. Adam and Evelyn remained at the table with Adam looking out the window, so Rose could not see if he wanted to whisper to Evelyn.

Removing his cell phone, Adam gave the restaurant phone a call and handed the phone to Evelyn. She answered several times to Rose's voice, but Rose never heard her.

Rose finally hung up the phone and made some comment about prank phone calls.

Adam wrote quickly on the pad, "That just proves what we already know — people can't hear you while you're near them. Let's try something else."

He called a number and gave the cell phone to Evelyn. "Okay," he said, "Talk to the person that answers."

She kept trying to get the person on the line to recognize her voice, but they behaved as if they were unable to. Adam had a look of astonishment on his face.

With a concerned look, Adam asked in a whisper, "Let's try one more." He gave the phone to her again.

Evelyn repeated in a loud, clear voice, "Hello, can you hear me?" A voice on the other end of the line kept speaking something in Mandarin. The line finally disconnected.

Adam stared at Evelyn—speechless.

"What is it?" she asked, worried at the expression on his face.

Adam felt chills go up his spine as he looked at Evelyn. Finally, he told her that the number was to an electronics repair company in China.

Whatever this thing was that Evelyn had, it could reach any part of the Earth. Adam found it difficult to wrap his mind around the concept. He knew a fair amount of physics, and this didn't seem possible, not at all possible. Could one person's brain produce so much power?

CHAPTER 21

ITH EACH PASSING HOUR, business became more and more dismal. Adam realized that he would be digging into his savings again to make payroll. He had to find a way to improve it before he ran out of money. His family's life insurance pay-outs would not last forever. Perhaps he should just close the place and go back to college.

The day shift did not end well as far as business was concerned. After Ralph relieved Adam for the evening shift, Adam sat next to Evelyn for a while at Rose's table. Rose would be getting off soon also. Clara, a part-time girl, would finish up with Ralph in the evenings and help close.

Adam and Evelyn listened to Ralph and Rose's good-natured bickering for a while before heading home. He asked her if she would rather eat out again or if she wanted to eat at home. She replied that she was excited about fixing something for him.

"After all," she said, "I have to work to earn my keep."

Adam responded, "Now you're making me feel like an evil taskmaster."

The day had been both wonderful and frightening for Evelyn. Every hour that passed, she fell more deeply in love. He was a sensitive and caring person and seemed to draw caring people to him as well. All but one, she thought. If Adam understood that the monster he had met in his dreams was Evelyn, and not some separate ghost, he might not feel the same about her. Or maybe he would. Maybe he didn't have a choice in the matter.

When Adam had explained to her that her ability could reach all the way to China, unlike him, she had understood the significance of it. If that thing inside her ever got out, no one on Earth would be safe — no one.

Arriving home, Adam cleaned up and tried to help Evelyn prepare dinner. She accused him of trying to keep her from earning a living and pushed him out of the kitchen. They were both trying to be upbeat, but something was bothering each of them.

She prepared dinner, and he made a real fuss over it, but her heart wasn't really in it now that she had time to think about the implications of the phone call to China.

After dinner, he sat at his bedroom desk, and she was on the couch next to the bed. He was talking about some advertising plans to help improve business when she decided to ask him.

"Can you ask me that question now? I've been thinking that maybe it will help me understand more about her and what she might be planning."

He set down his pencil and thought about it. "Are you sure, Evelyn? As you said, I can't be certain it was you and not her."

"But if not now, then when?" she asked. "I know you believe that she is not me, but I have to be honest with you; she is me. Maybe not consciously, but she is me. I try not to believe it. I don't want to believe it! But where did she come from? It's me, Adam; it's me!" Evelyn put her face in her hands and started crying.

He could not stand to see her like this. Walking over to her, he drew her into his arms and hugged her gently.

"Evelyn, it's going to be fine. I told you I would help you, and I'll be with you no matter what. I promise. I don't care that you and it are the same. I know your goodness is greater than that evil."

She looked at him, knowing that he had no idea what he was saying. She was like a paper doll up against a raging lion. How could she tell him? It would only frighten him, and maybe he would send her away. She may not be able to remember her dreams, but she could feel the evil, and it felt like it was plotting something horrible.

She straightened up and asked him again, "Please, Adam, what message did I send?"

"Before I could get the dream written down, I had forgotten most of the details, but what I do remember is the last thing you told me. You said that I should ask you about the day you lost your family."

Evelyn looked at him without saying anything in reply. Why would her subconscious mind want her to tell Adam about that?

Adam walked back to the table and sat down. "Evelyn, if you don't want to talk about it, it's okay." He watched her stare at him with no expression on her face.

"I've always tried not to think about it." Evelyn looked down at her hands gripping the armrests. Strangely, it did not feel like she was the one gripping them.

"Look, Evelyn, if it will make it easier for you, let me tell you about my own family and what happened a couple of years ago." Adam put down his pencil and looked at Evelyn. "My mother and sisters and I were going to attend a church play at our ward. It was one of those traveling plays, something that everyone got to be in if they wanted to try out. None of us were in it, but everyone said it was going to be entertaining. My father was late, so it was just us four. Since we were running late, I suggested my mother take everyone in her car; I'd follow after I finished dressing."

Evelyn sat as still as a rock, listening to his story and watching her fingers turning white from the pressure of her grip on the couch.

"The police said it was over quickly. Adam's family was traveling over the Industrial Canal Bridge at its highest point when a hit-and-run driver struck them from the side, causing my mother to lose control. When the rescue units pulled them out of the canal, they were gone." Adam was quiet for a few minutes before looking up. "The police never found the driver of that truck, but I think I'm finding it in my heart to forgive whoever it was, not for him, but for me. I won't let that sort of thing destroy my life too. I owe it to my mother and sisters to get on with it."

Evelyn felt disconnected with what her body was doing, but her heart was breaking, thinking of the heartache Adam was feeling now.

"My father quit his position at his workplace, Stone Labs, and purchased the restaurant. He said he had always wanted to have a restaurant of his own, but I could tell that something else was wrong. I don't think he could recover from their deaths. Of course, it was hard for both of us, but it seemed like, after that, he stopped talking to me about anything important anymore. We worked the place, trying to get it to pay the bills, and for a while, it appeared it was going to succeed. He worked as hard as I've ever seen him work, but I suspected he was only doing it for me. We even opened on Sundays, which had always been taboo in our family. The only time he took off was on Wednesdays, when he met with some of his friends he hung around with." Adam picked up a tissue and wiped his eyes. After gathering his feelings, he continued, "They were having one of their little get-togethers, probably playing cards or something, when this guy knocks on the door. Only one of my father's friends lived long enough to describe what happened to the authorities. This guy dressed in a black suit just stepped into the house and shot everyone..." Adam raised his hand to his face, covering the tears.

After a moment, he looked up at Evelyn. Her face was deathly pale, and his first thought was she might be going into shock. "Evelyn!" He jumped up and quickly moved to sit by her on the couch. He could not bear the look of anguish on her face as she looked at him and didn't know if she was going to strike out at him or start crying.

"Evelyn, it's okay! I'm okay! Talk to me!" He tried to take her into his arms, but looking down, he saw that her fingers were desperately clenching the armrests. He tried again, but still couldn't get them to release, and then chills shot up his spine when she screamed a sound he had not thought a human voice could produce. It was a sound of pure hatred and uncontrolled anger while at the same time, infinite sorrow.

Adam stood and looked around the room. It was getting late, and he needed to get to bed. He had thought about it some more and had to conclude that even advertising was not going to get the restaurant to recover from his two-month absence. It was going to be rough, but he needed to tell the bad news to Ralph, Rose, and Clara. It would be difficult; they had all tried to make this work. He had enough insurance money to give them each a decent severance. He hoped it would help while they looked for other work. He didn't see any other possibilities.

Reaching into his pocket to get his change and keys, he walked over to the dressing table and dropped them on it. When he looked in the mirror, he was startled to see his eyes were red and his face was wet.

"What..." he said out loud. He brought up his hand and wiped at them, not understanding what it was at first. He reached for a tissue and wiped his face, looking at his eyes still wet and a slight bit puffy as if he had been crying. He looked around the room again, his eyes lingering on the couch for a second before laughing out loud. "I guess I need more sleep than I thought!"

Getting undressed and into his pajamas, he climbed into bed and switched off the lamp. Yeah, he hated doing it, but he didn't think this was going to work. He hoped they understood. Turning on his side facing the window, he soon drifted off to sleep.

CHAPTER 22

THE GREAT OAK WAS DEAD. Adam walked around it hoping to find life somewhere, but it was so dry that whatever he touched turned to powder. Looking away from the tree, he saw that he was on top of a small hill surrounded by a desert, the surface dry and hard with nothing growing as far as he could see. It was completely lifeless. There was not even the slightest breeze or sound.

Looking up, he saw that the leaves were gone, leaving skeletal remains of the once life-filled branches. The sky was gray as if filled with a lonely mist that reached beyond the horizon.

This place was once beautiful and full of life; he was sure of it. But the joy he had felt here was gone. And there had been a girl; she had loved him, but he could not remember who she was. Maybe she was near; perhaps he could find her if he searched!

Running down the hill, he came to a dry streambed. It reminded him of something; he remembered the scent of her and her breath on his cheek. She had been here!

He began running, thinking he didn't know where to go, but knowing he had to find her. The only sound in the world was his labored breathing and the crunching beneath his feet.

Time passed, but nothing changed. The hill was gone and had been for thousands of millennia. It did not matter, he ran on and on as fast as he could, gasping for breath and listening to the crunch, crunch, crunch of the surface material.

Time passed, and he no longer knew anything except he must find her. There was no memory of anything but that. He remembered her scent and the feel of her cheek, and it guided him forward.

Time passed, worlds grew old, and stars died. Great galaxies twinkled out of existence, but he ran on.

And then — time stopped. There was no sound except that of his gasping breaths slowly becoming normal. He stood before a great ebony door and had the feeling he had been here an infinite number of times. What was it? Where did it lead? And then he knew. She was inside! Reaching for the doorknob, he turned it and pushed.

Stretching before Adam was a field of carnage he could never have imagined. The sky boiled violently, and lightning constantly flashed, the thunder causing the very ground to vibrate. A sickening smell permeated the air, and he realized it was the scent of rotting flesh.

Fear filled his mind and heart, and he felt desperate to escape through the door again, but her memory pushed him on. And then what he saw made him gasp in terror. The bodies stretched out before him, so horribly testifying of the limitless cruelties of some monstrous being, were all his! He had truly been here before, repeatedly, and each time he had ended up the same way. Bending over, he retched violently. He had to escape! But again, her memory returned, and he knew he could not. Just as he had done countless times before, he moved forward to search for her.

Adam felt the roar vibrating his chest and teeth before he heard it. It was so violent that its fury even muted the thunderous lightning! He turned.

A creature crouched before him and over his previously broken and shredded bodies, its red eyes dripping blood and hatred, its teeth showing viciously and screaming impossible rage. No demon of hell could be as horrible as this! Where hands should have been, dripping flesh-covered claws bore testimony of the carnage it was capable of. But as he considered the face of death, he recognized who it was that looked back at him, and his fear instantly ceased. How could he ever be afraid? Death would never still his love for her. No passage of time would change that. Nothing she could ever do or say would change it. It was a condition more permanent than creation itself. As he moved forward toward certain death, his hands outstretched to her, she stood.

And as he had also done so many times before, he reached to touch her blood-covered cheek...

But unlike the endless past, the deadly claws stayed locked at her sides, the scream of pure hatred and rage dying in her throat. And except for the distant thundering, all became silent. And then the creature called Evelyn fell to her knees, screaming out her anguish and sorrow, the blood-drenched claws reaching to the sky!

He quickly kneeled and cupped her cheeks in his hands. "Evelyn, I love you. I will always love you."

Again, the silence was deafening.

Covered in his blood, she looked at him.

Her eyes began to change, an emerald sea replacing an ocean of blood.

And then silence, complete and absolute.

And with the silence, all light vanished, leaving total blackness.

And in the blackness — she whispered, "It's finished. Please — take me home."

CHAPTER 23

A DAM SLOWLY BECAME AWARE of the sunlight streaming through the curtains. He felt strangely rested and happy. He noticed that Evelyn was asleep on the couch next to his bed. He tried to remember what had occurred last night, but couldn't recall anything after telling her about the death of his parents. He wondered if by doing so, she would now be able to discuss the death of hers.

Looking over at the clock, he knew he should be getting up, but looking at Evelyn, he couldn't bear it just yet. She was gorgeous; she was stunning; she was lovely beyond reason. How had he been so fortunate to have her come into his life? She was lying on her side with her palms under her cheek when her eyes slowly opened, and she smiled at him.

"Good morning," said Adam.

"Good morning," she said, and slowly stretched. Looking at him, she whispered, "I love you." She must have gotten up during the night and found a blanket to stay warm with; she now pulled it up to her throat and continued to look warmly at him.

"Are you feeling rested this morning?" Adam asked. "I feel great! In fact, I don't remember even going to bed last night."

"I feel wonderful too," she said. "Something happened... I feel as if a great weight has been lifted from me. Did you have any dreams again?"

Adam thought about it. "Not that I can remember; I think I slept like a rock. How about you, did you have any dreams you can remember?"

"I don't think so. But I do have this feeling of being... it's hard to describe. I know it must sound crazy, but with all the stuff that has gone on in my life, it's probably par for the course. For the first time since all this started, I feel whole, complete now. It's like I've been walking through the world as half a person." She looked at him. "Does that even make sense?"

Adam looked at her with a mischievous glint in his eyes. "It must be love."

A big grin spread across her lips making her look even more beautiful. "What shall we do today?"

Looking back to the clock, he said, "Ouch! If I don't hurry, I'm going to be late getting the place open this morning. Will you come with me again?"

"Don't even try to stop me." And then, looking under the blanket to make sure she was modest, she said, "Can I fix us something this morning?"

"We should probably skip it. I can prepare something at work," Adam said, jumping out of bed. "I'll just take a quick shower and dress in the bathroom, is that okay?"

Evelyn put on a big pouty face, before laughing and pulling her head under the blanket. Feeling her face blush, she called out, "I'm sorry about using your couch again last night!"

Remembering last night's conversation, he turned back to her with his clothes and said, "I know we're in a rush right now, but if you want to talk about last night before we go, we can do that."

Her head still under the blanket, she thought about it a few seconds. She needed to talk to him about it and tell him her theory, but there wasn't enough time right now. She remembered what he had told her last night, and she had seen a connection with hers that she needed to tell him, but it wasn't something that could be hurried. They needed time and privacy. Pulling the blanket off her head, she said, "I want to tell you; it's important to me, but we need some time. I'm not sure we have enough before you have to open."

"Okay then, we'll put it on hold for now, and I'll set aside some time during the day. Hey! We could go to the oak and discuss it there if you want."

"I'd love that!" she said excitedly.

"Good, I'll just be a few minutes." He headed down the hall.

Evelyn looked out the window and stretched again, feeling happier than she had in a long time. Getting up and picking up the blanket, she headed for her room. She smiled as she left, thinking about how wonderful it felt sleeping there. There was something about being close to him that made her feel safe, and in some unfathomable way, she knew he would always love her. Nothing could ever come between them.

The pre-setup went faster this morning because Evelyn jumped right in and helped. She even found the glass cleaner and went to the front door and several display cases. By the time Rose came in, they were sitting at the table eating a hamburger and fries.

"Good morning, Rose!" Adam said. "You look very nice this morning."

"Thanks, Adam. That's sweet of you to say." She went to the back and put up her things. When she came back out, and while checking the register, she said, "How is your friend doing?"

Adam turned around in surprise. "Do you mean Evelyn?"

"I don't know, you haven't introduced me to her yet," Rose said, still counting the money.

Evelyn and Adam looked at each other for a second before Adam said, "I'm sorry, Rose, Evelyn is my..." What was he going to say, my sweetheart, my soul mate, my eternal companion? And then, looking back at her, he looked into her enchanted green eyes and said, "She's my fiancée... if she will have me."

Evelyn smiled her most beautiful smile and said excitedly, "She will, and she does, and, yes to everything else!"

As Rose walked to the table, Adam could see nothing but Evelyn's eyes and eternity. And then, feeling as if he were afloat in a warm emerald sea, he felt her lips press against his, and they were no longer in the restaurant.

The world stopped, and nothing existed except the two of them. Reaching his arms around her, he held her gently and felt as if his heart would melt. But then he felt the warmth turning to heat and the heat igniting to fire, and very gently, almost imperceptibly, he felt her gently push against his chest, so gently that he wasn't sure she had exerted any force at all. But their lips separated, and he found himself breathing deeply to catch his breath. Opening his eyes, he realized that he was not alone in his feelings.

Suddenly, he looked past her and saw a field of unimaginably beautiful flowers stretching outward to meet with a deep blue sky, its color unaffected by the distance. And above him were the branches of a giant oak tree, so thick with leaves that the sun was barely able to penetrate it. Looking back to Evelyn, he saw that she wore a flowing gown, seemingly made of light and gently moving with the slightest breeze, reflecting the sky and fields around them.

He was stunned and knew he was not dreaming. This was real. It was not his world of dreams that he had told her about, or maybe it was. Maybe it was never a dream at all, but a construct of her mind.

Looking out over the fields again, he asked, "How is this happening? How did we get here?"

Evelyn reached up her fingers and let them rest against his cheek, watching him look out over the world they had created. She loved him so much. He was the very breath of her life, and she desperately wanted to be completely honest with him, but not yet. She could not tell him everything yet.

"We are still in the restaurant," she whispered, looking intensely into his eyes. But... we are also in another place... a place you have allowed me to bring you. Your love has allowed me to build this, and it is our love that allows us to stay here. I brought us here so that we could talk. The time we are here is not the same as the time we are in the world. Nothing will change there; time will not pass."

"It looks so real," Adam said as he felt the trunk. "I suppose it wouldn't do any good for me to ask you how you are doing it."

Evelyn concentrated a moment, trying to translate the process involved into something he might be able to understand. "I feel how much you love me... and multiply it by how much I love you. I then take the total and spread the void through it, contracting the energy needed to create a star down to our basic desires and emotions until a bubble of anti-matter forms. Once I have an infinite number of these bubbles, I stretch..." Evelyn stopped talking as Adam slowly waved his hands in front of her, gesturing for her to stop.

"I'm sorry," he said with a smile, "Obviously, I was right in my assumption."

"How is not important," she said. "We have to talk. I have not allowed myself to know many of these things consciously, but you need to know. First, let me tell you that I have been divided for a long time. Because of some things that were done to me, I have been... separate; that is the only way to describe it to you. Last night, you came to me."

"I don't understand," Adam interrupted. "What are you saying? What do you mean, I came to you?"

"Adam, please, I'm trying to explain this in a way you can understand. Please let me finish, and I'll answer any questions I can."

When he saw her staring at him in frustration, he said, "Okay, no more questions until you're finished. This can't get any stranger than the whole dream thing anyway."

"When my parents were murdered, I did some things in self-defense that caused me to appear invisible; that part you are somewhat familiar with, but there was something else I had to do that is harder to explain. And this strangeness about me that you think of as an 'issue' has been with me since birth. The reason it wasn't a problem then is because I was whole until the death of my parents... as I am now. When we met, I was divided into two personalities, the part you know, and the other. Looking back, I can see that I could have handled the problem differently, but at the moment, I was mindless with grief. I did what I could to prevent an unforgivable event, infinitely more serious than the stimulus would merit, one so terrible that it would have been better to terminate my existence than to allow it."

She told Adam about the death of her mother and father, leaving nothing out. "It was a deeply disturbing experience. In fact, it was so terrible that the only way I could stop myself from reaching out and... doing something unbelievably awful, was to divide myself. This is not something that is normally difficult to do, but I was not prepared. I split out that part of me, the part that would have gladly performed this unforgivable event, and I kept it locked away in another world. Unfortunately, as I said, I was not properly prepared. It was too powerful and completely obsessed with these desires for revenge. It also possessed certain critical information that I no longer had access to, that I lost access to during the split. After I met you in the park, I started trying to find your world. I left repeatedly, but each time, my divided self would find me and pull me back. It was when I found your world that I knew I would eventually be successful!" She paused, the sparkling joy in her eyes fading to an expression of dread. "But then... she found out about you. She knew that I loved you and knew you... for who you are. She thought you would somehow stop her from having the revenge she craved and therefore hated you. She hated you as much as I loved you. I didn't know what to do or how I was going to bring myself back together in such a way as to retain my virtue. If I were to have allowed myself to reunite while unprepared to do so, all the furious hate and anger would have consumed me, and all that would have been left would be her. And what she would have done then would have been unthinkable.

"She developed a plan to escape from the world where I had placed her. At first, she allowed you to feel my presence. It was very painful for her, but her desire for revenge was greater than her fear. And yet when you started "seeing" more than she expected, she could no longer take it and ended our communication. That was when I lost all hope." Moisture filled her eyes, and a lone celestial sparkle ran down her cheek. "I felt that all was lost, and I would never be free to love you and be together. I... I decided that I could not live without you. She was not able to stop me until she used you. She cared nothing about living, except if we died, she would not be able to get her revenge. She then allowed you to not only feel my presence but to see and hear me as well. When I heard your voice calling from the porch, I could not believe it was true, and I was so afraid she would take it away again. In time, I began to believe and hope." She paused and looked up into his face. "After that, she allowed me to bring you to your matrix and talk to you, not as a dreamer, but conscious. She told me if I got you to help her find out who had murdered my parents, she would allow us always to be together. Otherwise... she would not be pleasant; her hate was infinite.

"She was becoming so desperate that I didn't know what to do anymore. She told me to give you the message. She wanted you to find those responsible for the murder of my parents and tell me who they were. The fallacy of her hate was that she would destroy them and all who knew or loved them... Humans are all connected, and her solution would effectively destroy all humanity. I still thought I could stop her from doing anything so terrible if I kept her locked away. But when you told me what had happened to your family, I realized something... something that in my split matrix, I had not dreamed of before. It is something I can't tell you yet, but I promise that I will. As the full weight of that information crushed down on me, she attacked. Neither my conscious self nor yours remember it because she completely wiped it from our conscious minds. She overcame my control and pulled me to her. Her thirst for revenge became mine also. All the terrible, unthinkable things she was going to do became my desires as well. And then, something happened that neither of us was prepared for. You entered our world. As much as I loved you, we were coming together again, and she hated you. She hated you with such passion that I felt myself growing smaller and smaller. In the beginning, she fought you out of *hate. The hate changed to amazement and then to disbelief as you continued to fight for me. And finally, in the end, she understood and accepted that you loved not only me, but you loved her as well. Despite seeing her in all her naked evil, despite the horrible things she was planning, you always came back. You loved us despite that knowledge. Finally, she accepted it, and we joined completely, not as a master and slave, but as one complete person. And, it was because of your undying love for us."*

Evelyn watched him closely. Would Adam accept the truth? And more importantly, would he see what she had not told him, what she was hiding from him?

"Why don't I remember this battle you speak of?" Adam asked, getting more confused with each passing moment.

She looked quietly into his eyes before saying, "It is not something you would want to remember," and Adam felt a shiver go up his back.

She continued, "This morning when we awoke, I was so happy. There were things I could not tell my conscious self at first, but she could feel my joy! I am no longer divided. I am one again. Because of that, I can know the things I have hidden from myself these last couple of years." She looked at him seriously. "Adam, the same person or group that murdered my parents, probably murdered yours as well, and both our fathers worked for the same company, Stone Labs."

Adam's head was spinning. She was describing a nightmare to him. If he were not here now and had not experienced the things that had happened to them, he would not believe any of this. And now that he knew the story of the death of her parents, he had so many more questions, questions he had forced himself to bury. He had thought it strange that the investigation of the death of his mother and sisters had ended so quickly without success. Moreover, why had no clues developed as to who the man in black was? The murder of five men had quietly ended after a brief investigation. He suddenly realized that not only his father but his mother and sisters, as well as Evelyn's parents, were part of some organized plot. And Evelyn, having to experience this, broke his heart. He may not be able to help her have her revenge, but he would do everything he could to see to it that whoever was involved in this plot was brought to justice.

"Evelyn, I'm sorry about your parents and what you had to go through." Adam wrapped his arms around her, holding her to him. "I promise you that I will do everything I can to find out who did this. I promise I will."

"I do not want revenge anymore... No, that is not true, I do indeed want revenge and the most horrible kind, but I know it's wrong. Like you, I want him, and whoever else is involved, to pay for what they have done. But vengeance does not belong to me, and I will not do anything further except to protect us," Evelyn said, "Now that I am whole, I understand why I can do the things I can, and I understand how. But there are some things about me that I can't *share with you yet. I promise, when I can, I will tell you. Please believe me when I say that it's for your benefit that I keep it from you for now."*

Adam thought about it before asking, "Can I tell all this to Evelyn, I mean you... Oh, you know what I mean."

Evelyn smiled. "Much has changed, and I find I must allow a lot more to be known by my conscious matrix than I normally would have. What I'm not telling her are the things I haven't told you either. Trust me, there is a reason why we are separate, but circumstances have radically changed things. I promise you that I will take care of us both."

Adam wondered if that meant him and her, or her and her conscious self. He was confused.

"We are returning now." She held his face in her hands.

"Wait a minute!" Adam suddenly had a realization dawn on him. "This all sounds a lot stranger than you just having some psychic abilities! How can a human being do these sorts of things?"

Evelyn only looked at him for the briefest moment before softly kissing him; he again felt afloat in an ocean of warmth.

The brief contact Evelyn had made with Adam's lips set her heart on fire, and it was all she could do to separate herself from him. When she did, she felt her face flushed and knew she was blushing terribly. Opening her eyes, she looked up into his and saw a worried look on his face. She was immediately mortified and turned to the window in horror, thinking he had rejected her. But as she looked out into the traffic, understanding rushed over and through her, and she realized what had happened and where he had been. She didn't know everything, but what she did know made her feel relieved. If this monster that had been her alter ego was now gone, she should be able to live a normal life at least. But then she stopped and considered the fact that she was still invisible.

CHAPTER 24

IANCÉE!" ROSE SAID, STARTLED. She stopped at the table and stared at her coffee a moment before sitting across from them. She looked up at Adam for another moment before turning to look at the place where Evelyn would be and said, "Well, Evelyn, I want to tell you how much I appreciate meeting you! Adam is a wonderful boy, and I know if he loves you, then you must be a very nice girl. Just as I told him if there is ever anything I can do for the two of you, just let me know." With that, she looked back at Adam. "How was that?"

Adam looked at Rose, his mouth hanging open slightly. "You can see Evelyn?"

Rose shook her head. "I don't know how to take this... Either you're crazy, or I am. What am I supposed to believe? You've been visiting a psychiatrist for weeks, and then I catch you talking to an empty seat yesterday. Today, you tell me you're getting married to this invisible friend of yours! Is this supposed to be a joke? I told you yesterday that I think of you as a son, now that you have no parents of your own. As far as I know, I'm all you have! I know you aren't cruel; you wouldn't be trying to play some tasteless joke, knowing how much I care for you. So, which is it, the Happy Farm or The Twilight Zone?"

Adam could see that Rose was desperate. Her face was flushed, and tears were in her eyes. He had never seen her so upset before.

Evelyn touched his arm. "Adam, we have to talk to her and try and help her understand. You need to lock the store back up. Rose is not going to be good for anything in her condition anyway. Is there someplace we can go that will be out of the way, maybe in the kitchen?"

Adam had not looked at Evelyn as she spoke. Instead, he took Rose by the hand and spoke to her as kindly as he could.

"Rose, please listen to me. I'm going to try and explain everything to you, but it's going to take a while. Will you let me try and explain what's happening?"

Rose looked at him a moment more before gently pulling her hand from his and covering her face. "I'm sorry; I shouldn't have spoken to you like that! I don't know what's wrong with me!"

By now, Adam was next to her with his arms around her. "Rose, it's okay; everything's fine. I can explain it, I promise."

Adam left her and locked the front door, putting up the closed sign.

He wasn't sure what Evelyn had in mind, but he trusted her in a way that defied logic. He returned and knelt down next to Rose, holding her hands again. "Rose, come with me to the kitchen so no one will bother us. Maybe that will keep them from trying to breaking the door down."

Rose suddenly realized what Adam had said and started to object. "You can't do that; we have to keep the place going... we need every customer."

"It doesn't matter. Trust me; this is more important." With that, he helped her up and into the kitchen.

There was an office that connected to the back of the kitchen, which was used for storage and had a small desk for running the financial side of things. Adam set up two more folding chairs next to the one he normally used.

He invited Rose to sit, which she did, but she stared at the other he had put next to it — the empty one. Of course, Evelyn sat in that one, and Adam sat at the desk.

Rose looked up; her eyes were red and swollen. She looked terrible, and Adam felt sick that he was causing her so much stress. He had no idea how to begin.

Then Evelyn said, "Adam, tell her what I say. I'm going to try and explain it."

Now, Rose only stared at Adam.

He said, "This will not be easy to explain, but if you give me a few minutes and try to set aside your skepticism, I know you will understand." He reached over and patted her hand again in encouragement.

Rose said nothing.

"Have you ever looked for something that you knew was supposed to be in a certain place, but you couldn't find it? I don't mean that it was hidden from your view; I mean it was right there in front of your face, but you didn't recognize it as the thing you were looking for, and therefore, you didn't see it?"

Rose still didn't say anything. She just kept staring at him.

"When you look at something, you do not see it with your eyes. You see it with your brain. Your eyes only transmit electrical impulses to your mind, and it is there that you visualize the image. Do you understand what I'm saying?"

There was still nothing from Rose.

"Something horrible happened to this friend of mine. It was a tragedy much like my own, but she was in the middle of it. It was so terrible that this latent ability she has had all her life became active. Once it did, she was not able to turn it off, so to speak." Adam was quiet for a moment, wondering where Evelyn was going to take this. She had been feeding him suggestions as he explained the ideas to Rose.

For the first time, Rose responded. "And what sort of ability are we talking about?"

Adam picked up Rose's hands in his again. "This may seem impossible, but I know it's true, if only because it's been happening to me. All this time I have been going to the doctor, I thought I was going crazy. Now I know it wasn't me. To answer your question, the ability she seems to have is like ESP or something like that. She somehow able to turn people's attention away from her, and she is so good at it that no one can even see her. You can look straight at her, and your mind will refuse to believe she's there. She isn't a ghost or anything strange at all. She is just a frightened young lady that has been completely alone for the last two years. She needs our help, Rose; she needs your help."

The last part was Adam's comment. He knew one of Rose's weaknesses was a soft heart and a kind spirit. If she knew someone needed help, it was game-over on any resistance. He felt a little ashamed but knew he had to get her to believe.

Rose was quiet, but he could see she was thinking this through. That part of being needed was doing its job. He hoped it was enough.

After a moment, she said, "So if she were sitting in that chair next to us, I wouldn't be able to see her, not at all?"

Adam slowly shook his head.

Looking back at the chair, she said, "Is she sitting there now?"

When Adam didn't answer her, she looked back to him. He slowly nodded his head. "I said she hasn't been able to turn it off, but something occurred last night that may have changed that. She has not tested it to see yet. She isn't sure she can stop it, but now that things are better for her, perhaps she can. I can see her, but I am the only one, so far."

"I want to see her. Can I?" The question was so simple, yet also very touching. Adam could hear the desire to believe, and it was so mixed with the fear that it may not be true—that Adam might be crazy after all.

Adam said after a brief pause, "I don't know... do you want to?

A tear run down Rose's cheek when she said, "I have to, Adam, I need to."

Adam turned to Evelyn. "Evelyn, can you do this now? Do you know how?"

Evelyn thought a moment. "I'm going to try and say something she can hear first. That will be easier I think. Tell her not to be afraid."

Turning to Rose, he said, "Evelyn has asked me to tell you not to be afraid; she is going to try and speak to you first. Is that okay?"

Rose did not look like anything was "okay," but she nodded her head. Adam took her hands in his and waited.

Rose looked at the empty chair, and Adam looked at Evelyn sitting in it. She smiled at him and told him she loved him before she appeared to be looking through him.

"Hello, Rose."

Rose jumped involuntarily. Her eyes grew wide, and she stared at the empty chair.

"I'm Evelyn. Everything Adam told you is true. Please believe. I am so sorry for scaring you. I love Adam. This whole thing has been very difficult for him."

Rose looked back at Adam as if to confirm her sanity. "How?! Can this be true?"

"It is, Rose, and if you let her, I think she can allow you see her as well." Without taking his eyes from Rose's, he asked, "Can you do it, Evelyn?"

"I'll try."

Rose stared a moment longer into Adam's blue eyes before slowly turning again to the empty chair which was no longer empty. She gasped and put her hands over her mouth to stifle her fright. It was one thing to have faith that it was all true, but an entirely different thing to see with your own eyes and remove all doubt.

"Oh! It's true! How is it possible?" Rose knew it was true now, but knowing was not necessarily accepting.

Evelyn started crying, great tears cascading down her cheeks. "You can see me? It worked; you can see me!" Adam was now kneeling next to Evelyn, holding her in his arms.

Rose was stunned. She didn't believe it, but the young lady was right there. For a moment, she felt dizzy and completely disoriented. Without having a frame of reference, she latched onto the only thing she could, her compassion. She felt her heart ache to reach out to this poor child. She desperately wanted to take her into her arms and comfort her. "Evelyn, it is wonderful to meet you." She said this with the biggest grin Adam had ever seen on her. "I'm sure I don't understand any of this, but whatever is going on, I'm on your side, and I'll help. Everything is going to be fine."

Adam was patting away Evelyn's tears when he wasn't hugging her. Looking over at Rose, he passed some napkins to her as well. They all laughed for a moment before sitting in silence. It was incredible. It was a moment of intense togetherness, and they all felt it.

"You are such a beautiful young lady! I am so happy Adam found you." Rose pulled her chair up closer to Evelyn and put her arms around her in a warm hug. "It looks like I not only have a son but maybe a daughter too?" She said this as if asking for permission.

Evelyn hugged her in return with just as much, if not more, warmth. "Yes, yes, yes."

Evelyn told Rose about some of the strange things that had happened to her. She didn't cover the way they began but discussed things that Adam did not even know. At times, Adam felt he was being ignored, though it didn't matter. Seeing Evelyn happy was everything to him.

It was amazing how much ground two women could cover in a little over an hour. Rose seemed to have a good picture of Evelyn's life, and the two of them seemed more like mother and daughter than good friends now. Eventually, Adam brought everyone back to the present.

"We will have plenty of time to talk about this, but for now, we should go ahead and open up. There may still be a few hungry people out there that need our services."

Rose laughed and said she would get the doors open. They still had most of the day ahead of them. She looked at Evelyn and said excitedly, "There is still so much I want to talk to you about! Come help me open up!" She laughed as she started out the office.

"Okay, Rose." Evelyn smiled back at her. "I'll just be a moment. I have something I have to tell Adam."

Rose turned back with a stern look on her face that anyone could see was not real. "No making-out back here in the office. I'm the official chaperone now." And she laughed again as she left.

Adam looked at Evelyn questioningly. Then he saw Evelyn's face fall, and the tears start to fill her eyes.

"What's wrong?" he asked as his heart sank.

"Adam, Rose is wonderful, and I know I can love her almost as much as my mother, but... There is a danger of her knowing what she knows now."

Adam felt a whiplash from the sudden change taking place. "What..."

"There are people out there that want us dead. Rose is now a target also because she knows about me. They have been keeping a close watch on you for a long time, ever since the murder of your family. They are using you as bait to get me to come out into the open. That is why I cannot go visible. Until we stop them, our lives are in constant danger. As soon as they see me, they will kill both of us, and Rose will only be a matter of making everything tidy." Evelyn was wiping her eyes now.

Adam thought about this quickly. "I still don't understand. Who wants to kill you? Why? And why did they kill our families? Evelyn, how do you know this?"

"I think I know, but I need more time to work it out. We need to go home where we can talk in private."

"Why can't we talk here? Rose knows about you now and..."

Rose came back to the office door and said, "Come on, Adam, we're late enough opening the place up, and you have customers waiting for food!" She walked out without looking at Evelyn or even acknowledging her existence.

Adam looked back into Evelyn's eyes and saw the tears on her cheeks. "I'm sorry, Adam, it is better this way. If they suspect she knows anything, they will kill her."

He suspected it was like Evelyn was losing her mother all over again, and he gently pulled her close as she collapsed into tears.

Adam made a call to Ralph and asked if he could come in early. After Ralph grudgingly agreed, he told him he would pay him double time. That quickly brightened Ralph's mood.

Rose appeared to be perfectly normal, normal for her, that is. Along with no knowledge of Evelyn, she appeared to have no conscious awareness of his doctor visits; neither did Ralph for that matter. Adam suspected that everything connected with his medical issues was hidden from view now. He had no idea how such a thing could be accomplished, but he also did not doubt Evelyn's capabilities when it came to this sort of thing.

He didn't know how much of this was Evelyn's doing and how much was her subconscious. This thought brought another question to him. He remembered this morning when they had kissed, and he had been transported into her dream world or whatever it was. He had talked to a different version of her and had asked a question that she never answered. The question was an obvious one—all that was happening and all this stuff she could do; everything seemed humanly impossible. As he collected a few of his things, he looked at her and wondered how easy it would be for Evelyn to make him think, feel, and see anything she wanted. He felt the hairs on the back of his neck rise as he walked hand in hand out the restaurant door with her.

CHAPTER 25

EVELYN SAT QUIETLY. HER few attempts at talking to him had failed. He seemed to be settling into a strange mood, and she believed it could have something to do with her removing Rose's knowledge of Evelyn's existence. She tried again to explain, but he didn't seem to be accepting her reasoning.

He spoke briefly about the trance or dream during their kiss. She knew what Adam had been told. He appeared skeptical. She understood how he felt, of course, but she knew it was the truth. She knew that as surely as she knew she was human. However, she didn't know what it all meant, or how she was doing the mind control stuff. Perhaps she was insane. How could she know? He didn't seem to be angry, nor was he cold. He just didn't seem to have anything more to say. Eventually, the one-sided conversation lagged into an uneasy silence.

When they arrived home, she tried to stay upbeat. Could she make him something to eat? Would he like to talk about all the things that had happened today? He had proposed to her, after all. Shouldn't they be talking about that, making plans? No, he was exhausted and suggested they take a nap. Maybe they could get something to eat afterward. Perhaps Adam just needed time to accept the things she had told him; it was a lot to assimilate. It could be that, or it could be something else. She had seen him tackle the problem of her invisibility with zealous intensity. None of that was evident now. Did she sense mistrust?

"Adam? Is everything okay?"

"Sure, everything's fine. I just need to rest and have time to..." His statement drifted away as he closed the door to his room.

Evelyn stood for a moment in front of the closed bedroom door before going to his sister's room. It was all probably normal. He was just worried about what she had said about his father's murder. She had drawn a connection between Stone Labs and the death of both their families. It was a lot to consider. However, how did she know this in the first place? She knew it was true — she knew it as surely as she knew anything, but how could she explain her certainty to Adam? Of course, he would be cautious. Who would believe such a thing without some proof? What did she have? Just believe me, Adam. Just trust me. Sure, that monster is now part of who I am, but you can still trust me... Could he trust her? Could she trust herself?

Evelyn opened her eyes and watched the moonlit curtains move softly. It reminded her of a time long ago, a time now forever gone. Her bedroom had been a place of refuge. It had been a place where her imagination could soar, a place of princesses and castles, dragons and knights in shining armor. It had protected her from the world she now knew to be cruel and unjust. She choked back a sob as she thought about how she wanted to go back; she swallowed her anger as she thought of her mother and father, to be that little girl again, part of a family — loved.

She listened as she heard Adam moving around softly through the house. She considered her feelings. Before meeting him, she thought no love could be stronger than what she felt for her parents. Her love for them was a lifelong event, full of laughter, disappointments, and joy, all those things that make up a family. She would cherish those memories forever. However, her feelings for Adam were on a completely different plane. She wondered if every couple felt the same. If so, how did they ever have fights and abuse each other? How could these feelings end in divorce? How could something that felt so eternal, ever end?

Stepping into the hall, she noticed the light on in the kitchen. She entered the bathroom and splashed a little water on her face before briefly looking into the mirror. There was no reason to put makeup on. She had experimented many times, but it was never an improvement. She had never had the normal plague of skin blemishes. As her mother always said, her skin was as smooth as a baby's butt. She gently patted her face before leaving.

She found Adam sitting at the kitchen table with a worried look on his face, but it immediately brightened as he saw her come in. He stood.

"Hey, sleepyhead." Evelyn put on what she hoped was a lovely smile. "Can I fix us something?"

"That would be great, but it's too much trouble, as late as it is. Why don't we go out? It's only about ten. Have you ever been to Commander's Palace?"

"You mean the one next to the graveyard?" Evelyn's eyes lit up, but she put on a fake show of horror.

"Hey! It's a respectable place," he said defensively but smiling.

"The graveyard or the restaurant?" she asked.

They both laughed, and Adam responded, "Both."

He grabbed his notepad and in the process, knocked his pen onto the floor. Reaching under the table, he retrieved it but stopped when he saw something unusual. His first thought was of the gum stuck under his restaurant tables. He hated having to scrape it off all the time. He was never able to understand how some people would do that instead of just disposing of it in a napkin. However, this was his table. There was no way gum would have been placed here.

"What is it, Adam? Did you bump your head?" She was kidding, but also somewhat concerned.

Adam looked closer at the small blob and saw that it looked more like a piece of putty, and there appeared to be a small circular piece of plastic, about a quarter of an inch across, pushed into the surface.

"No, I'm fine. I just need to get this pen from under here." He had been on his knees but now rolled back into a sitting position. He looked up into Evelyn's eyes and placed a finger to his lips. From out of nowhere, he remembered a spy movie he had seen as a teenager. The room was full of people talking. The camera closed in on one of the people as they pressed a small, unseen device on the underside of a table. It was a bug used to spy on people's conversations.

Evelyn said nothing, but her eyes widened at the serious look on Adam's face.

He took another closer look at the gum before standing again. "Yeah, I think I should go to Commander's Palace. I haven't been there for a while."

At first, Evelyn did not catch Adam's change of the pronoun we to I. She watched as he tried to pantomime something to her. First, he touched his lips with his forefinger in the universal sign for hush and then tapped his ear.

"What's going on, Adam?"

Adam only shook his head as his mind raced to understand the implications of the bug.

Evelyn stooped under the table and quickly found the attached device. "Is that a microphone?"

Adam nodded his head once, before putting his finger to his lips again.

"It's alright; they can't hear me anyway."

Adam rolled his eyes and lightly tapped his forehead with the palm of his hand. "Well, I guess I should to go find some real company to enjoy dinner with. Maybe Ralph wants to go. Talking to myself all the time is getting to be a real drag." He said this while looking purposefully at Evelyn. She nodded her head in understanding.

They did not go to Commander's Palace. Adam drove aimlessly around New Orleans, trying to decide what they should do. If his house had listening devices in it, so could the car. How long had they been there? Was Evelyn's insanity contagious? Was he going insane as well? Living in his fantasy world with Evelyn was one thing, but having the real world join in was just too weird.

"Adam, if you are concerned about something in the car, we can park and go for a walk."

He nodded his head in the affirmative, but just as he turned off the boulevard, red and blue lights appeared behind them. There was no siren, and as he glanced into the rear-view mirror, he saw the patrol car was practically on his bumper. His stomach dropped, and he pulled over next to the curb but felt goosebumps dancing along his arms as he looked into Evelyn's face. She looked strangely different, but also ominously familiar — and she was angry.

Adam had been stopped before; he knew the routine. Just stay calm and keep your hands on the steering wheel. The police officer will approach the car from the driver's side and will have one hand on his pistol, though still in his holster. Being night, there will also probably be another officer at the rear of the car on the passenger side. It never failed to unnerve Adam when he was stopped for having a light out or expired tags. He understood the need for them to be careful, but it always made him feel like a criminal.

The patrol car had floodlights on, making it difficult to see behind him, difficult, but not impossible. What he saw made his heart jump. The officer was walking up as Adam had expected, but his handgun was not holstered. Although silhouetted, he could plainly see that the pistol was not in the officer's holster. In a moment of clarity, he realized that he was truly part of Evelyn's nightmare.

Adam's window was down, so he didn't have to remove his hands from the steering wheel. As the officer stopped just behind his left shoulder and just out of sight, he heard the request.

"Adam Yates?"

This was not a normal traffic stop. They already knew his name. The officer was not asking for his driver's license or insurance papers. What had he done? What was going on?

"Ye-yes," he stuttered. "I'm Adam Yates."

"Is there anyone in the car with you?"

What? What was that supposed to mean? Of course, they would not be able to see Evelyn, but why was he asking if Adam was alone? Surely, they had already looked inside.

"Sir?"

Adam froze as the officer stepped in front of the window and pointed his handgun at the passenger side seat. He had his finger wrapped around the trigger and was in the standard shooter stance. Without thinking, Adam threw himself over Evelyn to save her. His last thoughts were I'm insane! This isn't happening! I love you!

With his eyes squeezed tightly shut, he heard an unbelievable conversation.

"The vehicle has been abandoned."

"Maybe they took off on foot. Report it. I'll check around a bit. And turn off those lights. We don't want to draw any more attention than we have to."

"Hey, Sid, he's not going to be very happy about it."

"Just shut up and report it."

Adam lifted his face to look into Evelyn's eyes. There were tears in them, and he realized she was hugging him and gently stroking the back of his head. The anger was gone. She looked like his Evelyn again.

"What happened?" he whispered.

"They don't see us anymore. I don't know how I did it, but I must have covered you as well."

Adam moved his lips to her forehead and kissed her tenderly. Neither said anything as he sat back up and rested his head against the headrest. He watched the officer that had decided to see if he could find them lurking close by. When he returned to the patrol car, Adam was surprised to see that the vehicle no longer had the police lights on top and saw the other "cop" removing magnetic stickers from the doors and trunk. They were removing all indications that the vehicle had ever been a police vehicle.

Adam was shocked. "What is going on here?"

Evelyn didn't reply.

"I don't think those were real police officers," he finally said.

"Where are we going?"

Adam looked over at Evelyn. She had been very quiet since the incident with the fake police. "I thought we should find a place to hide. My house isn't safe anymore, and evidently, my car isn't either. I'm going to rent a motel room for the night. Are you okay with that?"

She turned to him. "I don't think we should do that. They probably have some tracking device on the car. Maybe, that's how they found us so quickly. It probably won't take them long to figure out what happened back there. Can we go back to Audubon Park and leave the car on some side street? I know a house for sale that we could stay in for a while."

"I hadn't thought of that. It's not far."

They abandoned his car a few streets north of Saint Charles and made their way by foot, south into the park area. Evelyn had no way of knowing if Adam was still being hidden by her. It would be safer to assume he wasn't.

As they progressed deeper into the park, Evelyn kept having the feeling that someone was watching them. She thought on several occasions that she had seen a man, but wasn't sure. She would have to check after making sure Adam was safe.

Separating the park's golf course from the residential section on the east was a line of large bushes and trees. One section had become overgrown due to a lack of maintenance. That was where Evelyn decided to make their escape from the park. If someone was following them, they should be able to lose them in the dark bushes.

CHAPTER 26

ONCE HIDDEN FROM VIEW, they hurried to the bordering houses that lined the perimeter. It didn't take Evelyn long to locate the one she had in mind, and they entered through an unlocked side door. Inside, she leaned against a wall to catch her breath. "I'm going to go back out to see if you were followed."

"Be careful," he whispered.

"That's no longer a big problem, but I promise I will." To his surprise and delight, she gave him a quick kiss on the cheek before heading out the door.

She did a quick survey of the property to make sure no one was near. Then she made her way back to the bushes, but before she could enter, a man dressed in casual clothing came out the same spot they had exited.

It was now completely dark, and there was little chance that he was there by accident. It was no coincidence. He carried a case that looked to be about half the size of a rifle.

Okay, so call me paranoid, she thought. This guy can't possibly be out for a nice stroll through the bushes. I wish I had more control of my talent. He needs to think he is in the wrong place or something like that. Come on! What's the use of being a superhero if I can't control it?

Then it happened. The guy set the case on the ground and moved back to the bushes and... "You have got to be joking!" Evelyn exclaimed. It was dark, but not so dark that she didn't know what he was doing. She looked down at the case he had left on the ground and waited for him to finish. Amazingly, when he did, he just left the case and walked back through the bushes the way he had come. She grabbed it and followed him to the other side where she watched him eventually make his way to Saint Charles Avenue. A vehicle was waiting for him.

Was this her doing? She didn't know, but it had to be. He would not have just abandoned the case—would he?

Back at the house, she found Adam beside himself with concern. "Where have you been?" He looked furious.

"I'm sorry! Someone did follow us, and I had to watch him. Don't be upset; I had to make sure we were safe."

His anger immediately vanished, and he took her in his arms. "Evelyn, please don't do that again. I thought something might have happened to you."

They stood there a few minutes in each other's arms trying to settle down the anguish both felt. Eventually, Adam saw the case on the floor where she had set it. "What's that?"

"The man that followed us set it down for a moment and just forgot to take it with him when he left. I picked it up and followed him back to the street where he drove away in a black limousine. It was really strange because he looked more like a tourist than one of those Men-in-Black types."

They both stared at the case for a moment.

Finally, Evelyn asked, "Do you think it's okay to open?"

Adam lifted it and answered with another question. "Why wouldn't it be?"

She placed her hand on his without taking her eyes off the case and just said, "boom?"

When she looked up at him, he was looking at her also. Neither said anything more until he had gently laid the case on a couch in the living room. They returned to the laundry room with the house's side door entrance and stared back at the case.

After a few minutes, Evelyn asked again, "Should we open it?"

Adam thought a second before answering. "Tell me what happened to make him leave the case. Did it look like he was placing it there on purpose?"

"Not at all, he just set it down and relieved himself in the bushes. Then he left without it."

"Now how likely is that? Let's look at this logically. If he was planning on somehow using a bomb to blow us up... No, this just doesn't make sense, maybe in a different situation like the car or the house or even the restaurant, maybe then, but not just keeping an eye on someone—right?"

"I do remember wishing I knew how to use my ability to make him go away, and it was just before he set the case down. Could it be me?" Evelyn wasn't sure but was hopeful that she was the cause.

Adam continued. "I don't think it's a bomb. That doesn't make any sense. It is much more likely, and yet insane to believe that you caused it or rather, your subconscious did." And then after a moment of deliberating, he said, "I say we open it."

He looked at Evelyn who said nothing at first. After a moment of indecision, "Adam, let me open it up. You go outside while I do it."

"What? No way is that going to happen! You go outside while I open it up."

"Adam, you know I can make you go outside. I have the power." She tried to put on as much bluff as she could muster. "I've done it before, and I can do it again. Don't make me do something we will both regret!"

Adam laughed softly. "Don't give me that baloney; you couldn't do it on a good day, and this isn't one of your good ones." He smiled.

"If you open it and get killed, I'll just kill myself too... and you know I will; I almost did it before."

"I can't believe we are having this conversation!" Adam was irritated but knew Evelyn was too stubborn and was not going to do this his way. "Okay, then we will do it together. If something happens, we can enjoy life in the Spirit World."

"Spirit World, what's that?"

Adam sighed and said, "Never mind, you'll find out someday, but hopefully not today. Let's just go do this."

They had been whispering for the entire time they had been in the house except for their brief outbursts as Evelyn had returned from following the mystery man. Now as they quietly moved toward the case, Evelyn whispered, without a hint of humor, "Why are we so quiet?"

"I don't know; it felt right, and you were whispering. I thought you had a reason."

"Oh." Evelyn raised her voice a little and said, "I think you're right. It can't hold a bomb or something like that. It's a strange shape for a briefcase though."

Adam said, "I don't believe it's a briefcase. It looks more like a gun case. My father had one he kept his handgun locked in. It looks the same, but smaller."

Evelyn followed Adam's lead as he knelt next to the couch. There was a combination lock. What were the odds that it was unlocked already? Not very good, he thought. Adam placed his fingertip gently on the release button. If the combination had been set to open...

Click!

D.R. Fuller

CHAPTER 27

EVELYN SAT ACROSS THE ROOM watching Adam assemble the rifle, complete with scope. She didn't know much about rifles, but it looked horrible. A fleeting thought touched her mind wondering how he could even touch the thing.

"Appears to be high powered from the look of the bullets," he said casually. His offhand remark was an attempt to calm Evelyn, but inside, his mind raced with the implications it represented.

From the moment she had seen the contents of the case, she knew for sure that all her suspicions were true. Along with the audible click, the world had changed forever. She knew her family had been murdered, as well as Adam's father, but the idea that they were still looking to kill them after all this time was no longer just a firm suspicion. It was fact.

Adam set the assembled rifle on the coffee table, and for the first time since opening the case, he looked into Evelyn's eyes. Neither said anything for a long time.

Finally, he stood, walked to the chair, and seated himself on the floor with his back to her, his head against her knee. He looked back at the coffee table with its ugly burden. He sighed, "You were right all along."

Evelyn said nothing. What was there to say? If this had happened to her last week, she would be screaming, but now, today, something had changed inside her. She was stronger, and she felt a little — dangerous. It was a very odd feeling. She almost wanted to go out and find the man and... NO! She stopped herself in mid-thought. No, she could not allow her mind to go in that direction. As deserving as it may be, she would not do it.

Adam continued, "I can't go back home or anywhere in public without the possibility of meeting another one of those. If you could make me invisible, it would probably be a good thing." He turned his head to look at her. "I'm just saying." He had a slight smile on his face.

Adam was incredible. His very life was in danger, and he could still joke about it. She stared into his warm blue eyes and felt a passion rise inside her. He was hers. The words — the very concept hit her with such an immense surge of almost violent determination that she knew she would destroy anyone or anything that tried to take him from her.

Adam saw a reflection of this in her eyes. "Evelyn, are you okay?"

She blinked as she suppressed the overwhelming emotions. She had to control herself; this thing that had given her more confidence was like some super drug. It would be too easy just to allow it to take over, and if she did, could she control it?

Adam stood in front of her now with his hands on her shoulders. She saw the uneasiness in his eyes, not fright, but concern for her.

"Evelyn, everything is going to be alright. I promise I'm not going to let anyone hurt you." He forgot that it was not her that was in danger at the moment. "We'll figure this out. I promise."

Looking at the determination in his eyes, she thought furiously, Yes, if I have anything to do with it, you will always be safe.

Looking as casual as she could, Evelyn smiled and said, "I'm starving."

Adam stared at her for an instant more before lowering his head, chuckling. When he looked back up, she noticed the tears in his eyes and a huge smile on his lips. "Now, what can we possibly do about that?"

"Not a problem for an invisible girl," she said with a touch of resignation. Give me a little while; I'll pick up something." Seeing his concern, she continued, "I'll be okay. I feel much more capable than I have for a long time. I know I can do this safely." She looked at him; he did not look convinced. "I'm better now." She put on a big smile and gave him a warm hug. "When our friend was sent home, I'm guessing he left with no memory of what happened." Her smile tightened momentarily. "And I'm guessing that his bosses aren't going to like that."

CHAPTER 28

THE HOUSE WAS OUTFITTED with a few decorative pieces of furniture, probably to assist in selling it. The electricity and water were connected for maintenance and showing it to prospective buyers. They should be fairly comfortable unless some realtors dropped by.

Evelyn had been uncertain whether to get take-out food or stop at a supermarket for something to cook. After searching the kitchen, she knew it didn't have the things they needed, but she could get them and organize their lives tomorrow. For tonight, they would do take-out.

Adam's first suggestion for food was his restaurant. Ralph and Clara would have closed already, and even if she turned on the lights and grill, no one would notice. Evelyn assured him that the purpose of her ability was to protect her. That meant if turning on a light would put her in danger, no one would see the light. This protection may have had problems before, but no longer.

Considering her confidence, Adam played the devil's advocate by asking her what would happen if there were an explosive device with a motion detector as an activator. After a moment of staring at each other, they decided against the restaurant. He gave Evelyn a twenty-dollar bill to cover the price. She would have to be creative about how she paid for it though.

It was late, but there were plenty of places still open. However, having gone so long without hamburgers and French fries, she felt she might be developing a hamburger fetish. Adam may have had his fill, but as she remembered the hot juicy aroma, she smiled and decided that for tonight, he was just going to have to be a man about it.

Evelyn stood on a quiet street-corner a few blocks from their house. Traffic was light, and it was late enough that many homes were beginning to go dark. She breathed in the night air, feeling more alive than she could remember. Her body felt energetic and strong. Although she had kept up an exercise program to stay fit, she had not run just for the fun of it in ages, especially not in the last two years. Being in public did not frighten her anymore either, so why not?

The place she chose was about three miles away and would give her a decent workout. She didn't want to overdo it though since her aerobics might not be up to par. She supposed she wasn't dressed for running either, but at least she had sneakers on. With a slight smile, she started off at an easy pace, keeping her eyes open for any dangers. She felt positive she could avoid anything dangerous she came upon, but she didn't want to be overconfident about her newly developed feelings.

Mostly she ran on the sidewalks. Although the streets were quiet, she loved the way the sidewalks were changed by the large trees growing between them and the street. Large roots had lifted and cracked the cement in many places along the way, something she was sure the homeowners probably hated, but she loved it.

She didn't remember growing up with any particular love for these wonderful trees. Perhaps it was because she had met Adam in one and they had spent so much time there. It felt almost like a symbol of their love; it was strong and seemed to grow forever.

The wind whipped past her as she increased her pace, filling her with delight. She felt like laughing, even yelling out loud. She was happy. At last, she was happy. She had Adam, and they loved each other; nothing else mattered. Elation filled Evelyn as she ran across the street.

Screeeeeech!

The sound of squealing tires and metal being scattered caused Evelyn to jump out of the street in terror! She immediately realized how careless she had been for not being more watchful crossing the street. A small pickup truck sat quietly with one of its front tires up on the curve. Damaged metal garbage cans were strewn in front of it, one still rolling with garbage trailing behind it. The driver, a young man, got out as several front doors of nearby houses opened, their occupants coming out to investigate. Several other porch lights came on, and curtains were pulled back, concerned neighbors looking to see what had caused all the ruckus.

One neighbor approached the driver and asked if he was hurt. He was in the process of trying to collect the scattered garbage cans and their contents. What had happened? Another neighbor approached who appeared to know him.

"Danny, are you okay?" he asked with concern.

"I'm fine. I don't know what happened!" He was almost in tears. "Pop's going to kill me!"

Both of the neighbors started helping him pick up the scattered trash. It didn't look like the property owners were home at the moment. "I'll let Ross know about the cans in the morning," said one neighbor. "You can get with him about paying for damages. It looks like you'll probably have to buy him a couple. What was it, a cat, a dog? I swear some people are so irresponsible when it comes to their pets."

Danny was calming down. His dad's truck didn't seem to have any damage. "I'm not sure... I don't recall seeing anything at all. I just lost control for a moment. I guess... maybe it was a dog or something. But all I remember is pulling hard on the steering wheel and hitting the brakes."

"It was probably a dog. I've seen a couple of stray ones running the neighborhood. In fact, I almost hit one myself last month. Well, just get with Ross in the morning and let him know you're going to pay for the cans. He's a nice guy with a couple of kids of his own. They're out right now, but he knows how you young'uns can be." With that, both neighbors laughed a little and headed back to their houses.

Danny breathed a final sigh of relief and said, "I will. And thanks for the help." He started up the truck and pulled gently off the curve. Alone again, he did not drive away but sat quietly trying to remember what had happened.

Standing no more than a foot outside his lowered window, Evelyn looked into his face. He was a good boy and was clearly upset. Evidently, he had almost struck her with the truck, and she had subconsciously caused him to turn away. He could have been hurt or killed! Tears came to her eyes as she imagined seeing his dead body slumped against the steering wheel after hitting a tree instead of the garbage cans. It would have been her fault. She realized now that even though she wasn't in any danger herself, she could easily cause others to get hurt or lose their lives. The thought horrified her. She had been selfishly letting go of her fear and caution. She was careless. She should have seen this and understood that she was now more of a danger to others than they were to her.

Evelyn stepped back and watched as the young man slowly drove away, shaken but safe. She stood alone in the street, listening to the slight sound of laughing coming from one of the nearby homes. She watched as the surrounding house and porch lights slowly started to go out. She knew this was a real turning point in her life; everything was different now. It was like she was invincible. Not only was she responsible for Adam, but she was also responsible for anyone that might get hurt because of her.

The sudden weight caused Evelyn to wonder if she was ready for it. It felt right to protect Adam, but to be the cause of someone else getting hurt was as fearful a prospect as getting hurt herself. She would not be careless again. She had to be just as watchful as she had been when she was the one in danger.

Continuing to be cautious, Evelyn jogged to her destination, a popular hamburger place she knew. There were a few people inside but no one outside. Three people were waiting in line. She took her place behind the last customer; though it made her feel silly, it also made her feel normal.

Before getting to the counter, a family came in and took their place behind her in line. They had a small toddler, but no one attempted to close the gap she took up in line. It appeared that they were aware someone was there but were not aware of them at the same time. She knew she had felt the same way in the past before her change. It was strange how people could stand right next to each other on a bus or in a grocery checkout line and never really "see" each other. Evelyn realized that in a lesser way, they were experiencing the same thing. She watched as the little girl pulled on her mother's dress trying to get her attention. There was a toy being offered if a particular meal was ordered and she wanted it. The child's hand unconsciously wrapped around Evelyn's finger, and although she was still ignoring Evelyn, her eyes filled with moisture. The human contact was incredibly touching. Evelyn wanted so much to pick her up and hug her.

"Next!" The young woman at the counter called to the family behind her, but the parents did not proceed to the counter as if uncertain about getting ahead of—what?

Evelyn stepped aside, and the family proceeded past her. She went over to the pickup counter and waited. A young man came over with a tray containing several hamburgers and a couple of bags of French fries. He called out a number over the intercom and two large guys that looked like they could be football players or pro wrestlers came over to collect the order. She took the tray from the young man and stepped aside to get some drinks for her and Adam. The two guys came up and looked at him expectantly. He looked back for a moment in confusion before asking them what their order was. Going back to another worker, probably a manager, he had a quick conversation before he came over and asked for their receipt. They produced it with a bit of irritation. The manager apologized and said it would be a minute more. They returned to their seats, and the order was restarted.

Evelyn finished up with the drinks and walked around the serving counter to get a large bag. No one paid her any attention, though they were careful not to run into or even touch her. She stood by the take-out section, and while still holding her tray, transferred the contents to the bag. Several workers walked around and past her, but no one touched her.

Before leaving, she took Adam's twenty-dollar bill and placed it in the cash drawer as the cashier opened it for another customer. As she left with her take-out, she was amazed by the different direction life was taking. If not for being in danger, she believed they could be very happy. She felt that most people had a lot of good in them and wondered how those that hunted her could be so evil. Well, they would not succeed. She was positive of that, but strangely, the certainty of that thought sent a cold chill through her.

CHAPTER 29

ADAM GREETED EVELYN WITH a hug that belied his calmness. She knew he had been worried, and it softened her heart for him even more.

"What have we got?" he asked.

"Your favorite cuisine, naturally," she said, putting the bag on the coffee table and taking out the hamburgers, drinks, and fries. "They may not be up to your high standards, but they should fill you up. The two guys I took them from looked like they could eat a bull all by themselves."

Adam looked at her with concern to make sure she was not hurting from the theft.

"Don't look so down," she said, "I put the twenty dollars you gave me in the cash drawer. It may not have been completely legal, but they were paid for, and we can eat."

Looking up at his no-comment reaction to her quiet humor, she recognized his concern. "It's alright, Adam. I accept who I am and what I have to do. What I worry about though is that it doesn't bother me as much as it did last week. I wonder if that has something to do with that evil personality I had inside me. From what I understand, it's not technically gone, only combined somehow to form a new me, or maybe I'm back to the old me—I don't know. Whatever it is, I don't intend to do any more than is necessary to keep us alive and safe. And that means feeding us right now, so eat up and enjoy." She smiled as he took a large bite and stuffed what room remained in his mouth with French fries.

"Well... they aren't as great as mine, but I could get used to them, I suppose," Adam muttered as he contemplated something.

"Yes, I can see that." She laughed. And then as she took a bite of her own, she asked, "Have you come up with any solutions for our friends?"

Adam looked at her a minute, his mouth still full, before answering. "Whatever happened to that delicate frightened young lady that needed my protection so much?" He spent just as little time saying this as was necessary before stuffing his mouth again, but he did watch her as if expecting an answer.

Evelyn pouted for a moment. "I'm still a delicate young lady... just not as frightened as much anymore, now that I have you."

That seemed to satisfy his male ego, and he smiled contentedly. They were both quiet for a while until he finished his first sandwich.

Taking a moment to breathe, he said, "The way I see it, we have two basic choices. We can run for the rest of our lives and try to survive by staying out of sight, or two, we can disguise me and go after them. The first option is probably destined for failure and the second is insane — how about you?" Adam picked up the second hamburger and attacked it vigorously.

Evelyn had also come up with those two choices, but was drawn ominously to the second one. She wondered if her evil mini-me might not be very much alive and making her desires known. As dangerous as it sounded, the choice of running forever had the feel of failure written all over it. "I think we should go with curtain two. If we run, time is on their side, and they probably have the resources to catch you eventually." As she watched him eat, an evil, but humorous joke came into her mind. "A third choice would be that I abandon you and go off on my own. They will probably catch you quickly because it looks like they are tired of waiting for me. Maybe they could tie you up and torture you for a while, thinking I would show up... eventually." She lowered her head to hide her smile.

Adam stopped eating mid-bite, looking at her for a moment, his face empty of expression. When Evelyn looked up at him, she had as serious a look on her face as he had ever seen. He casually put down what was left of his hamburger and patted his mouth with a napkin. Then, without warning, he attacked her, tickling her mercilessly, regardless of her pitiful pleas of "Stop, stop, stop!"

Eventually, he ceased the torture, and she was able to voice something besides her uncontrollable begging. With his face hovering dangerously close to hers, both their smiles slowly faded, and she whispered, "I hate you..."

"Yes," he quietly replied, gazing deeply into her tear-filled eyes. "I know."

Very gently, he pressed his lips to hers and...

Adam felt an unusually stiff breeze against his face as he experienced the sweet softness of her lips. The strangeness of this was swallowed up as his mind felt like it was fading into a blazing fire. But again as from a memory in the distant past, he felt Evelyn push gently against him until they were separated by just enough space that their lips no longer touched. He opened his eyes and gazed into a lake of molten emeralds. Her eyes had no pupils and were lightly touched by slight specks of gold.

He blinked quickly and looked again to find that they were the normal green he had come to love and desire. "Evelyn?" he asked, unsure of what was happening. Turning his head slightly, Adam was gripped by fear, and he clutched at her to keep her from falling. They both stood on top of a cliff overlooking a world of incredible beauty. Just as suddenly, the fear left him, and he realized where he was. It was enough to take his breath away. This place was not like the ones he had been in before. It was a world of valleys and mountains, high waterfalls that seemed to reach the sky, and full of forests as far as he could see, all of them seemingly oak trees. Where the trees did not grow, the ground and fields were covered with grassy flowers of colors he could not begin to describe, and the rainbows that stretched across the cascading falls displayed hues he was incapable of naming. This must be heaven, he thought. "Evelyn, where are we?" She had not said anything, waiting instead for him to get his bearings. "Adam, I love you."

The words he heard were simple words but seemed to carry an infinite universe of meaning. They held a promise of an eternity of happiness and a strange plea that he felt, but could not identify. This time, Evelyn was clothed in a shimmering rainbow of light blues and greens that he could never seem to focus his eyes on as they constantly changed, never appearing to have a surface.

"Why am I here?" he asked, but couldn't find it in his mind or heart to care about an answer. He was so full of joy in this place that the real world seemed far away and had no attraction for him.

Evelyn put her hands on his cheeks and drew his face close to hers. "Adam, can you concentrate on me and what I have to say?"

"Concentrate on you? Evelyn, I could concentrate on you forever. This place is incredible. I don't have the words to describe it. And you are even more beautiful in my dreams."

Evelyn thought about this a moment before trying again. "Listen to me carefully, Adam. Time is getting short, and you must make your decision soon."

Adam said, "I'm sure that the decision should be to go look for those losers that keep trying to kill us. Waiting around is not going to work for us."

Evelyn closed her eyes and shook her head. "It's like speaking to half a brain," she whispered in frustration.

"Huh? What was that?" Adam tried to focus his mind. He suddenly felt the importance of what Evelyn was trying to tell him.

"Do you have anything you need to ask me?" she said, her frustration still showing. "I know being here is difficult for you, but you need to try and understand how important this is. I can't believe you aren't supplying yourself with more resources!"

"Okay, what is that suppose to mean?" Adam's mind was starting to clear some. The more he looked directly at Evelyn, the easier it was for him. "Questions; do I have questions for you? Yeah, there's one, or ten thousand, I could probably jot down real fast. How about we start with how any of this is possible? And don't try to use all that weird bubbles of anti-matter stuff. And what is it with kissing you!? Can't we have a simple kiss without being shipped out to Oz?" He looked frustrated, but not upset.

The truth?" she asked.

"The truth... Yes, that would be refreshing, I would think,"

"Okay then, the truth... I can't tell you the truth." Evelyn suddenly looked defeated.

Compassion filled his heart as he looked at her expression. "Alright, how about something close to the truth?"

Evelyn took a deep breath. "You and my outer matrix are experiencing something that has eternal consequences. She needs you — I need you. We are the same. I know you love me, but you love without fully understanding, and I can't give you that understanding. How much do you love me? How much are you willing to sacrifice? I would not normally be communicating with you like this, but with all that has happened, I do not think I have a choice. I should just trust you to do the right thing, but so much is riding on you..."

Adam thought a moment before saying, "Well, that's certainly as clear as mud, and thanks for the vote of confidence. How about a second question? We are trying to keep these guys from killing both of us. I can see that she... you are acting differently now that you are not split, whatever that means. Should we try and find out who is behind this, regardless of the danger?"

Evelyn looked directly into Adam's eyes and said, "What danger are you talking about?"

Adam's mouth fell open. "I'm talking about the likely danger of a high-powered slug going through your pretty head not to mention mine!"

"Oh, that danger. Well, don't be concerned. It just seems dangerous because you don't understand." She appeared to suddenly understand that he was worried about something that wasn't a danger of any consequence or was nothing compared to another danger she wasn't telling him about.

Adam then stated the obvious, "And you can't tell me about it."

"Right," she said.

"There is another question I have. Several days ago in the restaurant, you let your — what was the term...your outer matrix — know that those that were trying to kill her are using me as bait. How can they possibly know Evelyn and I would come to know each other, and most of all... how can you know any of this if she doesn't?"

She lowered her eyes a moment and finally said almost in a whisper, "If I could tell you everything, I would. Please believe me; please have faith in me."

"Evelyn, you are incredible. You can't possibly exist as you seem. No person has a subconscious mind that is like you... and you ask me to have faith in you."

"Do you love me?" she whispered.

Adam looked deep into her eyes and whispered, "Yes. How can I not love you? You are beyond reason to me. My feelings for you have no logic. I just do." And then, "Are you making me love you?"

"If it were possible..." she whispered.

When Adam found himself tenderly kissing Evelyn, his eyes flew open and looked at her closed ones a full second before hers opened and she looked back into his. Jumping back, he said, "Wow! I'm sorry, Evelyn; I didn't mean to do that!" He moved away from her a few feet and put his back on the couch.

She sat up and blushed. "It was my fault. I teased you. We need to be careful. Living together and feeling as we do, it's too dangerous to let our guard down."

"Well, yeah... okay." He wondered if he should tell her what had just happened. Everything was becoming more and more confusing. Evelyn was not only an enigma but as he had told her in the dream, she was also impossible. "Evelyn, you are too real, but you are also impossible. You can't exist as you do." He then tried to tell her what had happened during their kiss.

After their talk, Evelyn had walked out of the room into one of the furnished bedrooms. He later heard her taking a shower, and still, later, he heard the door to the bedroom shut. After that, nothing; she had not said anything to him about the dream-trip, which was worrisome. They had not talked further about what they were going to do; they made no plans, created no future. He felt terrible.

CHAPTER 30

THE FOLLOWING MORNING, ADAM awoke on the couch and thought about the previous evening. If it were possible, her inner consciousness had said. It was the last thing, and he wasn't sure if it was a complete thought or if she meant to say more. Did she mean she would make me love her if it was possible, or did she mean, if it were possible for you to love me without me having to make you, I wouldn't have to do it? Thinking this over for a few minutes, he finally realized it didn't matter. Regardless of the reason, he was totally in love with her, totally and completely. He couldn't go through his life always second-guessing his feelings. In the end, it came down to the ancient proverb — fooled into believing you are poor and happy is better than knowing you are rich and sad.

He had to make up with her. He couldn't stand for her to be unhappy. Everything had been going so well before the dream.

He walked to her bedroom door and knocked. After several more taps and calling to wake her, he finally opened the door to make sure she was all right.

She was gone.

At first, he thought she might have just gone invisible on him out of spite, but that didn't make any sense. She wasn't like that. Would she have really abandoned him as she had joked about doing? She had been just joking. No, she would not do that. He trusted her and felt he knew her as well as he knew himself — except for the weird invisibility and dream things. Yeah, she had probably just gone out to grab some breakfast for them. That was all it was.

Sitting on the couch, he took a sheet of paper and began making plans on how they were going to get those people that were trying to hunt them down.

Who were they? They were trained killers who could cover their tracks well. They had access to good weapons and perhaps all the electronic goodies they needed. It also appeared that they could influence the local police to drop an investigation, so they most likely had people inside the police department in key positions. It meant they were powerful.

Where were they? They could be anywhere, and it was wise to assume they were everywhere. He was not sure where they were centrally located, but it could be close to, if not directly in the facility where their fathers used to work. That would be Stone Labs.

Why did they want to kill them? Unknown.

What would make them stop trying? That would probably be nothing less than Evelyn and Adam's deaths.

How much did they know about Adam? If Stone Labs was the source, they might have access to everything about him since his father worked there for years.

How much did they know about Evelyn? She was the main target, probably. Two years ago, they had tried to kill her and succeeded in killing her parents. Since her father also worked at the same place as his, he could assume that they knew all about her as well.

When did they take an interest in them? Unknown.

It looked like the biggest mysteries centered on why they wanted them dead and when this whole thing had started. But then again, wasn't the biggest mystery about how Evelyn could know that he was being used as bait to get her?

CHAPTER 31

VELYN SAT ON THE SEAWALL looking out over the brackish water of Lake Pontchartrain. She gazed at the stars, knowing their beautiful brilliance was greatly muted by the city lights. Hardly a breeze disturbed the quiet lapping of occasional waves against the concrete steps. It had been built in the 1930s and had taken about seven years to complete; she loved it. She remembered as a kid coming out here with her parents on picnics; there were watermelons on hot, muggy days and even fishing from the very place she sat. She could almost remember the smell of the shrimp he used as bait. Her father had been rather frugal in those days and had raided a dumpster used by a fish market in the French Quarter for bait. He always said bait was bait, spoiled or not.

She watched a lone city police car slowly patrol the road bordering the wall until it was out of sight. It was lonely here, lonelier than she had ever felt before. Even the previous two years had not been as awful as this. Last night had been wonderful — and tragic. Both extremes had combined to cancel each other, only emptiness remained.

With his lips pressed to hers so tenderly, she felt her heart would burst, but it had only lasted an instant. Opening her eyes, she watched him looking at her with a startled expression, before a sudden avalanche of information filled her mind. It was only facts and truths. It had little to do with the passion she felt or the emotions that filled her. Nevertheless, she now knew who she was — and what she was. Never would she have allowed this information to be consciously known, except for the extreme circumstances, at least not until the end.

Her mission was over.

Now, only the most important time of her existence remained, and that was in imminent danger — not only for her but also for Adam. Her mind told her that her mother and father were not, but her heart told her they were. Her life had been an act on a worldwide stage, with her as the star. It had all been a lie. Now, the only thing that mattered was Adam.

Evelyn slowly rocked on the rough concrete, her arms hugging herself in grief. Tears flowed endlessly, and breathless sobs racked her soul. She did not want to give up her mission, but she knew she had failed, and — she knew she was the cause. Lifting her face, she struggled to see the stars one last time as a young woman — as a young human woman, but her vision was filled with an ocean of regret, through which she could see only failure.

"I'm sorry, I'm so very sorry… please…"

After an eternity of grief, Evelyn felt an empty calmness envelop her. It was time to return. Her mourning was over; the loss of a lifetime was over. Her dreams, her desires — her humanity — everything was gone. Evelyn gazed one last time upon the gently lapping waves against the steps below, before closing her eyes. One last tear before...

She phased.

CHAPTER 32

EVELYN STOPPED BY A doughnut shop on the way home and picked up a gallon of milk and a dozen chocolate-covered, cream-filled doughnuts. Adam would probably be hungrier than a horse. She smiled. He was so sweet, and she knew he loved her dearly, but that was because he didn't know who she was. What would he do when he found out the truth? When was she going to tell him? With all the bluster and bravado about not caring if she were a demon or an alien or a ghost, he really was a delicate soul. Of course, that was the easy part.

As she approached the side entrance, she noticed him peeking through the blinds and wondered how long he had been anxiously waiting. When she got to the door, it opened before she could grab the knob, and he took her hand and ushered her in. The bag was forgotten as he hugged her close to him and told her how much he loved her and how sorry he was for last night. "I promise I won't let that happen again," he said.

"Let what happen again?" she asked.

"You know... the kiss!" He was blushing terribly.

"The kiss... oh, the kiss!" She smiled. "Now I remember. There was a kiss, wasn't there?"

"Huh?" He didn't know whether to be relieved or worried.

Evelyn stood up on the tip of her toes and put her hands behind his neck. "It's hard to remember it actually. Can you remind me?" She had the most innocent look on her face, but her emerald eyes sparkled as she purposely let her lips linger close to his.

Adam made a noncommittal noise and looked down at the bag she had dropped on the floor. "What have we got here?"

Evelyn looked down at the bag. "It's just a bunch of cream-filled, chocolate-covered doughnuts."

"Great! At least it's not more hamburgers."

Evelyn let her arms fall from his neck and put on a pouty expression.

"Come on," he said, "Let's dig in. I want to go over some stuff I've been organizing."

Picking up the milk and doughnuts, he set them on the coffee table in front of the sofa. For the next fifteen minutes, he showed her his notes and went over each point, discussing what he thought about each one. It looked almost like he was inhaling the doughnuts; getting a dozen was turning out to be a good idea. They had no glasses, so they had to share drinking out of the gallon container. She jokingly warned him not to allow any backflow into the jug, something she couldn't care less about, but it allowed her to break into his dissertation and make a comment. She was going to have to go along with whatever plans he came up with until she figured out how she was going to explain herself to him. It was not going to be easy.

The last point he brought up seemed to make him uneasy. "Evelyn, how do you think your subconscious knows that they are using me as bait to catch or... kill you?"

Evelyn averted her eyes from his and said, "I think everyone's subconscious collects and analyzes tiny bits of information that alone may not seem important, but together, describes a picture of much clearer events. Maybe my father said things that I don't consciously remember. Maybe I heard it somewhere or saw something... I don't know." She looked up into his eyes now that the lying was over.

"But how could your father or anyone else know we were ever going to meet?" Adam sat very still waiting for an answer.

"Uh, perhaps they..." She looked into his eyes, and tears started to cloud her vision. "I'm sorry... I..."

He sat still.

"Adam, I know why... I mean, I know why now. I didn't know before. But... Now I know because I... remember."

"What does that mean? You remember? What do you remember?"

She was quiet a moment. "I want to tell you, but I don't think I should. I'm afraid I will be doing something wrong by telling you."

Adam sat for a long time not saying anything. And then he said quietly, "Is she really gone?"

Evelyn knew exactly whom he meant when he said she. "No, she is not gone. She is still very much a part of me, but she is mixed in with the rest. That is why I am complete now..." She searched his eyes, pleading with him to understand.

"If she is still here... How can I trust what you say to me?"

Evelyn hated where he was taking this. He was pulling away from her at a time when he should be drawing near. "You trusted me before; you can continue to do that," she said desperately. "I know it seems like I am bad now that she is a part of my personality, but good can't exist without the possibility of evil. Good is—good because it resists evil. I can do evil just as you do, but we choose not to do it. You understand?"

"Yes, I think I do. When you drew me into your dream yesterday, I

184

asked if you were making me love you. You told me if it were possible... I think you had more to say, but you stopped with that." He was quiet for another moment before saying, "Do you think she is making me love you?"

Evelyn moved closer and took both his hands in hers. Looking deeply into his eyes, she whispered vehemently, "Adam, I have never been surer of anything than this — I, nor any form of me, could ever force you to love me. That is something you must do on your own, and you must do it completely and with full knowledge of who I am..." There it was! There it was...

Adam looked into her enchanting deep green eyes and said, "...And who are you?"

With her eyes glistening with moisture, she said quietly, "I am the one that loves you more than life itself. I am the one that needs you more than breath. I am the one that will be by your side for all eternity if you will have me, and I am the one that will never willingly allow you to be hurt. I am the one that..." Evelyn lowered her face into her hands and sobbed the remainder in a pleading gasp, "I am the one that, that..." She burst into tears, and he placed his arms around her shoulders.

"Evelyn, don't... please don't. You don't have to say anymore. If you have something you can't tell me, I will trust you to keep it a secret because I trust you with my life. Evelyn, I love you with all my heart. When you're ready, I know you'll tell me what you need to, but it will make no difference to how I feel about you."

Hiding her face in her hands, she did not lift it to him. She knew that he had no idea of what he was saying. If he knew the truth- She cried, desperately thinking that they were lost and that there was no hope for them.

CHAPTER 33

EING UP MOST OF THE night and emotionally spent, exhaustion eventually left her in a deep sleep. Adam covered Evelyn with the blanket and sat beside her on the floor, his head lay gently against her back. He didn't move for a long time as he just sat listening to her gentle breathing. He marveled at how much he felt like a part of her. *Why do I have to know all her secrets?* He thought, *What I know now is enough! I have never been with or seen anyone that loves me as strongly as she. Sure, there are plenty of questions, but none of the answers would change how I feel... ever!*

He knew she was putting on a brave front for him. Obviously, she did not want to worry him, something he was incapable of not doing. The real problem was that if he was around her, there was the chance that she would be hurt or even killed. He was the bait. At some point, they were going to set off a bomb or put out poison; he could not let that happen. Going after the killers would get them caught. He and Evelyn were fortunate they had not been discovered yet.

How long have they been following him? They had hidden microphones in his house and car. Was the restaurant bugged? Is that why one of them showed up yesterday? It was a miracle that she had been in the right place at the right time to see and stop him. Next time, they probably wouldn't be so fortunate.

Adam looked tenderly at her for a long time before finally making his decision. It had been the only decision he could ever have made anyway. He could see that now. If he had to sacrifice his life so she could live, he would do it. He would leave her, and they would follow him. He would never see her again—his heart suddenly broke, and he stifled a sob, his eyes filling with tears. This was the hardest moment of his life, harder than learning about the death of his parents, harder than anything he could remember. He walked to the door and looked back at Evelyn one last time before quietly opening it and slipping out.

CHAPTER 34

T WAS CLOSE TO 10:00 A.M. when he formulated the plan. Walking around town waiting on them to find him was just going to lengthen the whole ordeal. The best solution would be to gift-wrap and deliver him to their doorstep; that should end it quickly. He would get the car and drive to Stone Labs. He knew they ran tours for the public but didn't know when. He did not think it mattered though; he guessed that when they saw him, they would make a special allowance.

The restaurant was open when he arrived. He still had one more thing to do. He couldn't just walk out of their lives like he was walking out of Evelyn's, even though leaving her was so much harder.

As he entered, Rose looked up and gave him a friendly smile before calling out, "Ralph! Boss's here!" There was no business. The place was empty. It was like a funeral home before the grieving families arrived.

Ralph came out of the kitchen and asked if there was anything wrong with his car.

"No, I just decided to go for a walk, you know, get some exercise. But can you believe it? I fell asleep next to this tree in the park." He laughed. "When I woke, it was dark, and you guys had closed already." He hated lying, but the less they knew, the better. "I came in early this morning and went for a run again. That place is nice. You should try it, Ralph. Oh, and I'm not working today."

"What's wrong, Adam?" Rose looked concerned.

"Nothing is wrong. I'm fine. I just need to take care of some business. But before I go, I must do some paperwork. Do you two think you can handle all the business while I'm gone?" He smiled, and both looked at him like they had something on their minds. "What is it? Come on; you have something you want to talk about. I can see it written all over your faces." He tried to laugh, but couldn't find it in his heart to be convincing.

Rose said as kindly as she could, "Adam, a couple of guys came in looking for you earlier; I can smell bill collectors a mile away, and I think they were just that."

Ralph agreed, "Amen! We told them we didn't think you were coming in today. I hope that was okay."

Adam tried to make light of it, but the implications were so frightening that he paled a bit.

"You go on to the back and do your paperwork. If they come back,

I'll get rid of them good and quick. You just leave it to Rose."

This made Adam even more upset, and he told them not to rile these guys. "You can never be sure what some people will do. Everyone's crazy today! Look, I won't be long, just don't do anything foolish. I'll be back out in a few minutes." And with that, he went to the office and wrote two checks, one to Rose, and one to Ralph, $20,000 each. He then wrote out a smaller check for Clara. That was about all the savings he had left from the insurance money. He wrote a letter to Rose and asked that she read it to Ralph also.

Dear Rose and Ralph,

I must go out of town for a while, and I need to close the restaurant. I don't know if we will ever reopen, I seriously doubt it. Please accept this offering from me. You are worth so much more! You have been such good friends and have stuck with me when I needed you most. I can't tell you where I'm going, but if I'm successful, you will probably not see me again. You are both the best the world has to offer, and I love you!

Adam

P.S.
Please make sure Clara gets the check I made out for her. Thank her for her hard work. I appreciate it greatly.

He placed the checks in separate envelopes and put the letter in Rose's. Adam hated leaving them like this, but he didn't know what else to do. He couldn't give them any hints or clues. If the killers even suspected they might know something—He could barely stand to think of it. This was all he could do to protect them. Setting the envelopes on the desk in clear sight, he closed the office door. Ralph was in the kitchen preparing an order for a customer.

"Hey, Ralph..."

Ralph answered him, but kept busy preparing the meal. He was a good guy and would find another job for sure. The money would help though. "I put that extra pay I promised you in the office in an envelope. You can get it when you leave today. Thanks for everything."

At the last moment, as Adam left the kitchen, Ralph must have felt something wasn't right because he stopped for a moment and watched the kitchen door close, wondering what he was feeling.

In the main dining area, Adam walked over to Rose who was pouring some milk. As she finished and reached for a tray, he put his arms around her and gave her a warm hug. "Rose, thank you so much for everything you have done for me," he said quietly in her ear. When he pulled back, he saw the tears in her eyes and knew that in some way, she suspected there was a serious problem. She tried to put on a smile for him. He answered it with one of his own and turned to leave.

"You take care of yourself, honey," she whispered.

He held his breath as he turned the ignition and gave a prayer of thanks that the car didn't explode. Something like that would have likely killed everyone in the restaurant. In a few minutes, he was gone, gone from their lives, and from Evelyn's. He would do this thing for her. He would protect her in the only way he knew how.

CHAPTER 35

EVELYN TURNED A COUPLE OF TIMES on the sofa, snuggling under the warm blanket before gradually becoming aware that Adam must have put it on her after she fell asleep. She imagined his arms around her, holding her closely, protecting her from the world.

Remembering the conversation before falling asleep, she realized she had once again embarrassed herself. No wonder he thought of her as a helpless kitten instead of the dragon she was. Where was he anyway?

Opening her eyes wider, she looked at the milk jug and bag of doughnuts still on the coffee table. Her "mother's" advice came back to her again in the form of a warning, "Never let the milk set out and get warm; it's sure to spoil." Mothers were full of good advice. Evelyn smiled. There was something strange about the milk being out that did not seem right, besides the fact that it had probably soured. Adam could have put it in the refrigerator. It was wasteful to let it go bad like that; stealing it was bad enough. Slightly irritated, she closed her eyes again and snuggled deeper into the blanket.

Suddenly, as surely as she knew she was no kitten, she knew that Adam was gone. The knowledge that was as much a part of her as anything she had ever known. It was an irrefutable fact.

Pain clutched at her soul and radiated out through her heart until all parts of her body blazed with an unquenchable fiery torment. She screamed in terror as she threw the blanket away from her, kicking the table and its contents across the living room floor!

Running desperately through the house proved what she already knew; more information settled into her mind, he had gone to sacrifice himself. Another drawn-out scream filled the house as all the muscles in her body tightened in fear.

Desperately running as fast as she could, almost mindlessly back to the restaurant, she stopped and gasped at the empty spot where Adam always parked his car. There was a closed sign on the front door, but she could see two people, Rose and Ralph, sitting at one of the tables. Rose had her head on the table and looked to be crying; Ralph had his arm around her to console her.

Evelyn beat the door before realizing they would not hear, nor be aware that she was there. She stepped back from it before striking out with her foot hard enough to shatter the door in a thunderous shower of sparkling shards of glass and splintered wood! In the same instant, both saw her standing in the remains of the devastation. Ralph fell backward off his chair, and Rose stood defiantly, but with a scream in her throat.

"Wait!" yelled Evelyn. I'm Adam's... friend! Please, help me!"

"What?! What?!" Rose hollered. She couldn't think of anything to say as she desperately tried to understand what was happening. Ralph was crawling behind the counter in terror, all thoughts of protecting Rose gone from his mind.

In the next instant, Rose knew who this was; she remembered everything that had happened about Evelyn, Adam's "invisible" friend, with razor-sharp clarity.

"Evelyn..." she whispered. "Evelyn, he's gone! I think he's in trouble and someone's after him!" She was crying hopelessly now as she reached out to Evelyn.

In a second, Evelyn was holding her and trying to see through her tears. "Tell me, Rose! Tell me what happened!" She tried to calm her voice, but desperation drove her and colored her questions with insistence.

Ralph was on the phone calling 911. Rose may know this crazy girl, but she was crazy and dangerous.

Rose and Evelyn completely ignored him as Rose tried to let Evelyn know what had occurred. She let Evelyn read Adam's note and told her about the checks. "Something terrible is going to happen to him!" Rose whispered out in grief. "I just know it."

On reading the note, Evelyn's heart tightened within her chest, and the tears ran down her cheeks with abandon. He was truly doing it. He was giving his life for her!

She turned from Rose and looked out the empty hole that was the remains of the shattered doorway. Police cars were screeching to a halt outside with police jumping out and behind their vehicles, protecting themselves from possible danger. However, all Evelyn could see was boiling clouds of black and red. Pain stabbed through her as she moved out of the restaurant. Glass and wood were swept from before her as if pushed away by an orb of invisible force. The remains of the doorway and the surrounding structure buckled outward as the irresistible bubble passed through.

Reason and logic ended in the hearts and minds of the police officers. Here was obvious evil. Not a hardened criminal or murderer or even a senseless child killer—here was pure evil! It made no sense, but the guns that began firing were obedient to the laws of the universe, their deadly loads traveling across the finite space in a blink of eternity—only to pass through the emptiness where something had once been. What this thing was, they had no idea. Nor did they have any thought as to why they were firing their guns. When they stopped and looked at what remained of the restaurant front, they gasped in horror.

Several officers looked at a patrol car screeching away from the carnage and then returned their gaze to the catastrophe, all memory of the car deleted from their minds.

Inside the restaurant's shattered remains, they would find Rose and Ralph, she on the floor holding a clutched letter to her chest and Ralph with the phone clutched in his. Broken shards of glass and splintered wood covered everything except two clear circles around each unconscious body, neither with as much as a scratch or bruise.

CHAPTER 36

YOU'RE LYING!" ADAM SHOUTED. They had to be trying to manipulate him. For hours, they had interrogated him, and he had tried to tell them the truth, but they wouldn't believe him.

The interrogator spoke with sympathy, but his eyes were the eyes of a shrew. Adam didn't trust this one. He went by the name of Tom, but Adam had no idea if that was even his real name. He doubted it. He would never believe the things they were trying to make him believe about Evelyn. He knew her, and he knew who they were and what they had done. He would not be fooled.

Adam had arrived that morning to find everything quiet. There were no welcoming "men-in-black" waiting for him or any other indication that he was even expected.

From conversations with his father, he knew a few things about the place. The facility was built off I-10 between Baton Rouge and New Orleans. It covered almost forty acres and was surrounded by an electrified fence and topped with razor wire. Swampland surrounded the fence, and there was only one hardened shell road in or out.

The road led to a large parking area surrounding a visitor's center. Once inside the visitor's center, a large tunnel led into the facility by way of an escalator that went under the fence and into another enclosed building. From there, a company bus provided transportation to all points. Of course, no one could be unescorted while on the property.

When he arrived, the parking lot was empty. He left his keys in the ignition, not believing he would ever need the car again, and walked into the visitor's center. Inside the large glass doors, he found a security desk occupied by a smartly dressed woman in a dark business suit. She lifted a phone to her ear as he approached. Behind her desk, he saw a large hallway leading to the facility entrance. Before entering the hallway, a large heavy-gauge fence would have to be lifted by motor-driven cables. Even in Adam's depressed state, he found the courage to try a little humor on the straight-faced woman. "Security here is... intense."

Her face broke as she performed the expected smile and welcomed him to the facility. "Welcome to Stone Labs. If you are here for a tour of the facility, they are normally by appointment only, but we do offer special appointments outside the scheduled ones."

He forced himself to smile and said, "I'm Adam Yates." If he expected this to cause alarms to go off, he was disappointed because she did not even blink. "Well, Mr. Yates, what can we do for you?"

"I'm expected." With some small amount of satisfaction, he saw that this, at least, caused her to pause and even initiated a blink in response. Nice.

"I apologize, Mr. Yates, I was not informed about your appointment. Please have a seat in the lounge while I call your escort. Who did you say you have an appointment with?"

"I didn't actually. If you contact security and tell them I'm a friend of Evelyn Jefferson, I'm sure they will understand." The smile remained on her face, but now it had all the warmth of cracked concrete.

"Wonderful. If you step into the lounge, I will make that call."

She led Adam into a small room just off the main entrance. It had what appeared to be an unusually thick glass door, which she was polite enough to open with a keypad mounted on the wall beside it. He also noticed there were no handles on the door, again — nice.

There was only one sofa in the room with a small table in front of it, and a large mirror with a strange psychedelic pattern etched across it for art. There were no magazines, just the sofa, the table, and the mirror.

As he waited, he allowed himself to think about Evelyn again. She had a chance now. She was smart and would be able to stay away from them for the rest of her life. He was sure of that. He couldn't think of a better way to die than protecting her.

That had been his last thoughts until he awoke in the "interrogation" room. Instead of having a sudden end to his life, it was starting to look like it might drag on, for a little while at least.

Yes, they knew who he was, and they knew who Evelyn was. What they were trying to convince him of was that Evelyn was a foreign agent who was much older than she looked. She was a mole employed by an enemy nation to spy on the United States and had been getting national secrets from her father for years. She was trained in the use of psychological drugs and had used them on Adam for the last few months. Anything he thought he knew about her was a lie. She was evil and cared only about money and power. As a patriotic citizen, Adam should be grateful for the opportunity to assist his country in her apprehension.

Their techniques wore away at Adam and made him doubt himself. They were very good at what they did. Tom was only one of his interrogators. There were three others, one a very beautiful woman. All of them seemed like normal security people that were just doing their jobs, except for Tom who had about as much warmth as a snake. Adam wondered what could be in this for him. But he felt himself drawn to the others, especially the woman, and it appeared that she, most of all, believed as he did that Tom could not be trusted. Once, she had a fight with him about allowing Adam to eat something and rest a while. Tom had stormed out of the room in anger, and she had patted Adam's shoulder to let him know she was on his side. Everything about her said she could be trusted.

It felt like he had been in the interrogation room for hours and hours when she finally asked Adam to talk about what he thought Evelyn was, if not an agent.

"Tell me, Adam; you're a very smart young man. I can tell that, even without having read your file. This agent, Evelyn that is, might be shrewd, but she can't hold a candle to you. It is plain to see that you have been in contact with the drugs she uses to manipulate your thinking. The blood tests we performed on you were very clear about that. There is no doubt. But, what do you think she is, if not an agent of a foreign nation? I guess what I'm asking is what did she try to make you believe she was." Sandra sounded like she was trying to be sensible about it.

When Adam finally opened to her about Evelyn being invisible and not being able to shut it off, it appeared she might start believing him.

"But, Adam, listen to what you're saying To a smart man like you, does that seem possible? Isn't it much more likely that she has been drugging you somehow?"

"I know it sounds crazy," Adam said. "I've told myself that a hundred times. But, I've had... dreams... Yes, I've had dreams that... well, I'm so confused! They were so real, and if nothing else was real, the feelings I had for her had to be... right?" He looked at her, almost pleading for an affirmation.

Sandra looked at him with deep sadness in her eyes. "Adam, I'm so sorry for you. I can't tell you how many times I've seen this sort of thing. It's the drugs she uses and others like it. They separate you from reality and make you believe anything that is suggested to your mind. I'm so, so, sorry."

Looking into her eyes, he saw the moisture and a tear on her cheek. "But... it seemed so real..." he whispered.

"You rest a while. Are you hungry, thirsty? I can bring you whatever we have; how about some water or a Coke?" Sandra's eyes were tender as she tried to soothe his pain.

"I'm okay, but thanks anyway." Adam sighed.

"Adam, I have to go take care of some things, but I promise I will be back. I won't let the others harass you again. Okay?"

"Thanks, I appreciate that." Adam placed his head on the table and closed his eyes.

Sandra closed the door to the interrogation room and walked down to the adjoining room. Opening the door, she stepped into the observation area where the other three were talking quietly.

Tom smiled at her and said softly, "You're good... very, very good!"

"Everyone has a weakness; his is being a nice boy and having too much trust." She smiled humorlessly at Tom, and the other two laughed softly. Sandra continued, "I think I can get him to trust me soon enough to use him as bait to draw her here." Her lips turned down when she thought of her failure. "I was so sure that if we got him into that room, she would be with him. Filling it with gas should have put her out just as it did him, and that should have turned off this power to make us see things other than reality. I suppose it's a good thing that we didn't use the lethal stuff as ordered. At least we still have him. There is still hope we can draw her out."

"I talked to Senator Collins earlier, and he's getting impatient," Tom said. "He says that the committee is meeting next week. They need results."

"Yes, I know that! And he will get his results soon." Sandra looked worried though. Senator Collins had a funny way about him when it came to impatience.

"What's he doing now?" she asked, turning to the mirror.

"His head has been on the table ever since you left the room. He has probably fallen to sleep," said one of the other interrogators.

Sandra looked at Adam for a moment before continuing, "We can't give him too much time to think. We must keep him off balance. I'll head back in and continue the... processing." And she gave the others a curt smile.

As she opened the observation room door, an Army captain appeared, and requested Sandra and Tom accompany him to Senator Collins' office. It was not a request they could refuse.

In the interrogation room, Adam's head moved to a more comfortable position on his arms, and he finally drifted into a troubled sleep.

The world reminded Adam of what he thought a prehistoric swamp might look like. A thick mist covered the ground and drifted over pools of stagnant water. The vegetation looked limp and listless. Looking up, he saw that the sky was very much the same, low gray clouds hung down almost touching the trees and there was almost no movement. His view in any direction was lim-

ited due to the thick fog.

"Adam?" It was Evelyn's voice, but he couldn't see her. Looking around him for a possible clue as to where she was, he heard her voice again. "Adam, I can't find you... I'm trying, but I'm weak. Please help me!"

"How can I? What do you need me to do?" Adam was unsure of what was happening. Was this real or was it drug induced? Was he having a relapse? Sandra told him these drugs were so strong that even if you weren't taking them on a constant basis, they had lingering effects.

Evelyn was silent and did not respond to his request, adding to the feeling that the whole dream was drug induced. But then, "... I'm dying. Listen to me carefully and remember what I say. I am getting weak and will not be able to bring you here anymore. Always remember that I love you. Remember and keep that thought in your heart forever. I love..."

Adam awoke and lifted his head off the table. He didn't say anything. He didn't know what to believe, but his heart was hurting as if someone had punched him in the chest.

CHAPTER 37

S ENATOR COLLINS HAD AN intense interest in this special project, into which he had channeled an embarrassing amount of resources and his methods of doing so would not have been fully appreciated by the fact-finding committee, something he would stop at nothing to prevent. Elections were coming up, and none of this would prove beneficial. Quite the contrary, if he was not very careful, a future prison cell was not out of the question. He had trusted the Stone Lab security force to make certain everything was done right, but evidently, the job was beyond their expertise. Trusting them was a mistake that could cost him everything. He would not allow it to continue. There just wasn't enough time to be nice about it.

Captain Burns escorted the two interrogators into Senator Collins' office as instructed. Sandra Mitchell, the head of Stone Labs security, had taken personal responsibility to make sure the issue was resolved for the senator. She felt they were progressing nicely and was quite excited to report her results to him.

Upon entering the office, the captain closed the door and stood in front of it. Several other people were present in the room. Of course, she knew Senator Collins but had no idea about the other three. "Senator, I appreciate the opportunity to report on our progress, but I must say I did not expect you here today. Our progress report was not until Friday." She had walked briskly up to the desk he was sitting behind and had extended her hand in greeting. The first indication of trouble came when the senator refused to acknowledge it.

"Mitchell, I'm afraid your progress report is practically worthless unless you can report that the two targets have been eliminated. And, just in case you were not aware of what our contractual meaning of the word eliminated meant, let me clear it up for you: dead!" He raised his voice to accentuate the last word. "Were you aware of that definition, Ms. Mitchell?"

Sandra was stunned. The excitement of her progress felt like failure now. She hated feeling off balance, and the senator had just placed her at the edge of a cliff with nothing to cling to. She desperately attempted to take a couple of seconds to regroup and survive the encounter. There was little doubt that the senator was a very dangerous man.

"Senator, I understand the contractual interpretation of eliminated, and further, while I cannot report the two targets are... dead, I can report that we have one in custody and ready to serve as bait for the second. I am completely confident that he will do as we suggest. He is, after all, just a young man with very little experience. He is quite malleable." Sandra put on her most confident face and hoped he would not know how much she was pushing the truth.

"You have the young man..." He lowered his eyes for a minute before looking over at the other three sitting to his right, then back to her. "Sandra, I'm afraid we may not have given you all the necessary information. I hope this oversight will not prove to be — fatal." Senator Collins slowly rose and walked across the room before turning around to face her again. "How was he apprehended?"

Sandra sensed she was stepping back from the cliff and imminent danger. "He arrived this morning and presented himself to the security desk in the Visitors Building."

The senator seemed shaken a little bit by this, but said nothing.

"We followed the protocol set up by your people, and he was placed in the containment room. Once he was unconscious, we transported him to the interrogation room." She was feeling more confident now.

The senator's eyes widened a little, not much, but her training detected the shock on his face. "So, the young man arrived by himself, and after he was incapacitated, you did not discover the second target in the room with him? And am I correct in assuming that this interrogation room you have set up is in this very building where we are now having this pleasant conversation?"

Sandra was experienced enough to detect the threat in his tone, but she could not understand the source; what was he talking about? He made no sense. "Senator..."

Senator Collins stopped her with a look she could interpret in no other way than one that said her next few words might be her last. "Sandra... I only want one word from you: yes or no."

Sandra felt the ground crumbling beneath her feet as she said, "Well, yes and no."

Senator Collins said coldly, "For your sake, Ms. Mitchell, I hope you are a fast learner; otherwise, I will shoot you myself." With that, he turned to the three men and introduced them. "You and your staff will now be working with my people. This is Mr. Stern, the head of my personal security and his two directors, Mr. John Beck on the left and Mr. Steven Schumer on the right. As far as you are concerned, when they tell you to do something, you will assume it is coming directly from me. Are you clear about that?"

Sandra's face drained. "Definitely, sir. I will, of course, have to notify the head of..." Sandra's mouth shut with almost an audible snap.

"I don't believe you are clear about what I am saying, Mitchell. I don't give a damn about who you have to report to. You will say nothing to anyone about the operational details you are about to be briefed on. To do so will terminate more than your position with Stone Labs. Now, am I making myself clear?"

Sandra could feel her throat tighten in fear and the taste of bile in her mouth. "Yes, sir... I completely understand, sir."

With that, he turned to Mr. Stern. "Clean up this mess." Without another look at Sandra, Senator Collins left the room with the Army captain. Sandra took a second to look at Tom who was as pale as she was.

Mr. Stern had been talking quietly to the other two for a moment before turning to Tom. "Just to be sure, you also understand what Ms. Mitchell has agreed to, and you fully intend to cooperate?" It sounded like a question, but no one in the room understood it as anything close to a question.

"Yes... yes, sir," Tom stammered.

"Excellent. Now, won't you please assemble your staff for an immediate meeting? I will need to organize a few things and need to make sure I have their complete support, and, of course, understanding." He smiled congenially. "I have a few items of concern I need to go over with Ms. Mitchell first." Tom looked at Sandra for the briefest instant before leaving the room and closing the door.

Sandra's head was swirling slightly from the adrenaline rush she was experiencing.

With the same smile stapled to his face, Mr. Stern asked her to be seated in the chair. "The senator can sometimes appear to be overzealous when it comes to National Security matters; I'm sure you understand." He sat on the sofa across from her chair along with Mr. Beck and Mr. Schumer. We may not have much time, so I will give you as much information as you need in this matter. Not everything was technically spelled out in the contract. You understand — National Security."

Sandra swallowed and nodded her head, but said nothing.

"You were told that the young man you now have in custody would serve as bait to catch the second target, a young woman. You informed that the young woman would be hard to find, even impossible except for very good technology and a lot of luck. Something has happened with our target that has changed the rules under which we thought we were operating. You may be wondering how such an inexperienced, young woman, barely twenty years old, could have such a talent at evading overwhelming odds against her. What I tell you now, you will take to your grave and never reveal to anyone. You do understand that?"

Sandra swallowed, trying to moisten her throat so she could get the words out. "Yes, I understand completely."

"Good!" He looked at her for a full thirty seconds before continuing. "We have good reason to believe that our target is not human. Recent events over the past two years seem to have proven that beyond any rational doubt." He continued, "Approximately fifty years ago, we came into possession of a sphere about the size of a basketball. The technology required to make this was beyond anything we had then, or now. We contracted with Stone Labs on a Top-Secret Project to see if we could determine what it was. I'm sure you can appreciate the fact that the US Government does not feel comfortable with things it does not understand. Was it a bomb? Where was it from? Who had this type of technology? How could we obtain it? Are you still following me, Ms. Mitchell?" He did actually seem interested in an answer.

"Yes, of course," she said quickly.

Briefly looking at his two companions, he continued, "Stone Labs used a lot of resources to build some incredible devices to analyze and open the sphere, all of which failed. Nothing they could do would affect the device in any way. No amount of force, heat, vibration, radiation, or chemical contact affected it. In fact, the only way we could even determine we had possession of it was that we could see it with our eyes and feel it with our hands as well as move it around. We were not even able to produce a recording device that would detect its presence. The surface of the object was completely frictionless and harder than we have been able to test. It was invulnerable. This was the case for about thirty years. As you can imagine, that is a very long time and required some creative resource management for the funds to continue. Interestingly, but exasperating at the same time, we never did open it. One day while the lab staff was continuing to spend these considerable government resources to fulfill its contract, the sphere simply opened on its own. If the outside presented some very non-human-like questions, I could not begin to describe the complexity of the inside. We now arrive at our problem. The sphere contained a zygote and an extremely resilient one at that. All tests showed it to be of human origin and appeared very normal except for its resilience. Advances in the artificial implantation of fertilized eggs into humans were in their early history and often failed. However, this one readily attached itself and began a normal cell division. In seven months, our female target was born." Mr. Stern stopped and waited for Sandra to digest some of the facts.

The facts were straight out of a science fiction novel. If the threat of death in her present circumstances were not so real, she would believe the entire story a lie. What she was being told was that they were hunting some alien creature.

He continued again, "You may be thinking that this zygote must have been alien in origin, but there were no indications of this. Was this a normal human zygote that some advanced technology had preserved in this sphere? There are many possibilities other than an alien one. Well, that was the case until two years ago. Without muddying up the waters too much with unimportant details, let me just say that it was about two years ago that the decision was made to end the project as no useful information could be gathered from the living child. She appeared to be completely normal. The problem at the time was that Senate investigations were being conducted to determine more precisely, where certain money was being spent. This project became a target, or I should say the misuse of certain funds became the target of the inquiry. It was determined that the project would be scrapped and all evidence removed. That meant removing all material evidence to include living or otherwise."

Sandra was beginning to feel sick. "National Security, of course."

Mr. Stern stared at her a moment. "Of course."

He continued, "Incredible as it may seem, this clean-up operation provided proof that our little girl was not a girl at all. Indeed, if she was, she was a very, very powerful one. The reason she is so good at evading detection is that she can somehow redirect our minds."

"Yes, I know she is supposed to be invisible," said Sandra.

"Not really. She is still reflecting light and can still affect and be affected by the environment. The only thing that she appears to affect is our minds. We simply will not believe she exists, and we come up with other reasons for her presence other than the most obvious one, which is that she is actually there. If we take a picture of her and we are being affected by her presence, while she is in the photo, we will not see her. When and if she no longer affects us, we can once again successfully see her in the photo. The same goes for any other recording medium."

Sandra thought a moment while he waited and asked, "What happened to the original sphere?"

He smiled. "It disappeared."

"You mean it was stolen?" she asked.

"No, I mean it disappeared. Security locked it in an extremely secure vault and under some quite elaborate security precautions. It just disappeared."

"Where does Mr. Yates come into the picture?"

"Mr. Yates is the son of another Stone Labs employee. His story is not important at this time other than to say he was used in several tests with the subject to see how she would react to him. The test occurred while both were very young. After she displayed this amazing ability at seventeen, we tried to start the project back up again. Regrettably, certain senatorial investigations were uncovering too much and getting too close to our sources, so it was eventually decided to go ahead with the termination. Unfortunately, because of her new ability, the magnitude of the process of removing the problem had increased substantially. We tried to terminate what was referred to as the Adam-link, but fortune was on his side, and as it turned out, on our side as well, because we failed; only his mother and sisters were removed as collateral damage in the attempt to get him. Later, his father became an issue and had to be removed as well. Thus, we have our young man, Adam, as bait to catch our primary target."

"Evelyn," said Sandra. She was wondering if she would be able to finish their meeting before puking. The lack of justice and feeling was impossible to believe. Sandra was not beyond doing some terrible things herself and had done so, but this whole affair seemed wrong! However, regardless of how unjust it may be to the two kids, she realized that the senator was allowing her to know too much — way too much. Sandra Mitchel understood that she was never going to survive it.

"I beg your pardon..." Mr. Stern asked.

"I'm sorry; I just meant that her name is Evelyn."

He looked at Sandra for a few seconds as if he were trying to decide. She hoped it was not about her life. She had to survive long enough to get away, to live if she possibly could.

"Yes," continued Mr. Stern. "The subject's name is Evelyn, but you will do better to think of her as what she is — an incredible danger to our National Security. If she were to get into the hands of our enemies, there is no end to the damage she could do to this nation. Do you understand that?" He watched her closely for her answer.

"I completely understand. She would be that and more." She hoped that she was convincing. She didn't know who this young girl was, but if Adam loved her as he said, then she doubted the danger was to National Security. The real danger she represented was to some government officials that were about to be caught with their fingers in the proverbial cookie jar. The list of dead bodies was piling up. How could she keep herself from joining them?

Appearing satisfied, he finished up, "There are a few points I have left out, but this should be a good beginning. Will you see if your people are ready for that meeting? If not, please expedite it. I don't think we have very much time.

When Sandra opened the door to leave, but was met by Tom who quietly delivered a message to her. Mr. Stern turned from talking to the other two. "Is everything okay?"

"Yes, everything is normal. There was just an alarm malfunction; it's being attended to."

The three men immediately understood the implications.

"Lockdown!" Mr. Stern yelled.

CHAPTER 38

B LINDED BY RAGE, EVELYN exited the disintegrating restaurant and phased their minds. She walked to one of the patrol vehicles and accelerated away from the carnage. A portion of her mind screamed in agony at the danger her friends had been placed in, but she had no time to grieve; she had done all she could.

Time was short. She could feel her energy bleeding away into oblivion. Soon, there would be none remaining, and Adam would be doomed to the same fate. She wondered that her species' survival process was ever successful. Surely, the failure rate was high, but the successful consummations were eternal.

Her first stop was his home. Had he come here first? Was he hoping they would be waiting to kill him? Rushing through the house revealed he had not. Where would he go now? Standing in his bedroom, she evaluated the possibilities and likely vectors. She collapsed on her knees and screamed out in agony, "Adaaaaam!" Tears ran down her face as she thought of what he was doing. She knew he was not dead yet; she knew it because she was still alive.

Bending forward on her knees, she put her forehead on the cool floor and bawled. She cried for her mother and father. She wailed for her lost childhood, her friends, her world of humans — and she phased, shattering the windows and doors outward.

The world was gray and thick with a foggy mist. There was no sky, and all she could manage was a swampy surface. Visibility was limited to only a few yards. She reached out and transcended Adam's barriers.

"Adam?" she whispered. "Adam, I can't find you... I'm trying, but I'm weak. Please help me!"

She heard him respond with confusion, "How can I? What do you need me to do?"

Evelyn could feel the drain on her energy increasing. The process of transcending was accelerating her death.

Adam... I'm dying. Listen to me carefully and remember what I say. I am getting weak and will not be able to bring you here anymore. Always remember that I love you. Remember and keep that thought in your heart forever — I love you...need you! You will burn brightly for me if you concentrate — I must find you!

Evelyn collapsed on the floor in exhaustion. She had to conserve; she had to endure a little bit longer.

When she regained consciousness, his location immediately registered in her mind. She knew it as if she had been there a thousand times, and in fact, she had been there — more times than she wanted to remember. It was Stone Labs. That is where he was.

She pushed the police cruiser as fast as it would go, which was surprisingly faster than she thought they were capable of. There was no need to use the emergency lights or slow for traffic; every vehicle on the road had moved to the right lane and was driving safely and courteously behind the one in front. This condition extended as far before her as was necessary for her to continue at its maximum speed.

The normal chaotic conditions resumed once she exited the interstate. It only took about fifteen minutes to reach the shell road leading to the facility. Reaching the outer parking area, Evelyn pulled up next to Adam's vehicle.

She could see no sign of movement. There was no traffic inside the fence, and no vehicles were in the parking area except for Adam's. They were waiting for her.

Walking to the large glass doors of the Visitor's Center, she heard nothing but the soft crunch of her sneakers passing over the crushed shells. A wide sidewalk led to the glass doors where she put cupped hands over her eyes, trying to see inside the dark interior. It appeared that the Visitor's Center was closed. Looking back at Adam's car, she felt it was a bad omen, but she tried the door anyway. It was locked.

Turning her back to lean against the door, she realized how tired she was. In fact, she was exhausted. She understood the reason. She had to hurry.

Returning to the police car, she opened the trunk, looking for any tool and found the universal one, a tire wrench. It would do.

Thankfully, the glass door was not some super-plastic; it shattered nicely. Inside, she found that she had been mistaken about it being closed. It was so bright outside that, by comparison, it only appeared dark on the inside. There were a few couches, some hard chairs, and a central circular counter occupied by a dark-suited woman. Of course, she had not noticed the shattered door or all the glass shards spread out near it. This was the security desk.

Behind it, she saw the entrance to the facility. The memory of it became crystal clear in her mind. The heavy metallic gate was closed and would need to be opened before she could get in. She guessed correctly that the controls were located on the information island, but it also had a touchpad that required a code to be entered, a code she didn't have.

Evelyn looked at the busted door and the mess on the floor. What would happen if she showed the security woman the reality around her? Of course, she would immediately set off alarms and any chance she had of opening that gate would be gone. What then?

Evelyn looked at the woman and imagined a tour bus arriving outside. Seventeen visitors stepped off, and the tour guide escorted them into the Visitor's Center. Robert, the tour guide and a regular, walked over to the security guard, who now had a big grin on her face. It was common knowledge that they had a thing going.

Robert smiled and greeted her. "Good afternoon, Ms. Gonzales! How are you this fine afternoon?"

Putting on a front for the tour guests, she ignored his friendliness. "I wasn't aware of a group touring this afternoon." She opened up the schedule program and found the Nature's Heaven group listed for a quick tour at 3:00 p.m. "Ah! I see it now. She turned to the group of older ladies and gentlemen. "May I have your attention, please? Please. May I have your attention?"

As the talking settled down to a few whispers, Rita Gonzales gave a summary of what would follow, where they would be taken, and what refreshments would be served at the end of the tour.

An older and obviously senile lady in her 90s asked, "My dear, do you have a bathroom where I can freshen up a bit? I need to go. Please?"

"Of course, you will be able to freshen up as soon as you pass through the security gate. Someone will direct you once you reach the other side of the escalator. Are there any more questions? If not, we shall begin." She caught the quick wink from Robert and, while hiding her face from the others, blew him a quick kiss through the air.

Pulling up the security program, she put in her ID and password. After bringing up the security pad on the screen, she picked up the phone, gave a call to Visitor Point Two security, and announced the tour would be heading over. They quickly answered and thanked her. At that point, she put in the required code, which appeared on the other side of the gate at Visitor Point Two. They verified the correct code for the day and executed the command to open the security gate.

As the gate began to open, she said, "Please stay with your escort at all times and watch your step on the escalators. We very much appreciate your visit today at Stone Labs, serving our government faithfully for fifty-six years. Have a wonderful visit!"

The group had passed the heavy security gate and was now standing on the escalator as it moved them down and under the facility fence to Visitor Point Two. Robert quickly looked back and gave Rita a wave. She gave him a warm smile in return.

Evelyn ran down the moving escalator and up the next to enter Visitor Point Two. There were security guards with ugly-looking rifles standing at strategic points inside, but they were not on alert. Another security desk identical to the one outside was in the room, and a security guard was speaking into a phone. "Yeah, Sam Roland here. I received an alarm that the outside gate had opened. What have you got?"

Ms. Gonzales turned around and responded, "Nothing on my side. There must be an open in the detectors again. How about contacting maintenance, you know how they're going to love you calling them this close to shift change." She laughed.

"No problem," said Roland, "I can't begin to tell you how much I enjoy messing with those guys." They both laughed and hung up.

Roland called main security and let them know about the problem. This was passed on to Tom who also served as material support dispatcher. He called and reported the failure. With all the brass hanging around, he should probably also let Sandra know. He would finish getting the meeting together for Mr. Stern first, no sense in upsetting their new bosses.

Evelyn only took a moment in Visitor Point Two before exiting one of the doors leading to a small bus. The two security guards standing watch in front of the door didn't notice anything unusual, even when she bumped into the one on the right.

She had no problem knowing where Adam was now; she was being drawn to him like a moth to a brilliant flame. It appeared that he was housed in a three-story building in the center of the complex. It had no windows that she could see and was covered with black panel siding. A helicopter sat on the roof with several guards, its blades turning. There may have been more, but from her angle, that was the limit of her visibility. She could run there but was exhausted more than ever. She took the bus instead.

Naturally, no one noticed. She parked it in front and jumped out leaving the door and engine running. Quickly ascending the steps and entering the double doors, both with blackened windows, she found herself in a large room with guards stationed at the door and elevator. At the security desk, she heard the sergeant speak up. "Look smart! Senator Collins is on his way down." If possible, they straightened up even more and waited for the elevator door to open. When it did, a well -dressed senior man, sixty-five or seventy years old, quickly exited followed by an Army captain, no connection with site security. He talked in low tones to the captain as they exited the building.

Evelyn entered the elevator before it could close and pressed the basement button. That is where Adam was. Exiting the elevator, she ran down the hall and stopped at the door with a number pad. Someone would be needed to open it. A stalwart-looking security guard, sitting at a desk in the room, pushed his paperwork aside and placed his pencil on top of the stack. He took a second to stretch before walking to the door and entering the code to open it. Once Evelyn passed through, and the door closed, he looked at the clock, swore, and immediately went back to his desk to finish up before his shift ended.

Evelyn ran down a hall that seemed much too narrow until she arrived at a door that practically shouted out Adam's name. Again, there was a number pad next to it. How was she going to get inside? Feeling around her, she detected three people in the next office.

Tom finished making the calls needed to begin the meeting but still needed to contact maintenance. He wondered if it was a good idea to let the government people know they were having a slight detector issue. It was probably not worth the trouble to make them look worse than they already did. He turned to one of the other interrogators and said, "I'll be right back; keep watch on our young man and make sure he doesn't escape." All three laughed at that impossibility. The only way Adam was getting out of that room was in a box.

CHAPTER 39

TOM CLOSED THE OBSERVATION room door and stopped in front of Evelyn to punch in his code to open the door to Adam's room. He then continued down the hall.

Inside the room, Evelyn's heart almost failed her as she took in the pitiful sight. Adam looked like he was completely lost. His face showed pain and confusion. "Adam," she whispered.

As Adam turned to look, he could not believe his eyes. Inside the observation room, one of the interrogators saw him look toward the door. The interrogator swept his gaze to it but saw nothing. Unfortunately, the room's microphone picked up Adam's conversation just fine.

"Don't look, Adam, they're watching!"

He did as he was told and rested his head on the table again; his face turned away from the observation mirror. "How did you find me? Why did you come? You have to get away. They are looking for you and are probably setting up a trap." He was quiet for a moment as new tears filled his eyes. "You have to go... you have to allow me to do this, please!"

Evelyn sat against the wall across from the mirror so Adam could see her. "You never understood, Adam. You have never allowed yourself to understand! Why? I love you, and I know you love me. I'm dying... I don't know how long I have yet, but what you are doing proves that you love me completely! Please... please accept me. And Adam, I have..."

The door opened, and Stern and Sandra entered, followed by his two shadows.

Adam lifted his head and looked at each of them. Sandra tried to harden her resolve, but he looked so lost. This was wrong, so wrong.

"Hello, Adam," Stern purred. "It has been a long time."

Adam attempted to straighten up and act like he was completely in control, but his red face and swollen eyes could not support the claim. "I don't believe I've had the pleasure of meeting you," he said. "Perhaps in a sewer somewhere? I've heard they're full of rats."

Stern smiled, but hardly from humor. Sandra found she could keep her face severe but had to smile inside. Mark one for the kid!

Stern sat down at the end of the table, but Sandra and the other two gentlemen remained standing.

"Well now, Adam, aren't we just one happy family? There you are, our long-lost son, returning like the — what did they call him, the prodigal son, was it?" He smiled. "But we're missing someone, aren't we?"

"If you ask me, the room is much too full as it is," Adam commented.

"Adam, Adam, Adam, let's not quibble. You have become a disappointment. Here we were hoping you would be able to find your friend for us." Stern watched Adam's eyes with a fixated interest. "Now why is that? What have we done to upset you, my boy?"

Adam said nothing.

"Adam, I think it's time I told you a thing or two about your little friend, something you may not know. Do you need anything to drink, something to eat?" His voice was as silky smooth as a cobra's scales. "No? Well then, shall we begin?"

Stern covered roughly the same information that he had told Sandra earlier. He cut it a bit shorter but didn't leave out anything important. "So, my boy, you see... your little friend, I'm afraid, is a bit of an alien monster." He leaned back and smiled, still intently watching Adam's eyes.

Adam couldn't help it; his eyes shifted briefly to Evelyn before going back to Stern.

Stern caught it, and his smile widened into a toothy grin. "And, Adam, I need to tell you something really important that you also may not be aware of. Before I entered this office, I made sure that none of us inside would be able to open the door. None of us has the code. Isn't that wise of me?" His grin intensified to the look of a predatory beast, about to pounce on its prey. "What do you think would happen if I should put a bullet in your brain right now? There are so many ways of doing that; of course, it doesn't have to be with a bullet. Bullets are so messy. Aren't they, Evelyn?"

Sandra Mitchell screamed as she saw the mysterious Evelyn appear out of nowhere as if she had been there all along. The effect was incredible.

"Well, well, well, now we are a happy family," whispered Mr. Stern.

Evelyn didn't bother to look at him; her eyes were glued to Adam. She had no time.

Adam's face was unreadable. "Is this true, Evelyn?"

Evelyn looked into his eyes and said, "Adam, do you remember playing with a little girl when you were about seven? Do you remember your airplane and the places you flew with her?"

Sudden recognition flooded his mind and tears came to his eyes. "I... I thought it was a dream..." he whispered. Her hands reached for the sides of his face, and their lips pressed tenderly together in the sweetest embrace.

When he opened his eyes, he quickly looked around the room at Stern and the other three people, but they were motionless as if living statues. Astonishingly, as he looked back to Evelyn, she no longer appeared as human as the Evelyn he knew. She was dressed in a radiant gown tinged with blue. As usual, it did not appear to be made of any earthly material. Her skin glowed, as did her slightly golden eyes.

"Adam, I cannot bring us to your world or mine any longer; I am too weak."

"You look a little different from the five-year old I remember," he said.

"We do grow up, you know," she said.

"Yes, I can see that," he said, slightly flushed. "So, are you Evelyn or are you her subconscious? How am I to think of you? And…are you an alien?"

"Adam, I am Evelyn, she is me, and no, I am not human, but she is just as much me as I am her. We are one, but we have different aspects and purposes. Think of me as Evelyn-Prime. There is one thing we both share in common. We both love you as one. We are becoming one with you."

"But, Evelyn, how can you love me? If you are not even human and are so different from me, where are you even from?"

"Adam, you are not what you think you are—no human is. You are as alien to this world as I am. You are not a corporeal being as you think. You are a being of energy that controls a corporeal body. The body needs you, but you do not need the body to exist. Soon, you will understand completely."

Adam thought about this for a few moments, maybe for a lot longer because time did not seem to have any meaning now. "What you say… Do I have a choice?"

Evelyn saw the worried look on his face. She took a step closer to him and took his hands in hers. "Adam, you chose me before I chose you. But, you do not have to complete the joining if it is not your desire. There are consequences if you so choose though." A look of pain crossed her face as she observed the indecision in his.

"When must I choose?" he asked.

"The time is upon us, but you have a moment."

"I have so many questions yet. Where do you come from and why are you here? Why don't you let Evelyn know everything? I'm sure she does not know this. Does she?"

"Yes, she knows everything now. There is a reason we let our conscious minds have room to experience the physical world without the knowledge of the spiritual, but conditions altered one of the purposes of my presence here. I have had to abandon that mission."

Adam thought for a second and said, "Do I have an energy self like you?"

Evelyn looked at him for a while before answering. She had done so many things wrong, not the least of which had been disrespecting his Prime matrix by communicating directly to Adam. If Adam-Prime were not going to end his mission by telling Adam that he was not human, Evelyn would respect that, though it would mean their deaths. She would not compound her guilt by revealing it. "Adam, I am very old. The universe is a very old place. My kind merges only once. There can only be one for me, and that is you. It does not matter that we are not of the same species or that you are a new species. There can be only one for me. If it is not you, it cannot be anyone... forever." Lies and half-truths...

This took Adam's breath away. "There is so much to consider. Let me have more time."

A great sadness settled onto Evelyn's delicate features. He would not join with her; she could see it in his eyes. She did not blame Adam. His Adam-Prime loved her; she did not doubt that. He had saved her from the darkness, but he was not willing to give up his mission, even if it meant the end of their lives. He could end the mission by opening his conscious matrix to the reality of who he really was... She understood why he did not. They were Children of Heaven, the Eternal Swords of Light. Had she not had her mission destroyed by circumstances, she would never have forsaken it. He would not do what she had had to do. She would respect this and never tell him the truth, not even as the last of her energy dissipated.

"Adam, listen to my words and remember me as long as you can. This is all I have left.

I am Mouradyne. We are Children of Heaven, the Eternal Swords of Light. Billions of years ago, the Creator fashioned us from the elements. We were parasitic predators with only survival as our life-goal. He molded us into the Mouradyne. He gave us purpose and love. We serve only Him.

Just as he has given us Joy, we are charged to bring it to others. My mission was to live as a human, to feel what they feel, to love as they love, and to bring that life back to our world for evaluation. If it was judged that humanity was ready, it would be given the GIFT.

We arrived on Earth, ready to be placed inside mothers, to grow as human children and to age normally to their age of death. However, I failed my mission. When the tragedy of my Earthly parent's death almost caused me to do that which I would rather die than have done, I modified myself. Unfortunately, in doing so, I made mistakes, the results of which have proven fatal for us.

We are beings of energy and matter. As children, we are composed of one physical and one energy matrix. The energy matrix has been given a signature by our parents exactly matched with only one other signature. If those two energy matrices do not bond after a certain amount of time, both will perish.

My second mission on Earth was to find my mate and bond with him.

Bonding for a Mouradyne is becoming an adult Mouradyne. The adult is an immortal being of infinite power, its sole purpose being to serve the Creator. An adult is composed of one female and one male physical body, each with a separate outer matrix or consciousness. Between the two, there is a single Inner Energy Matrix that holds the collective knowledge of the experiences and wisdom passed on by each of our parents going back for eons.

The adult Mouradyne is immortal... if the children do not become an adult, their life force will continue to drain until it extinguishes.

I have failed my mission, and I have done that which is unforgivable. I have come between you and your... spirit. Though it means our deaths, I will not reveal the final knowledge that only you have the right to give.

I am Mouradyne, Child of Heaven, an Eternal Sword of Light... and I will love you until I am no more."

And with that, she released the flow of time and...

"Such a nice little family," said Stern. "What shall we talk about?"

Adam looked at Stern and saw that Beck and Schumer had taken out handguns and had them pointed at Evelyn.

When he looked back to Evelyn, he was appalled at how weak she looked. "What's wrong with you?" he gasped.

She said nothing for a moment. "It is a good thing that you are doing, Adam. I support your decision completely."

"What are you talking about? What decision am I making?" Adam was confused. He had no idea she was speaking to Adam-Prime. Stern was fascinated as well by the turn of events. Evelyn looked to be hardly able to stand, her features pale and sunken.

Stern smiled and looked at his two agents. "Perhaps we won't have to waste any money on those government shells after all... well, at least not on her." Both of them smiled.

Sandra had tears in her eyes.

"Evelyn, please help me to understand what is happening to you! What can I do?" Adam begged.

"You are doing the only thing you can do. We may never be together, but we will have this for eternity."

Stern's smile widened, and he said, "Aw, what the heck! A couple of shells aren't that expensive." Mr. Beck and Mr. Schumer smiled, and both fired a .45 caliber slug into Evelyn's failing heart.

CHAPTER 40

AS EVELYN WAS KNOCKED against the wall, Sandra Mitchell saw everything in slow motion, wishing with all her heart that she could look away. Time kept slowing down until it finally stopped, and yet she was as conscious as were the three government men. They could do nothing now except watch Evelyn at the point of death.

Terror gripped their minds. How long would this last? It seemed to go on forever. However, for Sandra, only grief filled her mind as she remembered the hurt and pain she had caused others. All she desired now was to end her existence. The pain was too great to continue, and yet she had no choice — none of them did.

Adam-Prime screamed!

He had stopped the flow of time inside a bubble around the immediate location of the Stone Labs facility, but it was too late. Every person inside this anomaly experienced the same contradiction; time continued in their minds but stopped for the physical world around them. There was a lot of time to think...

He watched, as Evelyn's energy grew ever smaller until it was barely a spark, a glowing ember in the blackness of time. He had tried to stop time before the bullets struck, but had waited too long.

He phased to a world of ice, a cold and bitter place of unbelievable sadness. He would not go on. He would not allow that ember to fade any further. For all of eternity, he would stay here and mourn her, his eternal companion or the companion that might have been, in a self-imposed exile from reality.

Adam-Prime did not know how long he had been sitting on the frozen ground. He didn't care. Endless loops of grief passed through him with pain and anguish in a never-ending sequence of events he would never feel worthy of enduring. He had failed her. He would not allow her to go into oblivion without him by her side. He had failed her. His pride and his failure to understand the full extent of the evil in human hearts had caused him to fail Evelyn. There was no way he could continue to exist, but if he didn't, that faint ember would cease, and he would never allow that. He had failed her...

Today is the ten-year anniversary of the world-famous Black- Sphere's appearance. Although the world-shattering event may have begun to grow stale as a news story, the phenomenon is still considered one of the wonders of the world. All that can be said about it has already been said, except of course, for the ever-popular conspiracy theories. It would not be proper to allow such an unusual event to go unmentioned on a slow news day.

After the existing exit on Interstate 10 was permanently closed to the public, many roadside gift and curiosity shops opened along the stretch connecting New Orleans to Baton Rouge. If one is searching for anything "Black-Sphere," they should find it there. From Christmas-time snow globes to flying saucers, they have everything.

Everyone knows the reason for the initial blockade around the Black-Sphere. Nothing like this has ever occurred in history. Is it dangerous? Is it an alien invasion? Which laws of physics can account for such an anomaly? From all over the world, scientists converged to study it.

Nevertheless, even today, on its ten-year anniversary, we have no clue as to why it is here, what it is, or where it came from. Bizarrely, the sphere is rather romantic. As the Black-Sphere stands proudly before the world, she defies all to understand her secrets, and on this, her anniversary—and much like Mona Lisa—she smiles with hidden humor at the world's futile efforts to understand her.

NEWS SPECIAL: as a curiosity, the very popular Senator Collins suffered a devastating stroke on this very day, ten years ago. Admitted to Stephen's Memorial Hospital where he remains today, he has been unable to move any part of his body except for his eyes. Even with his paraplegic status, Senator Collins has continued to serve his country. Many consider him a hero for this continued service. Although he was stricken, he has learned to communicate with eye movements and is said to be of great assistance in furthering Black-Sphere knowledge. For his great service to the country and his dedication, the government has expressed its gratitude by paying for his perpetual care.

An eternity of eternities had passed, and Adam-Prime was still unable to forgive his self. His sorrow had no limit, the depth of which was bottomless. The world was dead. No movement of the icy air, no change in the gray sky; nothing ever changed or varied. There was nothing to occupy his time in hell, but neither did he want it. He could never suffer enough. He would refuse to allow that precious ember that was Evelyn, to end.

As he had done a billion, billion times in the past, he thought of Evelyn. It had been such a different time. He thought of the two of them sliding along, running, playing as children do... the memory repeating, again and again, remembering it over and over. She had trusted him... He had failed her. There could be no forgiveness for this. The eternal loop continued.

In his mind, as he had done an infinite number of times before, he watched them slide across the ice, laughing, and playing. This time, however, the loop broke. How had he missed it? He realized that there was more to the moment. Why had he not seen it before? He remembered how they had sat looking at a great light in the distance. Evelyn had wanted to run to it. They had indeed done so, but never got closer. Adam had been the one to suggest they sit and wait for it to approach them. It took a long time, but time did not seem to matter.

Eventually, the light approached. It was the purest most radiant light he had ever seen. It was so wonderful that it refused to be described except in the grayest terms. A quiet, small voice spoke from it, and it filled his heart and mind with indescribable joy. He remembered crying; they were both in tears, not of sadness, but of joy.

As Adam sat on the icy plain of his endless torment, he saw that same light. He watched it for a very, very long time before asking it for help in saving Evelyn. The same quiet voice spoke to him now as it had then. "I have forgiven you from the beginning; now you have forgiven yourself. Is it not enough?"

Adam-Prime phased...

He looked at Evelyn, frozen in the act of dying. His mind filled with all he was and all he had been. He knew his purpose, and he knew his desire. The steel-coated lead slugs separated into their subatomic particles, breaking bonds held together by unimaginable forces. The incredible energy released was absorbed into the tiny ember, until it burned brightly. The molecules of Evelyn's physical body aligned themselves into their proper building blocks, her flesh, sinews, bones, and fluids returning to normal. Her eyes opened, and with a smile on her lips, she reached out to Adam...

Holding Evelyn-Prime in his arms, Adam looked out over the great fields of incredible beauty and then down to her. She was now dressed in a beautiful flowing gown of light and stars. Her hair was no longer dark brown but was as pure white as he could imagine. Her eyes also had changed. There were no pupils at all. Instead, the entire surface looked to be an emerald green with sparkling flecks of gold. Her skin was like silk and seemed to have a slightly greenish tinge. The color of her lips almost matched the color of her eyes except there was no gold in them. Her eyelashes were long, but she had no eyebrows, and he observed no visible ears. He took these changes in swiftly and slowly at the same time. The rest of her appeared to be similar to the Evelyn he knew except for the digits of her hands and feet, which did not seem to be joint-

ed like a human's. He watched her put her fingers around his arm to hold him tight, and it appeared that they were almost tendril-like. Overall, he suddenly realized, they looked exactly right, and he knew she was the most beautiful woman he had ever seen.

"Adam, you asked me if there was time left to make a decision. I cannot live without you. I do not want to exist without you. If you are not certain you want to be forever with me, then I will release you. Forgive me for not keeping my promise to protect you and forgive me for not trusting you... for disrespecting you."

"Evelyn, I don't care what happens to me. I only want to be with you, regardless of what that means. I will always love you."

Evelyn-Prime looked deeply into his eyes before saying with a whisper, "Forever then..."

She rose on her toes, kissed him one last time before taking his hands in hers, and looked into his eyes. "Forever, I'm yours." Evelyn and Evelyn-Prime melded and Evelyn was no more.

Adam looked down at her and felt his love for her increase a million-fold. All the knowledge of who he was and what he was, flowed into him, as he and his Adam-Prime melded, and Adam was no more.

Adam-Prime gently intertwined his own tendril-like fingers with Evelyn-Prime's and gazed deeply into her eyes.

And then...

A pale light appeared around each of their hands at the point of contact. At first, it was imperceptible but slowly grew outward until both of their bodies were surrounded with a pulsating glow, his, a brilliant, crimson-orange, hers, a soft, lavender-pink.

It paused for a moment...

Without taking her eyes from his, she slowly moved closer, rising on her toes until their lips joined. As their eyes closed and their bodies pressed together, the pulsing radiance increased and rapidly spread outward until they were both surrounded, two radiant forms standing beneath a great oak tree, making the rest of the universe black by comparison...

The World paused...

The Universe paused...

Time paused...

All energy, space, time, and the void outside of the bubble that was Evelyn-Adam collapsed into a singularity...

...and creation phased outward as the two orbs of radiant blue-white energy ignited like a new star and became one.

Evelyn-Adam no longer existed. In their place was born a single conscious-ness, infinite in power and obedience to its Creator.

Two physical beings formed within the small interrogation room. The final transformation into an adult Mouradyne was complete. They stood in each other's arms, eyes closed — feeling their hearts beating between them. Time no longer mattered, and whether they stood like this forever or created universes, their joy would be the same. Nevertheless, joy begets joy, and they desired to give it to others.

They separated and looked into each other's eyes. Neither had changed to their human forms. She looked at him for a moment, as did he to her. They then gazed upon Stern, Beck, and Schumer, and a terrible sadness came over them. She looked at Sandra and knew her through their combined memories. These and all who had been within the anomaly had suffered terribly. She looked into his solid emerald eyes.

We must release them and remove this memory. However, we will heal them first. This hate was not of their choosing. Look at those that surround them. They seek to destroy them even now.

What they shared of the guilt can never be paid by an infinite num-ber of what they have already suffered, but when they meet Him, He will know of what they have suffered and He will judge.

Before we do this, I want to...

He turned and gazed upon her, humor replacing the look of sorrow that had darkened his features.

She smiled at him and slowly changed. In a moment, she was in her human shape and personality, Evelyn.

Looking at him with mischievous eyes, she tapped a finger on the tip of his nose and said, "Come on, don't be shy!" and she giggled.

In a moment, Adam stood next to her. They were both dressed in jeans, sweatshirts, and tennis shoes. He now laughed with her.

"Wow! Now this is something to write home about," said Evelyn.

Adam picked her up in his arms and gave her a bear hug and kiss. "I love you so much!"

Evelyn smiled her most wonderful smile and said, "Ditto! Now, let's clean up this mess."

As they walked to the door, it opened before them, the very mole-cules changing to allow passage. At the next door, Evelyn said, "Wait a moment, if we want to be Evelyn and Adam, we have to do things a little differently, don't we?"

"Okay, alien girl, do it your way," Adam said as Evelyn entered the super-secret code into the digital keypad.

"Now wait a minute!" objected Adam. "How would Evelyn know the correct code to enter?"

She punched him playfully on the arm, and they continued to walk through the obstacles before them.

Eventually, they stood at the anomaly barrier. Adam turned to Evelyn. "Let's do it." They looked back and phased each mind, ending their eternal torment. In the same instant, the ebony sphere vanished.

CHAPTER 41

SANDRA STOOD IN THE interrogation room for a moment trying to remember why she was there. Mr. Stern, Mr. Beck, and Mr. Schumer stood beside her. Each of them seemed a bit dazed as well. Mr. Stern turned to the others and asked if they were all right and if anyone knew why they were in the room. "I appear to have had a memory lapse." He chuckled.

When they attempted to leave, they discovered the security pad had been disarmed; no code was required. "I guess we need to have maintenance look at this... Nah, who cares? I'm going home." And he did. In fact, every person at Stone Labs, Inc. quit that day. Of course, military intelligence had to process them first, but no one was able to shed any light on what had happened, why they had not aged, and why no one remembered anything. Obviously, there had to be explanations for abandoned wives, husbands, and children, but similar to the Black Sphere mystery, there were no answers. The one thing they all seemed to share was an intense joy at being alive.

BREAKING NEWS: OCTOBER 3, 2031

Senator Collins died today, ten years after the anomaly appeared. Oddly enough, his death occurs on the same day as the Black-Sphere's inexplicable disappearance.

CHIMBORAZO, ECUADOR - SATURDAY, OCTOBER 4, 2031

The honeymoon, following the most beautiful wedding she could ever have imagined, was over. They had traveled the world visiting one romantic spot after the next, each anchored forever in her heart. She understood that the "honeymoon" would never end, but this moment would always be special, and she was trying to hold on to it as long as possible.

It was the end of a life. She had loved and hated. There had been friends and enemies, the joys of discovery and the sadness of failure. Some may say it was sad and regretful, but it had been her life. She would have these memories forever, and whatever came in the future, they would always be special to her.

In the subzero temperatures, they sat quietly against the ice-covered rock, enjoying these last moments. Neither said anything. Evelyn slowly lifted a small handful of snow crystals and watched as the sun glittered off it like a million tiny stars. Indeed, it had been a beautiful life.

In the end, they had decided to spend their last few hours upon the peak of Chimborazo in Ecuador. They chose it because of the volcano's uniqueness. Although Chimborazo's peak had a height of only 20,564 feet above sea level and was only about 13,100 feet above its base, its uniqueness lay in the fact that its peak was 7,113 feet farther from the center of the Earth than Mount Everest. Due to rotational forces, the Earth is not a perfect sphere; it "bulges" at the equator. This unique equilateral deviation from the spherical provided what they had been searching for. There would be a critical instant when the Earth's rotation around the Sun and the Earth's own rotation around its center presented a point at which they would be as close to the center of the Sun as possible. While this was not necessary, wasting energy was not in their nature.

Evelyn looked up into Adam's eyes. "I'm ready. I have enjoyed our time so much."

Adam cupped Evelyn's hand in his, making sure he did not disturb the little handful of snow she held. "We need to report. Most of it is unpolluted, but I doubt it will be acceptable."

Evelyn moved her gaze out over the world below them, "I will miss them..."

Adam looked up at the sun and sighed. He stood up and offered his hand to her. "Yeah, I know what you mean."

Evelyn joined him, and together, as the last rays of the noontime sun touched their faces, they dropped their human images and personalities.

We will try to return if we can – and they were gone.

Before the surrounding air with its accompanying crack of thunder could even begin to react to the sudden vacuum created by their absence, Evelyn and Adam arrived at the exact center of the Sun. The time they remained at the nearly fifty-nine million degrees was an almost infinitely small fraction of an instant, but long enough to absorb the required energy without damaging the star. Then they were at their next accelerator point, and the next, and the next, ever accelerating, until they reached the far edge of the opposite side of the Milky Way galaxy. At this point, they had the exact amount of energy necessary to jump across intergalactic space to the Large Magellanic Cloud galaxy, 180,000 light years away. Here, the process of storing energy began once more, and again at an ever-accelerating rate. It would still take a while to reach their home. In the meantime, however, they had a place to go.

Adam looked into Evelyn's emerald green eyes and gently pressed his lips to hers. The only sound was the gentle breeze passing through the thickly leaved branches of the great oak. The world around them was full of beauty and delightful fragrances; they had forever to enjoy it, and they had each other.

EPILOGUE

ART SAT IN HIS CHAIR looking out the window at the setting sun. Jessie, his roommate, was joking with Betty. She was a good-natured nurse and put up with most of Jessie's foolishness, even when it was a bit off color. Art had tried on more than one occasion to convince Jessie that telling off-color jokes was not the way to impress the pretty ladies, but it was like preventing a sailor from getting a "Mom" tattoo. To Jessie, it was almost a religious obligation.

After a moment, Art returned his attention to the sun and thought about his life. He had spent most of it alone, never having married. He wouldn't say it had been boring, but more... incomplete. It always seemed like there might be something else for him to do, especially after discovering that silver sphere so many years ago.

He smiled at the memory. The gate guards had contacted the officer in charge and had removed it from his pickup. He filled out some paperwork and signed some forms, but other than a brief meeting with a serious looking officer the following week, he had never heard any more about it. Of course, Art understood the need for secrecy, and being warned that he was never to speak of it was only natural. Still, over all these years, he had retained a sort of possessive feel for the thing. He would surely have liked to know what it was and what had happened to it.

Betty laughed good-naturedly before telling Jessie it was time for his enema. Art tried to keep from smiling, he really did. If there was anything that his friend hated more, he wasn't aware of it. As Jessie put it, "It takes a man's respect away!"

"Oh, stop being such a baby!" complained Betty.

Art had to agree about one thing though. Growing old and having to have strangers stick things in your butt wasn't his idea of a good time. The Oakridge Nursing Home was a dead end, and for many, it was never a happy place where families came to visit. That is how it had always been for Art, but it never bothered him, as it seemed to bother the others. He had friends here, of course. Many had passed on, and some, like Jessie, were trying to keep their sense of humor about it all.

The sun was almost down when Art heard the voice. Although he could never remember hearing the silvery tone before, it did seem intimately familiar. Jessie and Betty's conversation gradually faded into the background as his attention focused, almost desperately, upon it. Everything in the room, including time, slowly settled into a small place in the corner of Art's mind—and Art remembered who he was and why he was on Earth.

Looking at the softly glowing hand covering his, he lifted his eyes to the beautiful face of his eternal companion. With her gentle touch, his mind opened to the life of their daughter, and her glorious success... and they were gone.

Betty looked over at the empty chair next to the window for a moment before turning back to Jessie. "I think you're spending too much time alone, Jess. How would you like to have a roommate?"

"Now you're talking Betty! I was wondering how long it would be before you decided to join me," Jessie said with a twinkle in his eye.

"Oh, you old fool! I'm not talking about me!" she laughed. "We thought that maybe Mr. Simmons could use some company. You know he hasn't got long."

"Oh well, I suppose if I can't have you, I might as well try to cheer up Sims. He's a good guy."

ABOUT THE AUTHOR

Daniel R. Fuller became enchanted as a child with stories about woodland creatures as they struggled to survive and flourish in a hostile world. As a teenager, he sailed with seafaring survivors crossing the world's great seas, man against nature. He came to love stories about romance and science fiction fantasy. He also loved Christianity and pondered how such things could exist. In time, he finally concluded that even in a natural world controlled by mindless evolution, God would eventually happen anyway and His story would be the greatest ever told.

Daniel grew up in New Orleans, Louisiana where he spent a lot of time at Audubon Park. The zoo, the lagoons, and the great oak trees all played a part in his childhood. New Orleans is rich in Spanish and French history, and seen from the eyes of a child, it was a wonderful fantasy world. "Invisible" was largely inspired by that world, and his sweetheart of 48 years, Florence, inspired the character of Evelyn. Today, Daniel lives in Utah with his 25 children and grandchildren. He has spent time in Europe, Vietnam, Korea, and has lived in five states. He has worked in the oil and gas fields of Louisiana and Texas and many years in computer technology. He is now retired and writes for pleasure and entertainment for himself as well as his family.

To find out more about this and other White Meadow Books authors and their works, please visit www.whitemeadowbooks.com

Or visit us on Facebook at www.facebook.com/WhiteMeadowBooks

www.ingramcontent.com/pod-product-compliance
Lightning Source LLC
Chambersburg PA
CBHW060547260626
47161CB00003B/1096